Whiter Than Snow

*Tommy!
You Rock!
Nate Ellis
Proverbs 3:5-6*

Whiter Than Snow

the Legend

BASED ON THE TRUE SNOW WHITE STORY

Matthew Eldridge

Copyright ©2014 Matthew Eldridge

All rights reserved. No portion of this book may be reproduced, stored in a retrieval system, or transmitted in any form or by any means—electronic, mechanical, photocopy, recording, or any other—except brief quotation in printed reviews, without the prior permission of the author.

Published by Matthew Eldridge
Conyers, Georgia
United States of America
meldridge@cheerful.com

Cover Model: Brittany Godwin

This young adult novel is a work of historical fiction fantasy. This story is based on the true life of Margarete Von Waldeck, also known as Snow White. Some of the characters are based on historical figures, while others are completely fictionalized. There was a great amount of research put into this story, and while I tried to stay true to the historical facts, events, characters, and timeline, many things had to be changed, condensed, or rearranged in order to keep the story interesting.

ISBN   1496112423
ISBN-13   978-1496112422

Printed in the United States of America

For the Love of my life,

Nicole

Matthew Eldridge

Whiter Than Snow

Prologue

The sky suffocated with darkness. Evil made his advances by sending out his mistresses to desecrate the innocent and pure. Among those, a simple woman, an aged woman, with a dark brown cloak and years of angst adorned as wrinkles on her face, made her way by the king's secret summer chateau.

The mother-to-be, the queen, screamed in anguish as the breech baby tried to force her way out of the womb. Because of the prophesies, the king wanted a private birth away from the castle and those expecting to see the newborn child. He didn't believe the prophesies himself, but he feared those who did.

A cold chill forced its way through the windows and the cracks in the door, swirling around the room and surrounding the new mom as if it was watching her. Three knocks quickly followed. The king was torn. He did not want to leave his love, who was suffering so greatly at what should be a joyous moment. And yet, what if the person at the door could help him save the life of his wife and child? He knew from seeing the feet of the child that he needed help. He could taste death in the air.

The knocker insisted. The king quickly made his way to the door and opened it.

"She needs help. I am a midwife," the old woman croaked, forcing herself through the doorway and into the kingly cottage.

"How did you know? Did God send you?"

She cracked a devilish smile and paused. "You can hear your poor wife scream for miles." The elderly woman followed the king to the bedroom, shifting her weight from her right foot to her walking cane and back.

The queen grimaced in pain. The midwife stared, smirking fleetingly as she recognized the noble figure, and yet, without a bow, took her place at the end of the bed.

The king waited for what felt like an eternity through screams and cries of desperation from his wife. Finally, with a piercing shriek from the queen, the child tore through her mother and entered the world.

The king, eager to see the child, rushed to the midwife's side to see his newborn daughter. The midwife turned away as if she was blocking the child from him and yelled forcefully, "She's not breathing! Help your wife!"

His beloved lay there pale and inert. He rubbed her forehead and she reached for him, trembling. He kissed her soft, sweaty cheek.

The midwife showed the baby to the queen for just a second and pronounced, "She's dead."

The child appeared lifeless. Her mother gaped at her milky white skin, ruby red lips, and black hair. Even dead, she was beautiful. "Are you sure?" the desperate mother cried, barely able to speak from exhaustion.

Whiter Than Snow

The old woman quickly took the child out of sight. "It's not good for you to look at it," she answered, moving out of the room, her voice trailing off. "She's as white as snow."

While the king attended to the ailing queen, the old woman quickly wrapped the child in rags and carried her outside. As the crooked witch headed for the forest, the mother thought she heard the sounds of a baby crying.

"My baby! My baby!" the queen screamed, trying to sit up in bed, her body convulsing. "Save my baby!"

The king heard nothing and tried to hush the sickly woman. Within a few minutes, his panic-stricken wife was dead.

The forest embraced the old hag, hiding her among the barren trees, enveloping her in the mad darkness that swallowed the sky. While most feared such a night, the wicked woman welcomed it. She felt warm by the invisible evil hands that held her, guided her, and drew her to the task at hand.

She scurried over tree branches, ducked below barren limbs, and hurriedly scampered through the forest with the dead leaves crunching beneath her feet. The baby cried again, and she walked a little faster. Her eyes were transfixed on the beautiful child in her arms. As a woman, she felt a tinge of sympathy for the child, but only for a moment. And while every motherly instinct would tell her to protect and nurture the infant, the calluses in this woman's soul blocked her from feeling anything at all. When motherly affection tried to resurface, she rebuked those feelings and remembered her assignment: kill the baby and save them all.

She stopped for a moment to catch her breath and heard the sound of leaves swirling about her. She closed her eyes to listen and the child cried once more.

"Stop it, I say!"

The precious baby ignored her. The wicked woman began running again, looking all around, unable to see from the veiled moon. She felt she was being followed. She found herself tripping over a large root, the child tumbling from her arms and into a pile of dead leaves.

A tall, dark figure scooped the child up into his arms.

"Give me back my baby!" the old woman screamed, not recognizing the man at first.

He kissed the baby on her cheek. With gentle eyes, he stared the woman down. She backed away, recognizing his face. She hated him, and yet he hated no one. Perhaps that's why she hated him. She hated him because she knew who he belonged to. She knew that the spirits and the moon she worshipped hated him too. She hated him because of his prophesies. After all, he did prophesy about this very night, about the birth of the child and her role in life, and about the old hag's attempt to kill the child.

"Samuel..." she bellowed, just before attacking him and biting his arm. Another firm hand grabbed her from behind and wrestled her away. Samuel buried the child under his cloak and began to run. The old hag chased him, crying and wailing, understanding that the safety of the child meant death to her future, for it had been prophesied.

Samuel's apprentice followed after her, and as the three made their descent down the mountain face on the other side of the forest, the witch lost her footing and tumbled down, hitting her body on a rock at the bottom.

"Should I go after her?" asked Micah, the young apprentice, as the two men of God watched from the top of the mountain.

"Let her be," Samuel answered. "Let's get this baby to safety."

The prophet and his protégé made their way across the forest and along the water's edge, watching the moonlight masquerade upon the small ripples on the water made from westerly winds. The cries of the little one increased as Samuel moved at a jogging pace into the remote village.

They approached a small cottage and Samuel knocked on the door. As a middle-aged woman, Lucinda, cracked it open, Samuel forced himself inside.

"She's the daughter of the king," he said matter-of-factly, as he laid the crying child on the bed.

The woman in bed clothes, forgetting she had guests, made her way over to the child, and picked her up, lovingly.

"Where is the king?" she questioned.

"You must keep her here for safety. Do not let anyone know who she is, or where she is. She is your baby now, by order of the king. You must make no attempts of contact with him. This is for the safety of us all." He paused and took a deep breath. "You must hide her identity. May God protect you."

A small infant began crying in the other room.

"But why me? Who am I? I have my own child to take care of!"

"You are nursing, are you not? Only you can feed this child!"

"Where is the queen?"

Samuel lowered his head, and the woman understood. She placed her face in her hands and began to sob, for she served the queen many years in the palace, and most recently at the summer chateau—the very place the queen died. She would have been there this very night had she not given birth to a son months earlier.

The prophet kissed the baby on the forehead. "Raise her as your own. You're a follower of the king, the true King! Raise her in his ways, for this is the child who has been prophesied about. The future of our country and our faith rests in her hands."

The men of God slipped quietly outside of the cottage, the sky as black coal consuming them, hiding them from the other villagers.

"I must go away for a while," Samuel told his student.

"Why? How?"

Whiter Than Snow

"What I did was a very dangerous thing. I did it to protect her—to protect our future. I will not lie to the king, but if he ever found out, it would be my life. I fear for the motherless child. The number of evil is great in our kingdom. There are many who would love to hurt the infant. Her light will end the darkness. God be with you. You've learned enough from me. Your job is to keep an eye out from time to time on this child. Make sure she is protected from the dark ones."

The year that Margarete was born, a young, Spanish prince named Philip entered his teen years. The boy knew nothing but a world of servants and the finer things in life. From his infancy, he'd been regarded as the golden child, the definitive heir to his father's throne; the child who would one day rule a great and glorious kingdom. His father, the Emperor, was the most powerful man in most of Europe, much like the boy's grandfather before him.

It was expected that Philip would follow in his father's footsteps, expanding his kingdoms even greater. Philip had been told this over and over—so much that the pressure he felt to fill such a role had stricken him like the plague. Anxiety ate at his soul in a way that it paralyzed him, leaving him bedridden for months shortly after his 13th birthday.

When he was well enough to walk again, he and his brother would walk to the market place, just outside the castle walls, and watch families enjoying themselves buying and selling.

Matthew Eldridge

Children laughed and played holding hands with their parents, fathers carried their young ones on their shoulders, and some played tag with their children in the streets.

The truth was, young Philip was miserable and heart sick, starved for affection from his mother and father. His parents were not in love, nor did they know anything about love. Theirs was an arranged marriage, and he was simply a by-product.

His father had a mistress, and her name was power. And as many times as he tried to introduce her to young Philip, Philip wasn't interested in power. The boy had but one interest, and one interest alone: to feel the love and acceptance of his father, to feel a warm embrace by the man, a hug, a kiss, and a kind word spoken. He longed to hear his father say he was proud of him. He was desperate to catch his father's attention. He wanted to feel secure and safe in the arms of his mother. He hungered for her affection.

Philip desired the life of a commoner. He ached for a simpler life where families slept within talking distance of one another, or even shared beds, where every day was spent as a family together, whether in the fields or in the market. He was tired of the nameless nannies and faceless guards who often watched him. He wanted to hold his mom's hand and hear her say the tender words, "I love you." And although he was already thirteen, he wished she would tuck him in at night and give him a kiss on the cheek. She had never done that.

He wanted love. He wanted a common family. He wanted a father who wasn't always traveling to other countries for weeks on end. He just wanted to *know* his father. He would gladly exchange all of his future riches for just a moment of family bonding, even if it meant without food or shelter or royal clothing.

His father, the Emperor, misunderstood the boy's desire for affection after the young lad tackled his mom with hugs and kisses at the dinner table one evening. Philip learned it from watching families in the village. The Emperor brought him a concubine the next day, not much older than Philip, himself.

"Today you become a man!" his father said.

The boy knew not what he was doing, nor did he want to do what his father expected him to do. The girl was beautiful, indeed, but the thought of doing something without love, without marriage as the priest said, seemed cold and disgusting. His sensitive heart ached for the girl, who proved to be somewhat experienced pleasing men.

She held him tight, and he paid her extra not to tell anyone what *didn't* happen between them as she left. He didn't want to disappoint his father, once again.

"Will you come back?" young Philip asked the girl.

She gently caressed the side of his face with the back of her hand. She was confident and comfortable. "If the prince desires me to."

"I do."

His father watched from afar and saw the look in the boy's eyes. He understood what must be done to dismiss any worry of possible attachment. He had a guard escort the girl to the outside edge of the property. As he pushed her off the land, he tossed a coin at her that bounced off her arm and landed in the dirt.

"Don't come back," the guard said, "or be arrested."

She crawled to the coin, picked it up off the ground and retreated into the market place, getting lost in the crowd, feeling much like a whore, even if she didn't sleep with the prince—it was the treatment of the guard that reduced her to scum.

When Philip asked for the young girl again, his father brought other women—older women, telling the boy to enjoy his youth; no attachments—the very thing Philip longed for. Eventually, he'd encounter numerous unattached relationships, enough to stir confusion into his love-starved soul.

While his brother would show a keen interest in his father's business affairs, Philip would grow to be the family disappointment, living life as a wealthy playboy who cared nothing for the temptress of power.

Chapter 1

Lucinda rubbed her calloused knees. She found herself kneeling on the bedroom floor, praying earnestly for God's provision in these dire times. And while he had never let her and the children go hungry before, it was hard to trust an invisible God as the food supply ran low and the hunger pangs raged against the bottom of her ribs.

Since the queen's death, Lucinda lost her main source of income, working as the queen's maidservant. And while gifts were periodically given to her by the kingdom to provide for her and her young children, it would seem as if they were all but forgotten in the latter years. Waldeck was becoming a wasteland by the abandonment of the king—and the small town struggled to survive in her own strength. Even Micah, the young servant of God, provided for the family while the children were toddlers. But his visits were further and further apart over the years.

Deep in prayer, Lucinda heard the pitiful moans of her prepubescent son in the next room. He caught the dreaded virus that plagued a third of their small village; a number of the children even dying from it. Ill with a high fever, he hadn't been in the fields to hunt in over a week—which meant they didn't have meat to eat. His coughing averted Lucinda's attention from her hunger and she focused on praying for the boy.

    Young Margarete found herself roaming through the woods in search of something—anything to bring home to her dear godmother and sickly brother to eat. Although she had just turned twelve, her godmother wouldn't allow her to find food on her own, claiming the woods were too dangerous for a domesticated young girl. Her overprotective attitude annoyed Margarete, who often felt smothered in the tiny cottage. The heart of an explorer, the teenager wasn't one to settle in and ignore the beauty of the world around her. Against Lucinda's direct instruction, the strong-willed girl left the cottage and the small village to discover the berry farm her adoptive brother always talked fondly about. As the young child braved the forest and found the wild berry patch on the other side, heavy clouds swam through the grey sky, forcing the late afternoon sun to retreat.

    Lucinda's uttered words were indistinguishable beneath the heavy thundering that boomed through the dimly lit sky. At one point, her son thought she was speaking another language and he wondered how she learned it so quickly, or perhaps his illness made him delusional. Either way, she was praying with fervor, urgently begging God to move on her behalf. And it was while praying so strongly that she paused mid-sentence and held her hands to her face.

    A vision.

    A clear vision came to her head.

Whiter Than Snow

"Margie!" she cried out loud, her nickname for her sweet god-child, Margarete.

Maybe it was God, or perhaps it was just her fears. She saw a vivid vision of the poor child hiding underneath a tree, curled up in a ball, tears streaming down her face—a black figure standing over the young girl. Perhaps the figure was a demon or a ghost, or perhaps he was a real person. Either way, Lucinda begged God for protection over Margarete. The dark figure looked to Lucinda through the vision and smirked at her, as if he could see her having the vision. If she wasn't mistaken, she recognized the eyes from a previous dream—the night before the queen died, twelve years previous. They were evil and soulless eyes.

"No!" Lucinda yelled, jumping to her feet, running to her son and feeling his forehead, hoping for a broken fever. She grabbed her kerchief and ran out the door in search of the twelve year old girl.

The heavy rains kept Lucinda to a trot. She screamed into the wind, "Margarete! Margarete!" while frantically searching for the girl.

She followed the usual path just outside the village until she came upon a much smaller one—the path often explored by her son and his friends while hunting. He repeatedly bragged about his discovery of it, and how he would follow the path through thick woods and fight wild animals until the witch's finger, where the path would turn and eventually spill into a meadow filled with fruits and berries on the other side. Lucinda was for certain Margarete was there.

"Margie!" she screamed again as she searched. She nervously stepped into the darker, much thicker woods. If she was lost, she would be stuck there for the entire night, which would be even more dangerous: for her, Margie, and her severely ill son.

"Follow the path straight," she repeated to herself. Her son told her that the path seemed to disappear, but that if she stayed straight, she would find it again, and eventually find the meadow. He warned her of a great tree—a wretched, old, decaying grey tree they called the witch's finger, because it looked like a finger pointing. They once found a rabid fox on the other side of the massive roots, so she heeded his warning and would avoid it—if she could even find it.

Lightning crackled all around, igniting the sky. Lucinda watched from the few cracks between the limbs and leaves that served as a canopy to the forest floor. It was when the lightning faded that Lucinda realized just how dark the sky had become.

"Please God, please," she pleaded.

As the lightning struck again and illuminated the trees, she saw one particular tree just fifty yards away—the weathered, wicked looking tree that stood taller than the rest—and she realized, it had to be the witch's finger.

She ran the almost non-existent path to the tree but then shied away from it, remembering her son's story of the rabid fox. Instead, she followed the direction of the boney, pointy fingers; the branches that leaned east. After fifty steps, she could see the rocky development of a path forming in front of her. Once she stepped into it, she ran with all of her strength, yelling the entire way.

"Margie! Margie!"

She exited the threshold of the forest and entered the clearing of the meadow. "Margie!" she screamed again, her eyes nervously darting around as she spun in circles for any clues or a glimpse of the missing child. She saw the plump, wild blueberries before her that her son spoke of, but no signs of disturbance. Margarete didn't appear to have been there.

"Please God! Show me where she is. Please!" she implored her Maker as she fell to her knees in the wet grass and mud beneath her, tears mixed with rain covering her face.

As she rested in the diluted dirt, hungry for the berries but refusing to eat, consumed with hopelessness and fear for the lost child, she remembered the vision of Margarete during her earlier prayers. The young child was in the nook of a tree…a tree with large enough roots to protect her.

Lucinda stumbled to her feet, her eyes wide open. "Thank you, Jesus," she prayed, her voice cracking as she ran back to the forest and to the path that would swallow her.

For a moment, the sky disappeared as the overgrown shrubbery consumed the space around her. She tilted her frame, running furiously towards the witch's finger—that great and glorious tree that was both majestic and frightening at the same time. She ignored the limbs that jerked her back and forth, sometimes pushing her or grabbing her clothes, sometimes cutting into her thin flesh as she ran by too feverishly. And although the limbs of the forest seemed as if they were alive, real hands grabbing, pulling, and shoving her as she ran, she ignored her fears and focused on the child.

"Margie!" she screamed again, the tree within sight.

As she reached the weathered tree, she paused, resting her hand upon its thick trunk as she worked to catch her breath. She placed her other hand on her chest, feeling the rapid beating of her heart which proved wildly overworked, so much that she thought she would pass out. She sucked the thin air deeply and stilled herself, trying to control her breathing.

She didn't see Margarete, and she was too exhausted to move on. She rested her back against the massive gray tree, her mind racing, her heart aching. It was over. She would have to find her way back. The sky was too dark to continue her search. She would pray for the girl's safety and trust that angels would watch over her through the night.

Lucinda stepped away from the dead tree, looking up at the direction of the fingers to find the opposite route—the way of the thinner path that would lead her home. Three steps into her journey, she saw an overturned basket on the ground.

"Margie?" she gasped.

She walked slowly to the basket and knelt down, ignoring the searing pain in her knees from the difficult run, and picked it up. A clump of berries fell from it as the broken handle gave way. Tears fell from her eyes as she tried to scoop up the berries and place them back in the worn, wooden container.

Whiter Than Snow

A coyote called to the night—or perhaps even a wolf. She estimated the distance and knew she needed to return to the village before the pack found her. Another one returned the call on the opposite side of the forest. Eventually the two would meet—somewhere near her location. She had to move quickly. And then she thought about the fragile child lost in the woods.

"Please, Jesus…" she begged again, her heart filled with fear.

Lucinda heard the growling sounds of an animal on the other side of the tree. Perhaps the coyote was closer than she realized. And although her mind said run, fear seized her as she stood motionless.

She waited…and waited. What she was waiting for she didn't know. Perhaps she was waiting to hear the sound again. Perhaps it was watching her and would chase her if she ran. She refused to believe it was a coyote. Something much smaller she convinced herself. If it was, in fact, the rabid fox, it would catch her for sure—and she would die from rabies if she was bitten, or perhaps spread the disease to her community. Whom the plague didn't kill, the rabies would, and she couldn't live the rest of her short life knowing she was responsible for infecting and destroying part of her village.

"God, protect me," she prayed silently, taking small, quiet, tip-toed steps towards the path.

And then she heard the sound again. Only, it sounded more like whimpering. The animal was injured. Her motherly instincts resurfaced and she turned back to the crooked tree, against all logic. She tried to still her breathing, but the panic inside refused it. She could barely hear above her own rapid breaths, but she heard the rustling on the other side of the tree.

She took two more steps toward the witch's finger; close enough to touch it, and paused. And that's when she heard the coughing. Lucinda stepped around the thick root to the other side of the trunk and looked down into the moist earth beneath it. A young girl was curled up in a ball in the crevice of the roots.

"Margie?" Lucinda said as she reached for the girl, her heart aching for the wounded child.

The somber girl ignored the woman, her body tremulous in the dampness and evil of the evening. Her eyes, once so full of life, were dark with torment.

The loving godmother knelt beside the girl and checked her body for wounds or visible marks, and after seeing none, scooped the hurting child up into her arms. Empowered by adrenaline alone, Lucinda drudged along the path in the wind and rain until they reached their small cottage.

Chapter 2

Six Years Later

The fair skinned, dark haired child spent many years hidden away in the remote village of Waldeck, and rarely left her home. She knew nothing but a simple life—a life of cooking, cleaning, gardening and books. Her brother, as she called him, was the handsome hunter, the teenage warrior who would bring home game for her to skin and prepare for the evening's meal. She never knew a father. And while Lucinda told her that she, in fact, wasn't her mother, she loved her all the same.

Margarete often fantasized about her parents as any adopted child would. She imagined her mom as a beautiful woman with a heart shaped face, perhaps with dark hair to match hers. She assumed that her mother was graceful, not the awkward klutz *she* was. She was told she'd outgrow her awkwardness as she aged. And although she was now eighteen and had blossomed like a beautiful rose, she still felt the gracelessness of a child.

Singing around the house as she cleaned, Margarete often imagined her mother cleaning with her, singing in perfect harmony. She pretended her mother had the beautiful, soft voice of an angel, and would hear her mother tell her she loved her over and over again. Many times her imagination got the best of her and she thought she really did hear a voice…followed by a feeling of warmth surrounding her. She never told anyone about it. It was her little secret to cherish.

She'd spend hours in front of the mirror, brushing her beautiful, thick black hair, and tried to envision her face as a woman—hoping to see a glimpse of the face of what her mother possibly looked like in the reflection. There was something magical about mirrors. They told a story. Not because they could talk, because they couldn't… yet the imagery created spoke a thousand words. What's funny is, Margarete could lie to herself about a lot of things, but she could never lie to the mirror. Whenever she tried to lie to herself, the truth was always revealed in her reflection—whether it be in her smile or lack of, or even in her eyes. The mirror reflected life. In some cases, it reflected death.

Sometimes as she would look deep into the reflection of her own eyes, she could swear her mother was staring back at her from the other side. And when she didn't see it, she longed for it.

Margarete glanced back into the mirror one last time on this cool eve. Her eyes sparkled like rich blue sapphires. She pinched her pale cheeks for color. Her lips were already a deep red and needed nothing for enhancement. They were the lips of a princess—full and luscious, resembling cherries. Although she would dream of being a princess and often pretend to be one in her younger years at play, her identity was kept a deep secret, even from her.

Whiter Than Snow

She puckered her lips and blew a kiss to the mirror. Perhaps tonight she'd get her first real kiss. After all, the boy who had stolen her heart for the past few years was going to be there.

She pushed the front of her black hair back with her hand, a strand tangling around her delicate, tiny ear. She practiced making faces at herself. At first she worked on her different smiles, then, tried several types of laughs. She played with tossing her head back and shaking her hair. Her thick, black, wavy mane was her trademark, and a dear friend taught her how to use it to her advantage—to flaunt it.

She gave herself one last glance in the mirror as the moon climbed the eastern sky, the sun retiring for the evening, stealing her light. She was ready. She had to be.

The villagers filled the square with dancing. It wasn't the dancing you'd see at a castle, and it wasn't the customary dances you'd find in places like London or Paris. No, this was the unique dance to Waldeck. Everyone knew it here—invented by Jack's parents. They were masters of putting on a good time. In fact, this festival, this celebration, was their doing. They were world travelers, touring the world as musicians. At the end of their travels, they would bring back the customary dances they'd learned and put them together to form an original, combined version for the Waldeck villagers. Tonight was a night for celebration—a wedding celebration of their oldest son Johan and his bride. Tomorrow they would begin their travels again, but tonight the young lovers would enjoy family, friendship, and drink love deep.

While the wedding itself was a private event, the reception was open to everyone in the community. Margarete fidgeted with her long dress while noticing the stunning scenery around her. The square was filled with the fresh fragrance of flowers—white, blue, and violet flowers that were as beautiful as they smelled. Torches lit the square at every corner. It was a simple, yet enchanting country wedding reception.

The closer Margarete got to the square, the butterflies fluttering inside of her danced wildly. She could hear him. She could hear his beautiful music. It wasn't necessarily a hot night, but she pulled out her fan and fanned herself anyway, probably because she didn't want anyone seeing her smile, or perhaps she just didn't want that one person seeing it—the person who caused her grin in the first place.

He was now within view. She watched from afar as he played his guitar, and she slowly glided across the square to see him, her eyes never leaving his.

It was his brother's wedding, but in her mind's eye, she was now walking to the altar where he played, eyes transfixed on him, her love to be, her man, her marriage. In her imagination this was her glorious wedding. Oh, sure, she was too young to marry, at least in her own eyes, but she could pretend and dream as every girl did.

She stopped just far enough where he'd have to search for her—hidden behind the throng of dancers who quickly passed her with the rhythmic melodies of the music. After all, every girl wants to be sought after, she thought to herself. She twirled her dress back and forth, continually fanning herself and staring at him with her piercing blue eyes that contrasted her black hair.

Admittedly, she was annoyed by his lack of knowledge of her presence. He was caught up in the song he and his family were playing. She couldn't hear it over the sound coming out of her heart pulsating in her ears. His music, on the other hand, well… it was just noise to her at this point. It was a masterpiece to him. He was taken by the melody. She was taken by him.

She turned and was about to leave when out of the corner of her eye, she caught Jack looking. He beamed at the sight of her. She smiled in return and grabbed at her dress nervously. He felt light headed and smitten. Embarrassed, the young man quickly turned his attention to his fingers and focused on the strings of his guitar.

He looked up again and his eyes widened. She wondered at the concern she saw in them until the issue manifested itself.

"Oh gosh!" she said, startled at the overgrown, hairy teenage boy now staring at her, blocking her vision of Jack.

"Care to dance?" the deep, husky voice said.

"No, I uh…"

He didn't hear her or didn't care and grabbed her hands and pulled her into the dancing circle. It wasn't considered good manners for a lady to turn someone down for a dance, even if his smell of sweat repulsed her.

She found herself enjoying it, even if it was Lawrence. More than anything, she watched how jealous Jack seemed to be out of the corner of her eye. Not that he had anything to be jealous about, but she could see he was, and there was nothing he could do about it while he played his guitar from the small stage.

She smiled at Lawrence, who was taking the dancing a little too seriously. His face showed stress and she could tell he was concentrating on his overgrown feet. Any moment he could trip on them and hurt them both. She knew that, and yet couldn't help but giggle.

He was an over-sized oaf. He wasn't bad looking. In fact, some girls in the village would probably consider him a prize. He had the strength of an ox. He had a beautifully chiseled face, light hair, and blue eyes like hers. But where he excelled in brute strength and looks, he lacked in the smarts department. She had never had a conversation with him, and didn't think he was capable of more than a few words. Sure, he could speak, but not at a level that would intrigue her.

Margarete was a thinker. She found stimulation in conversation and culture. Perhaps that's why she was so intrigued by the skinny, lanky Jack. He had been all over the world. He was intelligent. He would talk for hours about his adventures, and his face would light up with each question she asked. Her growing interest in him was a result of such conversations. It also helped that he spoke several languages. Who could turn down a man who was eloquent with his words?

"You're pretty."

Whiter Than Snow

She was interrupted from her daydream of her music man.

"Uh...thank you, Lawrence."

She felt him breathing on her neck.

"What are you doing?"

"You smell pretty, too."

"It's not me. It's the flowers."

She was a little embarrassed, noticing the other teenage girls watching them.

"When will you be my girl and marry me?" he asked.

She knew he had a crush on her—he made it pretty clear over the years. But this was the first time he had acted so boldly. She knew he wasn't serious, but it caught her off guard. It must be the wedding. Something about weddings give young men courage to talk about love and pursue eligible women for marriage. And something about weddings also made young girls lose their head for an evening and fall into costly relational mistakes. She was wise enough to know this, not that she was even tempted by Lawrence. Gross.

The song quickly ended—not quickly enough, and Margarete thanked the oaf for the dance and walked away from the crowd. She watched Jack put his guitar down in the distance. She could go to him, but decided to make him chase her. It was a game, of course. *Every girl wants to be chased.* Inwardly she wanted to run to him as fast as she could and wrap her arms around him. She wished it could've been him dancing with her, and that he was the proposer.

She kept her back to where Jack had been, hoping for a warm surprise—hoping he would come up behind her and offer her tender words, seeking her attention. Or perhaps he would just touch her back softly, letting her know he was there.

"Stay away from Lawrence. He's mine," the voice called out from behind her.

Margarete turned around just in time to see a monstrous girl with nostrils flaring, heading straight for her like a wild boar in attack mode.

Although Margarete had no desire for Lawrence, the spirit of competition welled up inside of her. The more she thought about them as being a possible couple, the more she felt nauseated. Nonetheless, she attacked back.

"If he was yours, then why is he asking to dance with me?"

Bad choice of words.

"Listen here, skinny rat, you stay away from him or I'll make you wish you were dead."

Although Margarete was terrified, literally trembling inside, she wasn't one to back down. Luckily she didn't have to.

"What on earth are you two girls fighting about?" the familiar voice rang out.

The heavy set girl quickly defused.

"We're supposed to all be Christians, remember? We're a team."

It was Jack. Sweet Jack—*here to rescue me.*

Whiter Than Snow

He wrapped his arm around Margarete's persecutor. "You know I love you, Kit Kat! But please leave my sweet Margarete alone."

Margarete tilted her head and made a face at the girl. *Yeah, that's right, I'm his girl!*

The girl crossed her arms.

Of course, Jack had to bring up the Christian thing. Margarete did see the girl at the meetings. Funny how she never even knew her name, and she figured Kit Kat, or whatever Jack just called her, was a nick name. The girl never participated in their prayers, but at least she showed up to the meetings. Some thought she was a spy. Others thought she was just curious or bored. She usually stood in the back and listened without participation.

Why did she come, come to think of it? Perhaps it was to see Jack? He was the leader, after all. It wasn't to see Lawrence—he was never there. He was so steeped in Catholic tradition his parents would skin him alive if he even got near those secret meetings.

Why did she come? Perhaps the same reason all the others came. Perhaps the same reason Margarete came. There was something magical, almost mystical about the meetings.

Perhaps that was the right choice of words considering the underground group meetings were growing larger every minute, sweeping through the country like wildfire and transforming lives. Perhaps the mysticism about them is why they were under such persecution from the Catholic Church in the first place.

People couldn't help but come. There was a power drawing them...an invisible force...and Jack and his family were responsible for this, at least in Waldeck, anyway. At the end of one of their journeys, Jack, his brother, his mother, his sister, and his father came back as different people—especially Jack's father. At their yearly festival celebration for the good people of Waldeck, his family took the opportunity to share why, and Waldeck had never been the same.

Their world travels led them to cross paths with a famous Protestant Evangelist named John Foxe, who shared the truth about the Holy Scriptures to them and opened their eyes. This new form of Christianity—this new way of thinking—was different than the traditional Catholic beliefs they accepted for so many years.

Jack embraced the new teaching and preached it to the young people of Waldeck, which drew Margarete to him all the more. He spoke of a faith built on the foundation of love, mercy and grace. There was freedom in this religion. There was forgiveness. No longer were they bound by rules like silly children. Instead, all were motivated by love, remembering that love had its fullest form in Jesus, who loved everyone so much he was willing to die on the cross for them. *He didn't die for rules. He didn't die for politics. No, he died for love. He died to save us,* according to Jack. He was an idealist sold on the ideology of love, and his passion and views of life won Margarete's heart.

Oh, and there was power. This new Christianity had power. Not political power or the power of the monarchy...no. This was a different kind of overwhelming power—the power of the Holy Spirit. There was power when they prayed. They could feel it consuming them, enveloping them. It was the power to bring healing. It was the power of comfort. It was mysterious and supernatural. It changed hearts and lives. The Catholics considered it witchcraft. But the power came from the name of Jesus, and was the strongest when they sang to God. Jack said he could even feel it in the strum of his guitar. It couldn't be controlled or tamed. It couldn't be manipulated for political gain. It was no respecter of persons or of age.

Jack said that it was this power that brought his dad back from the dead. Not literally, but his dad was an alcoholic. Jack calls those days the dark days. However, after this magical encounter with the famous John Foxe, and after the evangelist prayed for him and he was touched by the Holy Ghost, his dad has never been the same. It is this testimony that changed the entire village. Margarete often wondered if this power could bring her parents back.

Her mother and her father, as well as her godmother, were Protestant Christians. In fact, they were one of the few believers in the area before Jack's parents shared their testimonies. Now most of the town was saved. *Saved from what?* Saved from hell and Satan and all his demons. Saved from themselves and the sinful desires of their flesh. Saved from empty, hollow, lifeless, religious tradition. *Saved by grace.*

Yes, she too was a believer. But it wasn't until Jack that she experienced a powerful encounter with the Holy Spirit. It was like meeting God in the flesh.

Kit Kat walked away and Margarete twirled a lock of her black hair, smiling flirtatiously at Jack.

"Sorry about that. My cousin can get a little over zealous at times."

"She's your cousin?"

"Second cousin, really."

Jack took Margarete's hand and the two young love birds found their way to the woods, out of sight by the other wedding guests. Margarete couldn't understand the sweat on Jack's forehead, or why his hands were so clammy. And she didn't know why they were walking deeper and deeper in the forest, with no sense of direction, without a single word being spoken. She was not one for the woods…or for walks.

Jack stopped, twirled Margarete around, and looked at her endearingly. "I know we're young, but…I…I think I love you."

"You think?" she laughed.

"I…I know I love you." He looked away, embarrassed. "You're the most beautiful girl I've ever seen, and I've been around the world… okay, not the world, but at least all of Europe."

He was floundering. She batted her eyelashes.

"Please marry me, Margarete?"

"Jack, people always get excited to get married at weddings, only to later regret it."

"I would never regret marrying you. I am crazy about you—I have been since our childhood."

Whiter Than Snow

"You used to put sand in my hair!"

He laughed nervously. "Because I liked you."

"Why are guys so weird like that?"

"Please marry me…" He knelt down on his knee.

She paused and breathed deeply. "I can't."

Margarete ran off, her face in her hands, sobbing. She wanted to marry him, but the thought of marrying so young frightened her. Sure, many girls got married at her age, but only when they were forced to for financial reasons or for politics, and usually to men much older.

Jack chased her around a tree, stopped her and held her. Her body was trembling. He lifted her head by her chin, and wiped away her tears. She stared at him with her water logged eyes.

"Please, tell me why."

"Jack, I've always loved you. But what happens when we get married and you have to go tour the world playing music? I'll be left alone at home for months on end. Doesn't your brother's wife even care she'll be home alone?"

"Then come with us! I'm sure my parents won't mind."

"Your parents? Sounds romantic," she retorted sarcastically.

"You can tour the world with me. We'll experience the world together. You won't regret it. I'll make you feel like a princess every day!"

She lowered her head. She did love him. She would even fantasize about their marriage in her early teen years. He would come play with her god-brother, and she would fantasize he came to see her.

He lifted her head again and wiped away more tears. He rubbed the palm of his hand along her soft, youthful, porcelain cheek. She gazed into his eyes and nodded. He didn't know if that meant a yes or a maybe, or what, but he accepted it as a yes. He cupped her face with his hands and pulled her to him. Their lips met. She gasped and turned away.

Then she reached for more. His lips were tender. His breath was warm. She closed her eyes and thought she saw stars. *Her first kiss.*

The young lovers could hear the music starting again in the distance. Margarete pulled away.

"Don't you need to get back?"

"They can wait a few minutes. They aren't helpless without me."

Margarete reached for a few more small kisses.

He delighted at her enthusiasm. "I'll be back in just over a month..."

She rolled her eyes, sighing. It was already starting. She would have to wait on him as he toured. She placed her head against his chest. He pushed her back so that her eyes met with his.

"Hey... It's just one month—we've been waiting a lifetime for this. As soon as I get back, we'll make it official—we'll start all the wedding plans, too. I love you."

She didn't say it back, but rather, breathed it like a sigh, "I love you, too..."

Whiter Than Snow

Jack ran off without his bride-to-be to join his musical family. It happened so fast that she didn't have time to respond—to yell in his direction and ask him to escort her back to the square. Her mind was swimming in thoughts of matrimony, but her spirit was on edge by the dark forest that surrounded her.

A cold chill breathed on her neck and she wrapped her arms around her body. She was alone. The realization stung. There was a darkness there, darker than the darkness she could see with her eyes—a darkness she could only sense with her spirit. It paralyzed her. In fear she trembled, slowly placing one foot in front of the other, letting her ears guide her out of such a murky place.

"Just follow the music," she whispered timidly to herself. She heard Jack's guitar in the distance and it soothed her.

Still, a small tear leaked from her left eye. She removed her hand from her body to wipe it and the cold air seeped in where her arm once covered her side. She felt naked and exposed.

The forest seemed to work its evil wonder, and as much as Margarete wanted to push those wretched thoughts out of her head, she couldn't. She looked up and saw the trees looming over her, choking the moonlight, whispering softly, yet forcefully—retelling the horrible events she tried so hard to forget.

Her jaw quivered as the tears began to pour. She was now swimming in this nightmare. It consumed her just like it did so many years before when she was just a child.

"Don't be afraid just pray...Don't be afraid just pray..." She repeated the words like a mantra. They were words of wisdom from Lucinda that she learned as a child. They weren't working in these heavy woods.

As the fear preyed upon her mind, the thought that Jack may never want to marry her if he knew the secrets of this forest floor threw her legs into a sprint so fast that she found her way out of the woods and crashing into Lawrence—who happened to be standing just a stone's throw away from the path.

Margarete didn't recognize the oversized hands that touched her at first, and she screamed such a blood curdling scream that made the young man tense up and hold her tighter, returning a scream of his own. Before she knew what she was doing, the palm of her hand went up and slammed into the oaf's nose, forcing him to let go. Blood gushed out as he fell to the ground.

"Lawrence?" she cried out.

He sat there holding his nose, looking up at Margarete, wiping blood on his shirt.

Chapter 3

It should have been a serene night's rest. The young man of her dreams just proposed. She just shared their first kiss—*her first kiss*! Not only that, but he wanted to take her around the world. *How romantic!*

However, it seemed the ghosts of the forest followed her home—to remind her—to make sure she didn't forget. How could she? Most people have nightmares. She only had one, and she lived through it…and in her dreams she relived this same nightmare over and over and over again since the tender age of twelve.

How a boy like Jack would still love her if he only knew. *Knew what?* That she was scared? That she lived in fear most of her life? That she didn't trust adults and she was terrified of the forest? Surely there was much more to it than that. She would love to share this nightmare with someone, but if he only knew he would abandon her she assumed.

The pretty young woman rested in her bed, her hair spread out above her as she combed strands with her fingers. Tears flooded her blueberry eyes.

Lucinda walked in with a brush and started gently brushing the young woman's satin hair. Margarete covered her wet face.

"Your hair is so beautiful," Lucinda complimented her.

The girl sniffed.

"What's wrong, dear? I saw you with Jack. Everything ok between you two?"

"Jack's wonderful," Margarete blurted, which threw her into a series of heavy sobs.

"Sweet child," Lucinda said softly, "then what's wrong?"

"I have to tell you something."

Pause.

"I'm listening, dear."

Sitting up on her bed, staring at her surrogate mother, the young woman sniffled and cried out, "Jack asked me to marry him!"

Lucinda laughed. "Then those are happy tears, I presume?"

Margarete fell back to a lying position. "Noooo…"

"I thought this was what you wanted? You've played as if you were marrying Jack since you were a little girl."

"I know."

"Then what is it?"

She propped herself up on her elbows and whimpered. "I'm not good enough for Jack."

Lucinda stood up from the bed and stared at the young woman, concerned. "You can't be serious?"

Whiter Than Snow

"I'm being serious."

"Dear child! That boy is lucky to have you. You are an amazing young woman who can cook and clean—you're intelligent, and you're beautiful. You are every boy's dream."

"You wouldn't understand…"

Lucinda sat back down. Margarete turned over on her stomach. The lovely woman gently touched the teenager's back.

"Tell me, dear child, what's troubling you?"

The beauty sat there silently, her lips sealed as if a demon itself were clamping it shut. Her eyes searched back and forth, hoping for words to spring forth from her mouth, but nothing came out.

Eventually, under the sweet finger-tipped tickles on her back by her surrogate mother, Margarete fell asleep. Perhaps she wouldn't have the nightmare tonight—perhaps not this time.

Morning came quicker than expected. The blinding rays of sunlight penetrated the window and kissed Margarete on the face. She sat up, yawned, and rubbed her eyes groggily. She heard Lucinda stirring in the kitchen downstairs and lazily rose out of bed, walking over to the mirror and looking into it. She gave it a *drop dead* look, rolled her eyes, and walked away.

"Good morning, darling," Lucinda said as she brought Margarete a tray full of food.

"What are you doing?"

"I'm bringing you breakfast in bed."

"No…I mean, you aren't supposed to make me breakfast."

The kind soul placed the food on the foot of the bed.

"Margarete, honey, you've been so good to me, cooking for me and your brother all these years. I think I have the right to spoil you if I want to."

This drew a smile from the black haired maiden.

Margarete fell back on her bed and munched on a piece of toast.

"You know what I think you need? I think you need to get out of here."

"What?"

"Go for a walk in the woods," smiled Lucinda.

This stung. Margarete didn't answer, nor would she. She wanted to tell Lucinda about her horrible, traumatic experience, but she didn't have the courage. How would Lucinda see her then? Would she want to throw her out?

"No…" Margarete spoke softly, after clearing her throat. "No!" She said it again, bolder, in case she wasn't clear the first time.

"Alright, then. How about you and I take a special trip to a special wedding?"

Margarete shrugged her shoulders. A wedding would make her miss Jack all the more.

"How about a special wedding at a special castle?" Lucinda added.

Whiter Than Snow

Margarete's reserves disappeared and joy exuded from her face. "Really? They're finally getting married? Which castle?" the teenager asked eagerly.

Matthew Eldridge

Chapter 4

The Wedding

"But still, it's a little odd, don't you think?" Margarete asked as she stood behind the throng of people in the cool morning air.

"I don't know."

"But why not the big palace in Brussels? Why so close to Waldeck at a palace half its size?"

"I assume she wanted a smaller wedding; perhaps much like the queen before her."

"It just doesn't make sense. Why come to a castle that's been abandoned and a town who doesn't know you anymore to celebrate your wedding day?"

"Silly child, you're wearing me out," Lucinda answered. "Besides, if it wasn't here, we wouldn't have been able to come. I thought you'd be excited."

"Oh, I am! I am!"

"Perhaps one day you'll get to see the big castle in Brussels."

"Perhaps!" Margarete smiled, imagining Jack taking her there on one of their many future travels.

The palace courtyard was crowded with hundreds of souls, surrounding a purple carpet where the king and his new bride would ascend to the altar. It was the end to the king's lonely years after losing his first wife and child. And while Lucinda and Margarete may never know the truth about why the wedding was so close to Waldeck, their assumption about the queen wanting a smaller wedding was partially correct.

The truth was threefold. While her new husband was king over the land from Brussels to Waldeck, and everything in between, there was a great political war of power taking place. A new queen meant a new threat—and a largely publicized wedding could be the very end of her life. What better way for a competing kingdom to flex its muscle than at a wedding ceremony! The queen also had secret relations in these parts of the woods, and her husband wanted to re-establish his authority with the smaller areas of his domain, connecting with the people—his deceased wife's people.

How he chose his royal bride, no one knew. But her charm won his heart, or his flesh, so they say. The kingdom had not seen her yet, and this wedding ceremony would give both the Aristocracy and the peasants an opportunity to witness her beauty for the first time.

The altar was stuffed with an assortment of colorful flowers and candles. A sea of tulips waved in the wind as the gentle breeze blew their fresh aroma towards the crowd.

Whiter Than Snow

Margarete and Lucinda watched from fifty yards away through cracks between the crowd and soldiers that outlined the carpet and the altar.

"I wonder what it looks like in there!" day dreamed an excited teenager, Margarete, pointing to the entrance of the castle.

"It's beautiful!"

"I wish I could go in."

"Be careful what you wish for, dear."

Margarete beamed and stood on her tip-toes to see. "I can't believe you lived there!"

"I was serving the king and queen. That's hardly living. And I spent most of my time in the bigger castle, in Brussels."

"I couldn't imagine being a queen, living in such an enviable place, having people serve you...all these people watching you!"

Lucinda paused for a moment, then, grabbed Margarete by the arm, forcing her to stand flat-footed and look into her eyes.

"Margie, look at me. That's not what being a queen is about. A good king and queen are to be the greatest servants of all. Their job is to serve the people in this kingdom—to make sure they are provided for, well fed, educated, and protected. The queen I served was a woman who understood that. She was compassionate and loving. She would give all she had for the people in this kingdom! She hated living in such a place."

"She hated living here?"

"She hated that she had so much, and there were so many without. That's why she loved the summer cottage in Waldeck. It made her feel more like a commoner."

"What happened to her?"

"She died, giving birth, long ago."

"Oh dear…"

"I'd rather not talk…"

Lucinda was interrupted by the cheering crowds as the new queen approached the castle in a horse-drawn carriage.

"She's here! She's here! The queen is here," Margarete gasped. "I can't believe it!

Young flower girls painted the carpet with soft rose petals as the queen exited the carriage with the help of her chauffeur and began her glorious march to the altar.

Margarete gasped, "She's so beautiful!"

The bride walked with elegance; her head was held high and poised. Her face was long, her high cheek bones full of color. Her skin was as soft as rose petals. She was breathtaking. It was obvious why the king chose her, if based on beauty alone. He was graying; she was twenty years his junior, at least.

"She looks like she's gliding on air," Margarete observed. "She's wonderful!"

The commoners bowed as the majestic couple walked by.

"Look at the way she holds her head—I've never seen anything like it!"

"You're young," Lucinda responded.

"Have you ever seen such a sight?"

Whiter Than Snow

"As a matter of fact, I have."

The wedding was like a magical fairy tale dream world to Margarete. The voices faded from all around her. The sounds subsided in her head and the crowd seemed to dissipate in this vision of hers. Perhaps it was only a daydream, or perhaps it was a vision. She saw herself in a beautiful wedding dress—she was royalty, and a prince, yes, a beautiful prince was walking with her down the aisle. Ah, the fantasies of a teenage girl.

Margarete talked non-stop on their journey home, questioning Lucinda about castle life, kingdoms, relationships, royal fashion and more. She couldn't help but notice that the king and queen weren't an exact fit, and Lucinda's explanation that marriage for the wealthy was usually for political reasons and not for love just wasn't comprehendible to her.

"Well thank God I'm not wealthy."

"Why's that dear?"

"I would hate to marry for the wrong reasons."

"And what's the right reason?"

"You know…love," she said with a soft smile.

Lucinda returned a smile of her own. "Well, I wish the best of luck to you and Jack."

Margarete looked down at her feet. She wanted to smile, but guilt overwhelmed her. There was a cold nip in the air, and the sun began to set behind the distant hills. They would've stayed in town a little longer, but Margarete requested they return before dark. Unfortunately, it appeared that darkness would beat them home. The child walked nervously with her adoptive mother.

"So tell me, how did Jack propose?"

Glancing around the forest, the young bride-to-be fidgeted with her lips, trying to distract herself from fear. "Are we lost?"

Lucinda answered, "We'll be fine. I know my way through these forests. If we just had more daylight—that would help."

Margarete's fear grew in her stomach like a cancer. She wanted to vomit. She never ventured into the forest at night. Never. Not since she was twelve.

"Jack's proposal?"

"Oh..." The child had been distracted. "It was...different really."

"Uh-huh."

"He...well...he took me into the woods and told me he loved me and that he wanted to marry me."

Lucinda grinned. "He kissed you, didn't he?"

Margarete gasped and relaxed. "Yes!"

"Kissing always leads to crying," her godmother said, laughing at the teenage beauty.

Before Margarete could respond, the two were enveloped in light, which was odd for this late of an hour. The glow appeared to come from a group of miniature lights floating by which resembled fireflies, and yet...they were smaller than any firefly Margarete had ever seen. The tiny lights led them to the heart of a village. It was as if they were blinded by conversation until now—but a small village surrounded them. People encircled them from every angle, almost oblivious to their presence.

Being strangers and women, the two should have been frightened by the odd little village which resembled something ancient, but they weren't. There was something about these people. Their faces were kind, and although none of them spoke a word, Margarete could tell they were all friendly.

"Hello. Are you lost?" the sweet voice called out.

Lucinda turned around to see a beautiful woman with fiery red hair and soft milky skin standing before her.

"Um. I don't think so."

"Would you like a place to stay for the night?"

"Well, if you could just point us in the right direction…"

"In the morning," the voice commanded. "Tonight you need your sleep. The forest is a dangerous place. You'll be well protected in the village."

"Um…might I ask," said Lucinda, "just where are we? What village is this? I've lived here all my life and I've never seen it before."

The red-headed woman with gentle eyes sighed and said, "You're not far from home. Now come—"

"Thank you, but we really aren't far…"

Margarete interrupted Lucinda, "I'd like to stay. Please? It looks like a cute little village."

"Very well, then," Lucinda answered.

The red-headed woman nodded, then disappeared.

A young cobbler emerged and took the women to a cabin and said, "You may stay here for the night. May I have your shoes please?"

"Our shoes?" returned Margarete.

"Yes. They need a-fixin'. Your shoes take you on your journey. If your shoes aren't right, they may just take you on a journey you aren't supposed to be on—and they can cause you a lot of pain on that journey."

"Will we have them back by morning?"

He chuckled. "Why yes, dear woman. It won't take me long to fix them."

The two women slipped off their shoes, gave them to the cobbler, and entered the home. It was a tiny cabin with one warm, cozy bed for the two women to share. A candle flickered on the bedside table.

There was an overwhelming feeling of love in the room. The girls couldn't explain it, but it was there, consuming them with warmth, and within minutes of lying under the covers, they were fast asleep.

Morning came without warning. Margarete woke to the sounds of a gurgling brook singing a lullaby, just yards away. The air was silent, except for a few caws by a crow flying by. She slowly opened her eyes to view it. Seeing the bare, blue sky overhead, the young woman quickly sat up, and looked to Lucinda who was lying beside her on the bare grass. The cabin they fell asleep in no longer existed. Margarete nudged the woman she called mom.

"Wake up!"

Startled, Lucinda quickly opened her eyes and sat up. Confusion didn't quite describe the look on her face. She took a cursory glance around the open field surrounding them.

"What…where…?"

"Yeah…" Margarete answered, knowing what Lucinda was thinking and wondering the same thing.

Lucinda looked down, shook her head and exhaled. "What did I drink last night?"

She took a longer look at the field around her. No trace of homes, livestock, or people. The field was empty—with no signs of the previous night. The village was gone.

"Nothing…"

"How did…whoa!" She shook her head again and looked up at the sun. "I must've had some crazy dream."

"You weren't dreaming," answered Margarete.

"How do you know?"

"Fireflies? A beautiful redheaded woman? A cobbler? A house?"

"I guess you do know," she said, shaking her head again. "But how'd we get there…I mean, how'd we get here? Where'd it all go?"

Margarete inspected the ground. "Maybe it was all just a dream, and we were both in it."

Matthew Eldridge

Remembering the cobbler, Margarete quickly reached for her shoes and noticed that they were, in fact, fixed as new, with no explanation.

With one final look, Lucinda inspected the place, only to find that they were in the field just a few feet off their path, and only an hour's walk from home.

The shrubbery thinned and the trees peeled back, exposing the blue morning sky above as they walked. Margarete pointed to the thick cloud of smoke billowing before them, a few hundred yards up the trail.

"Looks like someone's burning something."

Lucinda answered, "Probably just clearing the woods for a new home."

As the girls approached the area, they saw the smoke coming from a charred home.

"Oh dear," Lucinda commented. She stepped closer. There was no movement in the blackened house covered in ash. "I don't like this at all."

The women continued their journey.

Ten minutes later, they came upon another partially charred home. This time, a man was strapped to a tree. An arrow pierced his cheek and struck through the other side of his mouth, and into the wood, leaving the man's head pinned against the tree. Lucinda approached him cautiously. He appeared unconscious…or dead. She kept her eye on the man while speaking to Margarete.

Whiter Than Snow

"Check the house, make sure no one's inside!"

Margarete nodded and scampered to the door. It was already cracked open.

"Hello? Hello? Anyone home?"

Lucinda tapped the shoulder of the man stuck to the tree several times. He remained unconscious. She felt his hand and it was still warm. There was life. She didn't want to untie him. She feared him falling from the tree and tearing the skin on his face even more. The weight of the arrow couldn't hold him.

Margarete pressed the door and it squeaked. She peered in, taking a few steps towards the light shining through a window. The home had been destroyed as if a tornado ripped through the insides.

"Hello?" she called again. No one was there.

Lucinda carefully inspected the arrow in the man's mouth. Should she try to remove it while he was still unconscious, passed out? Or should she wake him? She gently placed her hands on the arrow and closed her eyes. She took a deep breath and tugged. The arrow didn't budge. It was penetrated too deep into the wood. She looked again at the man's mouth, this time taking a closer look at his wounds. She wanted to throw up. She didn't know how she was stomaching this. It must have been God's grace, she assumed—because in this moment, she was the only one who could save this man. She wrapped her hands on the arrow's end again and pulled. The man moaned. Still, the tree gripped harder.

"Dear God," Lucinda prayed out loud. By now, Margarete made her way out of the house and back to Lucinda. "You don't want to see this. Was there anyone in there?" she addressed the teen.

"No," Margarete answered while trying to look away, but yet she couldn't peel her eyes from the poor man's face.

Lucinda yanked one last time, grunting as she pulled. The man's head dislodged from the tree as the arrow came loose. The jerking woke him.

He opened his eyes warily. "Help me," he said with a mouth full of dried blood, and then shut them again.

Margarete couldn't fight the tears streaming from her eyes as she watched the helpless man. She reached behind the tree and quickly untied his hands. He fell limp onto Lucinda, who lowered him gently to the ground. Luckily, he was a skinny man.

The man touched his face and started crying. His body convulsed in shock.

"Shhhhhhh. You're going to be okay," Lucinda said in a soothing, motherly tone. "Let's get him inside!" she said to Margarete.

The two women helped the man to his feet. Margarete propped his arm up around her. Lucinda did the same thing on the other side. They pulled the man inside the home and laid him on the bed.

The man was still incoherent.

"Do you have any liquor?" Lucinda asked. "Do you have any liquor? Hello? Do you have any liquor in the house?"

He slowly lifted a finger and pointed to a cabinet. Margarete scurried to it and opened it. She pulled a bottle from the shelf and gave it to Lucinda. Lucinda ripped the lid off and poured it on the man's wounds. He grimaced in pain.

"What are you doing?" Margarete asked.

"This'll clean his wounds."

"I'm sure if he drinks it, he won't feel them, either."

"Poor soul, I don't know if he's able to drink at this point. Magarete, I need you to run to the house and get me a sewing needle, and some…"

"What? I don't know how to get home from here," she interrupted, terrified.

Lucinda could see the anxiety in her eyes. "Just stay on the straight path, you're less than thirty minutes away. You can do it. You're almost a grown woman. I commandeered these woods as a young girl."

Margarete looked to the door teary-eyed, then back to the man. "What are you going to do with him?"

"I need to sew him up, which is why I need you to hurry. The longer we wait, the worse it's going to be. And maybe by then he can tell us who did such a thing to him."

Matthew Eldridge

Chapter 5

A few days had passed, and the young woman couldn't stop thinking about castle life—and her future husband, Jack. It didn't seem real. She felt like a child about to play house with a boy.

She counted the days until his return. At the same time, she rehearsed in her head over and over telling him it wouldn't work. She was torn—as any girl would be. Why wouldn't she marry him? She would never tell. She *could* never tell.

Margarete busied herself cutting potatoes when a knock from the front door echoed through the house. "Open up by the order of the king!" The voice shouted from the other side.

The king? Margarete ran around in circles, unsure of what to do. She truly wasn't presentable, she assumed. *Oh dear, what to do, what to do!* She quickly untied the apron around her waist, forgetting the bonnet on her head, and scurried towards the door. *Oh dear!* She felt the bonnet. Her black hair was a mess beneath it.

Lucinda smiled at the nervous teenager and walked calmly towards the door and gradually opened it.

"Madam, the king requests your services at his summer chateau! You will serve him immediately, beginning Monday morning! That is all!"

"Summer chateau? The king hasn't been there in years," she responded, her voice trailing off as she closed the door behind her.

Margerete grabbed her hands and began shouting, "Oh my gosh! The king? The king! You're going to work for the king again?"

"No dear. You are."

"What?"

"I'm too old for this kind of work. You're young and full of life. It's your turn. You will go in my place."

"Godmother! I don't know what to say? What if I mess up? What will I do?"

"Dear child—you already know how to cook, sew, and clean. What more is there for a king?"

"Oh Godmother, I'm scared! I've never been in the presence of royalty before!"

"They're no different than anyone else. The king is very down to earth; he'll like you."

"What about the queen?"

"Well, I don't know her, dear. But if she's anything like the first queen, she'll love you. She was a charming, sweet soul. She loved children, and she loved God. I miss her so. Sometimes when I look at you…I…"

Lucinda stopped in mid-sentence, and turned to the blanket she was folding.

"You…what? Godmother?"

Whiter Than Snow

She paused for a moment, took a deep breath…"Well, you just remind me a lot of her, that's all."

"I remind you of the queen? Really?"

"The king's first wife; you have similar eyes to her. She was a very beautiful woman!"

"So is the new queen! She is the most beautiful woman I've ever seen!" Margarete responded, picking up her apron and twirling it around the room like a school girl pretending to be a princess at a royal ball.

"Well, if she's as sweet as she is beautiful, she'll love you, dear one."

Lucinda spent the evening sewing a proper dress for the new servant of the king. It was as cheerful as the child herself. Margarete worked on setting the table for royalty, pretending she was serving the king and queen.

"Oh dear, Godmother, I can't do this! Do the blades turn in or away from the plates in a royal home? I can't seem to remember!"

"Calm down, child! You'll do fine!"

"And I'll never get this curtsy down! Oh, I'm doomed! I really don't want to go! All the things I can normally do—suddenly I can't do them… or remember them."

"Margarete, dear, all your life you've asked me questions about the king, queen, and their palace. It's time for you to experience it."

The teenager laughed. "I don't believe the summer royal cottage is quite a palace!" She began setting the table again. "Oh, I just can't believe it. I'm going to be in the presence of royalty!"

"Child, don't forget—you're the daughter of the true King. You *are* royalty!"

"What?"

"Jesus! You're a Christian, child! That makes you a child of God! And he's the King of all kings!"

"That's true, Godmother," she giggled. Her face sobered as she looked to Lucinda. "What about Jack?"

"What about him? You'll be back before he is. This is just a small get-away for the royal couple, perhaps."

Chapter 6

The summer estate was anything but a kingly cottage. In fact, it was an undersized castle nestled deep in the trees, just a stone's throw from the homes of commoners in the village. Sure, there were a number of summer homes owned by the aristocracy nearby, but all were settled very close to one another, and only separated from peasants by a thick hill, a stream, and a thin forest.

With anticipation, the young teen of Waldeck made her way into the oversized chalet and inspected her room, which was about three times the size of her room in the village. It took great restraint not to scream from her excitement. She danced around the space, rubbing her hands on the beautiful bedspread, then to the window, humming a tune that matched the birds singing outside. It was a new morning—a new beginning!

After unpacking her things, she readied herself in the kitchen, as instructed by the king's driver who picked her up just before sunrise. It was quite shocking that the king and queen had such few servants at the cottage, but understandable at the same time. They wanted privacy. This must have been their honeymoon, she assumed.

The child nervously began her duties, anticipating her first meeting with the royal family. As she set the table, she could hear the king discussing breakfast with his wife as they traveled down the royal hallway. She scuttled out of the dining hall and watched over the eggs. Listening intently through the doorway as the king and queen approached their chairs, her heart was beating faster than she thought was possible to still be alive. Time stood still. The moment she'd been waiting for and dreading at the same time was upon her.

"Does she not remember to have our breakfast on the table when we arrive?" Margarete heard the queen bark at her husband.

"Lucinda!" the king called. He addressed his wife, "She's really very good."

Margarete walked out, head low, and placed a dish of hardboiled eggs on the center of the table.

Both the king and queen watched the tense child.

"Hello," the king said, staring at the girl in wonder.

"Hello," Margarete answered, in a soft, almost non-existent voice, just before disappearing into the kitchen and reappearing with a plate full of toast.

The king couldn't help but laugh. He was addressing the child. Lucinda would've understood to stop and pay attention to her king when spoken to.

"You aren't Lucinda," said the king, bemused.

"No, I'm not…I'm really…" her voice trailed off as she exited the room again, anxiously trying to relieve her shyness.

"Young servant! Do you not understand to stop in a king's presence and listen to him?" the queen yelled to her.

Whiter Than Snow

Margarete walked out of the kitchen slowly, this time with a special French pastry she hand-made for the king, the recipe and idea a hint from Lucinda. She placed the pastry on the table.

The king's eyes were dreamy with delight. "Who are you, child?" the king addressed.

"I'm...I'm..."

"Do you not know who you are?" barked the queen.

The woman was already proving to be difficult. Margarete inhaled a wisp of air and answered, "Lucinda is my mother."

"Your mother? I didn't know she had a daughter," the king responded. "Did she remarry?"

"I'm her goddaughter, really."

"What's your name, child?"

"Mmmm...Margarete."

The queen ordered without even looking at the girl, "Well Margarete, I'll have buttered eggs. Whites only!"

"Yes, Your Highness."

Margarete retired to her room after the kitchen was clean and sulked for the next fifteen minutes on her bed. She replayed the morning's events in her head, and wondered how she could have screwed everything up so badly.

I just wanted to make a good impression, she thought to herself. She had hoped to redeem herself with a wonderful lunch. The king and queen were traveling and had requested a picnic basket. She assumed this would be a much easier task since she wouldn't have to physically be in their presence serving them, offering her another opportunity to falter.

Ah, and then the dinner preparation would start, intertwined with cleaning. To royalty, this was the most important meal of the day. She better not screw this one up! They would beat her for sure, or worse yet, hang her! She had heard horror stories about royalty abusing servants from other kingdoms, although Lucinda assured her that the king had always treated the queen's servants like family. Besides, they were no longer living in the 1300's!

The setting sun's rays painted the dining hall through the windows and silhouetted the queen's frame with a glorious amber glow. Margarete was captivated by the woman as she made her way to her chair. Her eyes followed the royal bride.

The table was dressed with a fine meal: turkey, fruits, nuts, eggs, vegetables, bread and soup. Ah, and let's not forget the king's favorite wine.

"What do you think we are, swine? We can't eat this much food, child! You have stuffed us today! This is preposterous!"

Margarete ignored the comment by the queen, dipped her ladle in the pot, retrieved the soup, and gently poured it before her in a bowl. It was a special soup, one that Lucinda taught her to make for the king; his favorite. She had hoped to please him. She couldn't help but to glance at the queen's striking face as she served her.

"It's not polite to stare," the queen said flatly.

"I'm sorry. You are very beautiful," Margarete said timidly.

"Do you not know that you are not to speak unless we ask you a question, child? I simply made a comment, not a question," the queen replied, then, addressed the king. "Why didn't this Lucinda of yours show up?"

Though her words were harsh, the queen reveled in the girl's response. A smile cracked from her lips, but was short-lived as she watched the king gawking at the beautiful young woman serving them.

Margarete walked over to the king, poised and graceful (for she had been practicing), and poured soup into his bowl as well.

She watched him closely as he smiled at the meal before him, recognizing the mushrooms and onions swirling around in the soup before they settled on the sides and bottom of his bowl.

"I haven't had this in years," he said with a jolly laugh.

A hint of a smile slipped through the sides of the girl's mouth, and the exasperated queen took notice.

"Spppppppptthhhhhhht," the queen shouted as she spewed her soup out. "Are you trying to kill us? That tastes like poison! Where did you find those mushrooms?"

The king sipped the delicious soup from his spoon.

"Don't eat it! It's poison!" the queen yelled.

However, it was too late. He savored the taste, swishing the soup in his mouth before gently swallowing.

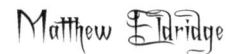

"MmmMMmmm," he sighed.

"I said don't eat it!"

He placed the spoon beside the bowl. "Well if I die, at least I'll die a happy man. The soup is fine, dear," he gently corrected the queen, while looking to Margarete.

With eyes narrowing, the queen threw her napkin down and accused, "And just who are you calling dear? Me? Or her?" She threw back her chair and stormed out of the room, and out the main hall of the cottage. Margarete and the king watched in silence.

The king picked his spoon back up and continued sipping on his soup. It was obvious that Margarete was upset, fearing that the king would be disappointed with her as well.

"The meal looks wonderful. Why don't you have a seat and share it with me?" he addressed the teen.

Margarete just stared at him, terrified.

"No sense in letting it go to waste. Come on, have a seat," he prodded.

"In the queen's chair?"

He nodded to the chair adjacent to him. She slowly walked over to it.

"Have a seat…and don't worry about the queen. She'll warm up to you. She's had a rough day."

She slowly pulled the chair out from the table, folded her skirt under, and sat down, uncomfortably.

"Please eat!" he suggested. "Everything smells delicious. You did a marvelous job. Lucinda taught you well."

Whiter Than Snow

Margarete took a few small bites of her bread, uncomfortably watching the king eat his meal. Lucinda was right—his eyes were warm and inviting.

"Your hair, child…are you a Sicilian?"

"I am a Christian…"

The king chuckled. "No dear, I mean are you from Sicily?"

"Oh," she answered, embarrassed, "I'm not sure…"

"Well either you are or you aren't."

"I was raised by my godmother," she answered.

"Lucinda? She's a wonderful woman, isn't she? She served me and my…well…she served me for years. She was like family."

"She is my family. She's all I've known."

"Well, if you are anything like her, you will do well serving the king."

"She told me you are a Christian."

"Hmmph," the king almost choked on a turkey bone, peeling the meat off with his teeth. After releasing some of it from his mouth, he answered, "I gave up on God a long time ago…"

The young girl looked down at her plate, discouraged. She didn't know what to say.

The king twisted his head to the side as if he received a new revelation. "Or…perhaps God gave up on me?"

As the sun descended, the naked moon climbed the sky, providing a veiled light to the coven of witches who met deep within the womb of the woods. A pot brewed in the middle of them. One stirred while another rang the neck of a chicken, smearing its blood over her, then, dumping the remains into the pot. A third chanted a message…

"Moon and stars and guiding hands, show us how to win this land. Kingdoms come and kingdoms fall, who's the fairest of them all? Let our queen take the throne, and with her power, this land we'll own."

The coven of witches cackled in laughter, dancing around the fire and brew. Each took turns sipping from the stew, their eyes reflecting greed and trickery scheming in their minds.

"Speak to us now, spirits of old, how to tame the weary soul. The king—he must lose all he can, what can stop our master's plan? His bride—who is—now takes this land."

The witch with the chicken blood on her face poured letters in a silver bowl and mingled the blood of the chicken and a frog. She broke an egg over it, the chicken's child, and twisted the bowl to see the signs from the dark one.

"Oh witches! Do beware—a princess, coming here… She is our doom, she is our nightmare!"

Whiter Than Snow

The queen sat in the midst of the witches. She gently spoke, "A princess? There are no princesses here! And I have no sons to find such a princess!"

"Unless the king…yes, the king—he had a daughter once, had he not?" One of the wenches addressed her, "Has he not told his bride of his child?"

"He won't talk about her. Only that she died long ago."

"She lives. Where she lives we do not know. But she lives."

"We must find her…and kill her. I won't have my throne or my power challenged," the queen raged.

Matthew Eldridge

Whiter Than Snow

Chapter 7

The week seemed to pass by rather quickly to the servant girl, who had mastered the cleaning and cooking for the royal couple. And while she hardly spoke five words to the queen, the gorgeous royal woman seemed to grow accustomed to the quiet teenager.

Margarete learned their preferred meals and portions, but always made a point to add something extra special of her own recipe for the king. Not only was she a wonderful cook and homemaker, her timid, humble attitude pleased the king, too. And while the queen felt threatened by the beautiful child by looks alone, she knew her husband and king well enough to know that he would never go after someone, or some *thing* so young—especially a lowly servant. The king had too much integrity for that. However, she did catch him from time to time staring at the child. She questioned him once, only to hear him say that the girl's eyes reminded him so much of someone he once knew. The queen assumed he was speaking of her godmother, Lucinda.

Cottage life was becoming a comfortable routine. Her duties weren't much different than her duties at home with Lucinda. Margarete would use the early morning hours to do her dusting and cleaning, just after breakfast, and before making the royal lunch. And although she listened to the king and avoided the room just east of the kitchen, something drew her to that very room. Perhaps nothing more than curiosity mixed with teenage rebellion, but drawn she was.

She pushed the door open, which creaked and popped—dust falling from the crevices where it had settled over the years. Through the crack she could see a bed covered in beautiful linens. She pushed her way in, and her body began trembling. It was as if the weight of the world crashed upon her. Perhaps because she knew she wasn't supposed to be in there. Perhaps there was something more.

Her knees buckled under her and she found herself in a chair next to the bed, dizzy. She wanted to touch the bed—she wanted to mourn. Her heart was heavy as if an invisible elephant sat upon it. Tears trickled down her cheeks, and yet she didn't know why.

The door creaked and startled the young woman. She quickly stood up, broom still in hand, and the king entered the room. He wanted to yell at the girl, but after witnessing the tears that covered her face, he couldn't bring himself to it. He had already warmed up to the girl, and he realized that she had a gift—not just any gift, but a God-given gift. It was a gift he had seen in his previous wife. It was compassion mingled with discernment. It was the gift to feel the pain of the wounded—the gift of love for those who were hurting.

Only to Margarete, it was so much more. She felt something beyond discernment…she felt connected to this room. Both compassion and pain consumed her. How could it be that she felt such strong emotions over a room—over a place she'd never been? Or had she?

"This is a private room," the king said gently.

"I'm sorry, I was just…"

"I understand," he interrupted.

The king wanted to hug her, but refrained. Even with the purest of intentions, if the queen were to see him, it would mean trouble for the young girl. Still, her tears touched him. She was a gentle soul, and her presence during the past week had comforted him—not just with wonderful food, but something about her spirit. The queen could be very strong-headed at times, but he felt that Margarete's soothing presence brought a peace to the small castle that wouldn't be there otherwise.

"I wanted to thank you for your service this week. Lucinda will be compensated well."

"Thank you, Your Highness."

He turned for the door, then, turned to face her again. His eyes began to water as he focused on the beautiful bedspread.

"My wife…my *first* wife, died in this room long ago," he said, choked with emotion.

"I'm so sorry, Your Highness," she said as she bowed her head.

The ruler stepped out of the room, made his way towards the main hallway, turned around and smiled at Margarete. For a moment, he saw his first wife walking out of the room—in the form of Margarete. He could swear his wife was staring back at him through the young girl's tender eyes. He knew that his own eyes were playing tricks on him and he dismissed it. But at least now, he understood why Margarete's eyes seemed so familiar, and why he'd warmed up to her so quickly. She reminded him of the first queen, minus the black hair, of course.

"Dear…," and then he realized he accidentally called her by such a name, "Margarete, we leave for Brussels on Tuesday. Would you be willing to serve us at the palace?"

She put her hand to her chest, unsure.

"Your duties would be shared by others, of course. It's a beautiful place. I think you will enjoy it," the king said.

Chapter 8

The young, blue-eyed woman sat on her bed daydreaming about Brussels. She weighed her options carefully. She had dreamed about being in a castle ever since she was a little girl, and although, as Lucinda said, she'd be there to serve, it would be a welcome new experience all the same.

It did occur to her that the queen wasn't exactly the easiest person to work for, and that her situation might worsen in the castle. At the same time, there was more room to hide—she could get her duties done (which would be considerably less, overall) and then retire to her room, far away from the voices that carried through the hallways.

Ah, and then there was Jack; Jack, her love; Jack, her first kiss. Jack, the boy of her dreams who proposed to her on a warm night. Oh, how she wished the two dreams would mesh together, and Jack could be with her in the castle, and that she was there to live, not serve.

But she had to be real. Young love doesn't always last, she believed. People grow and change. She thought perhaps one day she would fall in love with an older man who had reached a level of maturity. Such a man wouldn't change, not much anyway. Perhaps such a man could take care of her and provide security and safety. Jack was in no condition to take care of her. He still lived with his parents, for heaven's sake. Besides, he was a touring musician—she couldn't take that away from him. He loved the road, and it wasn't fair to expect him to drag her along—nor could he afford it. And she didn't want to be home alone without him for nine months out of the year. What kind of marriage was that? And although she always loved him, the back of her mind wondered if there was another, perhaps if she was out of Waldeck? There was a great big world out there to discover—so much greater than her tiny village…which made her wonder why Jack would choose her. He was blessed to see the world and all the beautiful women in it, and yet, he loved her. It made her feel special.

Who was she fooling? She was madly in love with Jack. Jack—the boy so full of life and color, the boy who knew more about the world than most men three times his age. Jack: the boy who spoke as a man and loved God with his entire being. Jack, the young melody maker who played the guitar like it was an extension of his arm. Jack—the perfect catch. Yes, perfect; too perfect…*too perfect for me.*

It was as if a cold, moist draft worked its way into her room, around her bed, and seized her body. She shivered. She saw nothing, but felt something—icy, boney fingers grabbing at her head and heart.

It was the forest—or the memory of it, anyway. It came up through her gut and expelled the warmth in her soul. She turned on herself.

Whiter Than Snow

Why was she even daydreaming about Jack? What was she thinking even entertaining such an idea of marriage? Jack was perfect, and she was…tainted. How would she ever tell Jack?

The invitation to serve at the castle now seemed like a blessing. Margarete saw it as an escape—a way out.

"*Run away, run far away,*" the voices told her. She didn't know if she really heard them, or if they were only in her head, or perhaps it was just her voice speaking subconsciously out loud, but she agreed to obey. Yes. She would go to Brussels and start a new life. She was unworthy to be a wife of such a beautiful creature as Jack, but she was an excellent servant for the king, and the perks of living in a castle were a bonus.

The journey was long from Waldeck to Brussels, and the travelers were fatigued. Margarete hardly slept from anticipation on the voyage. *The castle!* She was finally going to see the inside of the castle! She could hardly wait. Although she was going to serve, she felt much like a princess already, traveling for days from the king's summer cottage in the cool mountains to his castle in a velvet-lined coach, drawn by several horses and a funny man who drove it. A dream come true! The castle!

Her head bobbled against the velvet lined walls, weary from lack of sleep, then came crashing to the bench she sat on. A bump in the road awoke the sleeping beauty. She couldn't see outside, but she knew the carriage stopped.

She heard the neighing of a horse.

"This is not good," she heard the driver say to himself as he dismounted, carrying the lantern with him, the thin light barely piercing the darkness around them.

She poked her head out of the carriage window and could barely see through the blackness of the night. A funny smell infiltrated her nostrils. *Smoke.* Old smoke mixed with new smoke.

Margarete stepped out of the carriage. To her right, she could see a home that had burned, smoke still rising from it. The smell was putrid. She heard voices in the distance, the sounds of crying echoing off the charred trees of the forest. She looked to the other side of the carriage and saw a home still burning, in the same direction of the loudest cries.

"My child!" a woman screamed in the distance. With that, Margarete quickly ran the hundred or so yards towards the burning house.

"Stop! Stop, young woman. Stop!" the coach driver cried out in an attempt to protect Margarete from doing something foolish.

The area was still dangerous. It was obvious arson was involved, and whoever the perpetrators were could possibly be enemies of the King of Brussels.

Margarete reached the woman whose face was covered in ash and tears.

"Please, my baby boy," she babbled hysterically, staring at the burning wood house—helpless and desperate.

By now the driver caught up with Margarete, out of breath.

Whiter Than Snow

"Don't just stand there! Go in there!" Margarete ordered him.

"Are you mad?"

"If you don't go, I will!"

He knew the king wouldn't be happy if he returned empty-handed, with a dead servant girl on his hands. And he couldn't let her die—not since she was in his care. He hesitated, took off his coat, rolled his eyes at her as if to say, *I can't believe you are making me do this,* and ran into the burning inferno to search for the missing child.

The walls were engulfed in flames. The second he entered, part of the roof fell in.

The child's mother screamed.

Margarete and the soot covered woman watched in horror for what seemed to be an eternity. They weren't coming out. The mother continued to sob and the scared teenager held her.

An explosion blew the rear wall out of the wood cabin, exposing the insides. Margarete squinted into the fiery furnace, hoping for a glimpse of the driver or the boy. She entertained the idea of entering the cabin herself.

Could it be? They heard coughing from within.

The driver came out of the opening in the wall carrying the woman's six year old son, who had been too frightened to make it out on his own.

The woman ran to him and grabbed her son, weeping. "Oh, thank you! Thank you!" she cried out to the man as she kissed her boy. "God bless you!"

The man dropped the child, collapsed on the ground and coughed uncontrollably from smoke inhalation.

The woman scooped her child up into her arms and kissed him repetitively.

"He'll have to see a doctor," the driver said in between coughs, noticing the boy's burns on his body. "Where is your husband?" he asked, holding his chest, looking up at the woman.

The woman looked down to him, fresh tears flooding her eyes. "They took him!"

"Who took him?" Margarete interjected.

"I don't know. Soldiers."

"Soldiers? Why?" asked the driver as he struggled to get up off his knees.

"They said because we worship the devil."

"You worship the devil?" he asked in ignorance, still coughing.

"No. We are Christians. My husband's a pastor."

"Then why would they say this?"

"Because we aren't Catholic. They said they were removing evil from the land, just before they kidnapped my husband and burned our house down...all of our houses." She pointed through the landscape towards the burning trees.

Margarete hugged the woman. "I'm so sorry, but aren't we still in the king's jurisdiction? The king would never send soldiers to accuse families of devil worship."

"How far is the doctor from here?" the driver interrupted.

"He was taken too," she cried.

Whiter Than Snow

"Dear God. We'll have to find the closest town, and hope they weren't ravaged as well. Let's get in the carriage."

The woman stood still, fearful to enter the carriage.

"You're the wife of a pastor. What do you take the king for?"

"Isn't the king responsible for this?" the mother asked.

"No, this isn't the king's doing. And there are powers over him as well. The lines are messy in these lands."

The woman was still hesitant, kissing her son on the forehead and surveying his wounds.

"The king's not Catholic," Margarete interjected, coaxing the woman into the carriage.

Matthew Eldridge

Whiter Than Snow

Chapter 9

The weary travelers made their way through the forest and down the dark and winding path. The smell of smoke clung to them and inhabited the carriage. The boy coughed and wheezed until Margarete thought he would pass out.

"We should be there shortly," Margarete spoke softly. She wasn't certain, but thought that reassurance would help the frightened mother.

The mother nodded, gripping her son tightly and kissing him on the head.

The morning sun peeked through the trees, kissing the forest floor as the wagon approached a new town. A ray of light pierced through the curtain window, shining on the boy's hair. His mother pressed her lips against it.

"Burtscheid," the driver said softly to the crew in the carriage.

The boy's mother answered, "We should probably keep going then. That town is run by the Abbess. It's an entirely Catholic town."

"Nonetheless, it's probably a lot safer than Aachen, and I'm sure the nuns there will know how to nurse a wound. It's their job to help people. Besides, you're more likely to run into soldiers in Aachen, in search of some free thinkers. Good news is I heard word that King Ferdinand might be in town! He's a hero here, and people may just assume we are part of his entourage. "

"And how is that good news?" asked the boy's mother.

"Well, King Ferdinand, or whatever his title is now-a-days, may be staunch Catholic. But he is also good friends with my king, the King of Brussels! They fought together against the Ottoman Empire years ago!"

In the distance they could see the Burtscheid Abbey, the Cistercian Nunnery, which happened to be the largest building in Burtscheid. They could view the ornate domed roof poking through the trees.

The carriage followed the narrow dirt road encircling the perimeter of the small town, which finally led to a small entranceway that pumped visitors into the heart of the tiny settlement. It was early morning, and for the most part, the town looked like a ghost town. However, gawkers could be seen looking out their windows, hoping for a glimpse of royalty.

For devout Roman Catholics, the abbey was probably the most beautiful nunnery in the region to visit. However, in order to keep the town truly secluded from the world, there was only one road in and one road out, and that road was hard to get to. It was rumored that several attempts were made to build a closer road leading to Aachen, but secret militia were brought in to destroy the work and would kill any man who tried to continue it. It was a silly

Whiter Than Snow

order, but to a leader thinking they are being devoted to their God by protecting such a place, a sword in the gut of a peasant was nothing—even a peasant hired by the Abbess.

Still, other political figures in the small town region believed it was a secret way to keep economic control over Burtscheid. It was clearly a central town to so many other villages or cities. The town had no ruler or authority over it other than the Abbess. It was subject to the Holy Roman Emperor, but from hundreds of miles away, he had no control. It was a free village. Perhaps that's why he gave the Abbess control. He knew a woman of God would keep order.

However, that still didn't answer why there was only one road in, and a hard road at that. It was a way to keep travelers out, and on their way to Aachen to spend their money. The livelihood of Aachen was dependent on the oppression of the other local cities or towns. That was the political assumption. Then again, Burtscheid held a deep secret…a secret the locals wanted to keep from the rest of the world.

The path curved around the town, and after an exhausting tour of the small city, the road-worn travelers finally found themselves at the door of the abbey.

The coach driver quickly dismounted and poked his head in the carriage. "Wait here! I'll find help!" he said, and ran for the door of the abbey.

He knocked, but then without waiting, forced the front door open. It was a large and heavy oak door, and the fact that it opened slowly gave the nuns in the room time to respond.

"It is improper for a man to enter the abbey!" one of the nuns chastised.

"I'm sorry. We need help. I have a hurting boy!"

The nun quickly jumped from her seat and followed the driver outside to the carriage.

The boy slowly opened his eyes, whimpering in pain as the nun stood over him, looking at him through the open door of the carriage.

"Burns over most of his body…" the driver said.

With a heart of compassion, the nun reached out to the boy and prayed for him in Latin. The travelers didn't know what she said, but they could tell it was a heartfelt prayer by the concern on her face and the tears forming in her eyes.

"I need you to bring the boy to the south side of the city."

"That's a good ten minutes or so away!"

"I know. Trust me. It's what the boy needs."

By now, several of the nuns had gathered around the carriage.

"I will go with you. Your son will be fine," the nun reassured the mother of the boy. "What is your name, dear?"

"Mine? Clairece," answered the boy's mother.

"That's a beautiful name," the nun said in a soothing tone, taking her hand. "And who is this tough young man with the blonde hair and blue eyes?"

The boy was in too much pain to answer.

"This is John."

"Oh," the nun said, "like that John Foxe fellow."

Whiter Than Snow

"Yes...he's my cousin."

The driver shook his head emphatically in an attempt to shut the mother up, as there was a price on John Foxe's head. The fact alone that she was his cousin suggested that she was probably a Protestant. The driver feared this revelation could end the nun's hospitality.

There was silence for a short time as the horses trotted down the dirt street once more.

"How do you know about my cousin?" Clairece asked, breaking the silence.

"Oh...we hear things from time to time. He actually stopped by here once and tried to interview me. Interesting fellow. I hear he's writing a book against the Catholic Church?"

"Not exactly..."

"Not exactly?" the nun raised her eyebrow and questioned softly.

"I think it's more about people dying for their faith."

"Hmmm. A book of martyrs."

"Yes," Clairece answered.

The nun nursed the boy's wounds with some oil and the tip of her robe as she conversed. "I take it you are a Protestant?"

The mother looked nervously at Margarete, fearing the truth could result in unwanted trouble and worse yet, that the boy wouldn't be attended to.

"Don't be nervous dear, your secret's safe with me. I won't tell a soul."

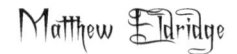

The new awkward silence ate at Clairece. "And who are you, again?"

"I'm the Abbess of Burtscheid," the nun said politely.

More silence.

The carriage arrived at the secluded, south end of the village. It appeared to be protected by a thick wall of trees and shrubbery, but the travelers could hear the sweet sounds of a bubbling brook through the green mesh.

"There's a path to the right—it's narrow, but we can make it," the Abbess offered.

The driver steered the carriage to the right and followed the path for a good hundred or so yards before the terrain became too difficult.

"This is as far as we can go," he said, pulling the reins and drawing the horses to a halt.

The Abbess responded, "It's not much further. We can walk the rest of the way." She quickly jumped out of the carriage without the escort's help, and reached a hand to Margarete, who then offered to help the mother with John.

The Abbess led the way down the worn path into the woods, the sounds of rushing water getting louder. Finally, the path narrowed and the travelers had to duck below branches to make it through to the other side.

"Wait a minute!" the Abbess said as she stopped the entourage. "Are you lost?" the driver asked.

Whiter Than Snow

"No." She pointed to the huge spider web that blocked their path, inhabited by a mammoth spider. "It's the cross of Saint Andrew."

"You're saying this spider is a sign from one of your saints?" the driver smirked. "No wonder people are breaking free from the Catholic church."

"No, that's the name of the spider. It's in the shape of a cross. It's the wasp spider," Clairece answered, defending the Abbess.

The Abbess picked up a stick and carefully tore down the web and let the spider crawl away. She quietly began her journey again with the visitors following closely behind.

At the end of the dirt path, where the trees parted, was an oasis of some sort. Several beautiful blue pools of water were before them with bubbles forcefully coming from the center—steam protruding from the rapid suds.

"Hot springs," the Abbess explained.

"So here are the mysterious springs. I've heard about them. I heard they have healing power," Clairece said in wonder.

"They will help heal your son."

Clairece swiftly walked into the water carrying her child.

The Abbess yelled, "Go to the bubbles!"

Clairece trudged through the thick sandy floor, the water encompassing her knees and then lapping at her waist. The boy trembled as his wounds touched the water.

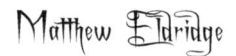

"You're almost there," Margarete called to her.

The entire team watched anxiously.

Clairece reached the massive bubbles and placed her son in the water over top of them. He winced, but the steaming water was in fact bringing healing. She laid him on his back so he floated on the water. He tipped his head back as the steam bubbles worked their wonder. His mother's tears streamed down her face and painted his. Was it working? Who knew? But she prayed diligently that it did.

"Dunk him in!" the Abbess cried out.

They arrived back at the nunnery as the morning sun climbed the eastern sky.

"The boy and the women are welcome to stay here until the boy recovers. He'll need us to take care of his wounds properly. He'll need to bathe in the springs every day."

The driver interrupted, "The young woman and I need to continue our travels. Thank you for your hospitality."

"You've had a rough night. You all need some sleep. I can get you a room next door at the inn. Wait here..." She started to walk away.

"We appreciate the suggestion, but..."

"That wasn't a suggestion, it's a command. You need your rest, and you need to bathe. We'll make you a nice warm meal. Now wait here as I requested."

Whiter Than Snow

The Abbess went inside while the guests waited for her return. The driver chuckled at the commanding presence of the Abbess. She was almost as demanding as the Queen of Brussels, but filled with tenderness and mercy.

"Look at this," Margarete suggested as she pointed to a sign attached to the front of the abbey.

Her escort read it out loud, "In Honor of Saint Nicholas, Saint of Orphans and Sailors."

"Is that Saint Nicholas, as in, the Christmas gift-giver?"

"I do believe so," he said warmly, his arms folded behind his back.

Matthew Eldridge

Chapter 10

"I can't believe I'll have to live in such a hideous place as this," the inebriated prince said, staring out of the carriage window at the gloomy sky, the damp air biting at the travelers. "I must be out of my mind."

"England's not that bad. I think it's beautiful," said the made-up woman sitting beside him.

The prince took another sip of his wine. "And if you had brains as big as your breasts you'd realize that we've been out of England for quite some time now."

"I thought you were moving to England?" she said, innocently and confused.

The prince rolled his eyes. "Just do yourself a favor and don't talk. You're prettier when you aren't talking," he said.

The blonde-headed woman leaned back against the seat and turned her head the other way, hoping the prince wouldn't see her tears as they trickled down her cheeks. She suppressed the fact that the prince was using her and would soon toss her out as a nobody, once they arrived in Spain. And although she was the daughter of an Aristocrat, she felt as worthless as a servant by the degrading words of her master, Prince Philip. She willingly accepted the prince's offer as a traveling companion, hoping to experience a sliver of the life of a real princess, albeit, she was far from being one. Still, being with the prince made her feel special.

Chapter 11

The blue moon exposed herself in full glory above the abbey. It was a beautiful night, and Margarete enjoyed the gently stroking breeze blowing through the window as she braided her hair by candlelight.

The sound of horses' hooves pulling a series of carriages echoed in the street. Margarete walked to the window of her second story room and peered out at the visitors who made their way to the front of the abbey—their faces glowing by the torches they held. It was royalty, she was sure of it!

The carriages were ornate with Spanish design. It made the king of Brussels' carriage look like it belonged to a peasant, if peasants were to own carriages. The men with torches made their way over to the inn where Margarete's escort was staying. She watched breathlessly as they entered.

She heard a commotion, and fear seized her. What if these were the very men responsible for the burning of homes? What if they were there to capture and torture Christians? What if the Abbess told them who they were—that they were in fact, Protestants, not Catholics? What would be their fate? Could she trust the Abbess? Should she try to escape?

Then again, since when did soldiers travel in such luxury? She laughed at the foolishness of her own fears, even though some of the men appeared to be soldiers—but perhaps they were bodyguards for royalty.

She heard loud voices coming from the inn and watched as her driver was dragged out of the front door. Did they know who he was? Did they know he was sent from the king of Brussels? Who were they? They obviously came from a powerful kingdom.

Her shallow breaths almost caused her to hyperventilate. Would she be next? What would happen to her escort? How would she make it to Brussels? More importantly, what would happen to the poor mother and child now safely resting at the abbey? She would protect them—even if she had to lie, she would protect the child. *Where are these crazy thoughts coming from?*

Margarete continued to watch as her driver was tossed into the streets, and then as one of the escorts opened the door of the middle carriage. A man—a very handsome man—made his way out of the carriage and surveyed the scene. He was beautiful she thought—if men could be beautiful. It was no longer the fear that took her breath away, but this man with his piercing eyes…looking up at her. *Oh my gosh, he's looking this way!*

She quickly hid behind the curtain and blew out the candle at her bedside. She was shaking, yet, her heart was aroused at the thought of this man, this prince, whomever he was. It's funny how some people have such an attraction that you can see just a glimpse of them in the dark and it sends your heart into a catatonic state. She had never felt this before. She was curious, but she knew that curiosity could lead to her death, especially here, especially because of the nasty rumors of Protestant Christians being murdered all over the region for their faith.

She sat quietly on her bed, sensing her pulse beat wildly through her veins. She leaned back on her pillow trying to breathe, but she couldn't stop thinking about him—about that smile and those eyes. *I must be delirious from lack of sleep*, she thought.

Knock, knock, knock!

The sounds at the front door of the nunnery startled her. She glanced back out the window as she heard the door creak open. She couldn't exactly make out the conversation.

The Abbess mumbled something that wasn't too clear. "Tell the prince we have no room for his girlfriends here…"

A prince! He's a prince after all! Margarete thought to herself.

"She's not a girlfriend, she's his, uh…cousin."

"Does the prince really think he can hide his sins from God?" the Abbess said with conviction.

The door slammed shut, and Margarete watched as a guard opened the door of the middle carriage. A beautiful woman stepped out. Her blonde hair was astonishing and ornate with jewels. Her dress was stunning, and the broach, well, big enough for Margarete to see from her upstairs window. It was obvious that the woman had enough cleavage to hide a town—perhaps that's why the prince liked her.

Margarete looked down at her own chest…flat. Okay, not completely. But she was small enough to feel self-conscious. In an age where the only part of a woman a man could see was cleavage, she felt pretty inadequate.

The woman glanced to Margarete's window, a hint of sadness in her eyes, and then, turned away as she was led to the inn by the guard. Why she wanted to stay in the nunnery wasn't clear, but Margarete could tell by her face that she was disappointed. If she was, in fact, the girlfriend of the prince, why wouldn't she stay with him? Perhaps because somewhere inside of her soul she desired purity, as all women do—and there was nothing more pure than a nunnery. Perhaps she had heard about the famous abbey and wanted to stay the night there? Or perhaps the prince was protecting his image by trying to make her stay at a different location. There were few princes who traveled through this area, and if one was betrothed to be married to a powerful queen or a princess, he had to do what he could to dispel rumors of infidelity.

Margarete rested back on the bed, her eyes heavy from the long day. Her heart fluttered at the thoughts of the man she saw. How silly, she thought, to have such feelings for someone she witnessed only for a moment. *And what about Jack?* Was she betraying him by acknowledging how good looking this other man was? He made her blush, after all.

Then she thought about how ridiculous any girl would be to fall in love with a prince—if he even was a real prince. A prince was a pleasure seeker. A prince was powerful, rich, and usually good looking. They could have any girl of their dreams, but instead, they married for political reasons and had a hundred or so mistresses on the side for their own pleasure. The thought nauseated Margarete. Of course, she only knew this from the stories Jack told. Stories he learned through observance while playing music for royal families.

She used these thoughts to push the warm feelings of the mysterious prince out of her head. When she succeeded, she finally fell asleep, but not before imagining that she was the beautiful woman staying at the inn…big breasts and all.

"Sisters of Brussels," the queen pronounced, her face aglow by the burning embers before her. "The Sisters of Waldeck saw our future…your doom."

"The prophesy?"

"Yes," the queen said. "The child, she lives." She took the moment to stare at each and every one of their faces—twelve in all. Some were old and wretched, while some were as youthful and beautiful as the flowers that surrounded them, no older than the princess herself.

"She cannot live. If the prophesies are true, she seals our fate for *The Sisters*," answered the wise one.

"You're worried about *The Sisters*?" The queen said with a hiss. "She threatens my kingdom!"

"May the spirits of old tell us where she is," another witch answered.

"May the spirits strangle her and drag her to her death," the queen said through a clenched jaw.

The Sisters of Brussels hooted at her remark.

Matthew Eldridge

Whiter Than Snow

Chapter 12

3 Months Later

Margarete stood at the window talking to the birds that nested on her window sill. Of course they didn't understand her, and they never really talked back except with an occasional whistle or chirp, but it was the only way to keep her sanity. They were the only conversations she had in the last few months, besides talking to the king every now and then. Even the other servants would ignore her...or perhaps she was too shy to engage in any kind of conversation with them. Or perhaps they were all too busy, frightfully and dutifully serving the queen. There were consequences to pay for any casual conversations the servants had with one another. Conversations meant they were neglecting their duties, at least in the eyes of the bitter queen.

Margarete liked the king, and would imagine at times that he was her father. She would have make-believe conversations with him.

"Father, what do you think of this? Father, care to dance? Father, do you think I'm pretty? Father, do you love me?"

She would've never said it out loud for anyone to hear, but she did get carried away at times. "Father, aren't those flowers beautiful?" she said one time while watering plants on the terrace.

"Excuse me? Who are you calling 'Father?' You twisted child!"

Margarete was startled. She twirled around to witness the queen standing over her.

"Uh... No one... I was just..."

The queen was curious for a moment. "You don't have a father, do you?"

"I don't know him."

"I'm sure he's not worth knowing." The queen smirked, then, turned away.

Margarete bowed her head. Her father was a war hero, she was told by Lucinda. But responding to the queen could mean twenty lashes—or worse yet, her death. She had learned over the months that even a look at the queen could result in harsh punishment. So far, in her short time as a servant, she had been whipped, slapped, beaten, verbally slaughtered, locked in her room, forced to eat all the leftovers until she vomited, skipped meals, and, oh yes, forced to wear oversized rags to represent her humility as a servant when the queen felt threatened by her beauty.

She was living a life of hell. How the king put up with the queen, she had no idea. It had become apparent that he was the absent king—a king who disappeared into his work and study. He was hardly the king Lucinda spoke of. No, instead his wife ran the kingdom, at least on royal grounds anyway, and she did as she pleased while he retreated to his private chambers, leaving Margarete to fend for herself at the wicked, yet beautiful woman's abuse. The queen even spoke harshly to her husband at times, and Margarete was certain any other queen would lose her head for it. However, the king endured it.

It seemed the king died long ago—along with his first wife. He was nothing but a shell; an empty, tired soul who lost his passion for love and life. Margarete's heart broke for the man, and she prayed for him often in her room. He needed to know God's love all over again, she'd tell herself.

Then again, she too, lost life's passion. She knew what it was like to be unfairly robbed of something so precious, and while she forced smiles for years, her past hung over her like a dark rain cloud. Her current situation didn't help. Her soul was being stripped, like a rainbow being robbed of its stripes, one color at a time.

"Make sure the guest bedrooms are clean with proper linens. We'll have royal company tonight. I expect you to look your best as you serve us, understand? We don't need our servant girl looking like the peasant she is. It's time to make a good impression."

Margarete wanted to ask who was coming, but feared the consequences. She lingered for a moment, wishing, hoping the queen would tell her.

The queen began to walk away, spun around and answered, as if she knew Margarete's thoughts. "Prince Philip from Spain will be our guest tonight. I expect you to do your job with precision. Don't be seen, and when you are, look your best."

As Margarete lit the candle on the dinner table, the sounds of strangers in the hallway sent flutters through her stomach. She quickly retreated to the kitchen and adjusted her clothes and the scarf on her head.

She glanced down the other end of the hallway as he passed through. He didn't even notice her, but she noticed him. It was HIM! The prince she saw in Burscheid! She fought the smile that invaded her face.

He may not have seen her now, oh, but he would at dinner. She would make sure of it.

Margarete entered the dining room with the beauty and swagger of a princess. She was poised and stunning. She bowed before the king, queen, and prince, and carried herself into the kitchen. She didn't always have to do that, but around guests it was encouraged, especially since the guest was royalty.

A few moments later, Margarete returned with the appetizer. Her hand shook nervously, and she was sure that the queen took notice, or worse yet, that Prince Philip noticed.

Whiter Than Snow

"Thank you," the handsome prince said as she placed his soup before him. "What is this?"

It was odd that he would thank a servant, but Margarete accepted it as a positive sign. However, she was nervous to respond, knowing the unwritten rules, and knowing the queen wouldn't like her talking to the prince. But he did ask her a question, didn't he? What was more rude, to answer royalty in a casual manner, or to ignore him altogether?

She answered apprehensively, "It's…it's a specialty. The king's favorite."

She tried not to look him directly in the eyes under the careful gaze of the queen, but couldn't help herself. His eyes were wide and engaging. He locked in on hers and she felt exposed, naked. He smiled.

"Hmmm. Smells delicious. Did you make…"

"We have a chef," the queen interrupted.

"This is my recipe," Margarete answered him.

"Well, if it's as good as it smells I'm in for a treat, I can see." He winked.

She was flustered and clanged a dish on the table, spilling some of its contents. She quickly took a rag from the front of her apron and, after brushing up against the side of the prince, leaned into the table and dabbed the spill until it was gone.

He swallowed. "Or perhaps it's you who smells good," he said to the girl who stood too close.

"Must be the food, I'm sure of it!" the queen answered, eyeing the servant, simmering in the thought of the prince's words.

He was forward...*too forward!* Margarete's face flushed as she walked briskly into the kitchen for retreat. *He noticed!* She perfumed herself lightly with a homemade fragrance just for him.

"Stupid servant girl! I'm so sorry," said the queen to her guest.

"It's perfectly alright. If I had a servant like that, well...I'd consider myself a blessed man," Prince Philip answered as he took a sip of his warm soup. "She could spill as many things as she wanted, and I would grant her forgiveness."

The queen smirked sarcastically. "I'm sure you would tire of it."

Margarete reentered the room, smiling of course, because she heard the prince's comment. She carried a dish around the back side of the queen so the woman couldn't see her. She caught the prince looking, and as he did, in a gutsy move she threw her head back to toss her beautiful black hair like a wild stallion tossing its mane. It was her signature move, one she practiced in mirrors since her childhood. Only, it was at that point she realized her head was mostly covered by her scarf and her hair was up, and she assumed she must've looked pretty funny without her hair flying around. She quickly retreated back into the kitchen without even placing the dish she was carrying onto the table.

"Oh dear," she cried to herself, realizing the dish was still in her hands. She assumed she'd look even more awkward taking the dish back out to the guests. Her face reddened with embarrassment. She assessed that she made a total fool of herself.

Whiter Than Snow

How could she go out there again? How could she face this gorgeous man? Ugh!

"I wonder where the dessert went?" she heard the king say.

She looked down at the bowl she was holding…yes…the bowl she forgot to leave the first time: her delicious homemade tarts.

"Oh dear," she said softly to herself again.

Matthew Eldridge

Chapter 13

Margarete brushed her thick hair while thinking wonderful thoughts of the delicious Prince Philip. And of course, her foolish mistake of trying to flip her hair in front of him while her head was covered…and forgetting to leave the dessert dish on the table. She wondered what he thought of her now, or if he even thought of her at all. Ah, but he had flirted with her at dinner—she was sure of it!

Small flurries filled her heart. She had never felt this way about a man before. Foolishness, she assumed. He was royalty, and not just royalty. He was one of the most prominent men of modern times. He was the son of the Emperor, and a war hero, not to mention breathtakingly handsome! He would never choose her. He *could* never choose her. But he was flirting. Why? Ah, yes. And then she remembered the big bosomed woman at the Abbey. He merely saw women as objects, did he not?

She tried to dismiss her thoughts, but couldn't resist her feelings. *If he only knew.*

She stared at the glowing candle on the night stand, watching the flame flicker brightly as the wind gently pushed air through her window. She sighed happily at her thoughts. *Yes, that's what he had done.* She was dying in this castle, inwardly. She had thought about ending her life many times—because serving the queen was the same as living in a dungeon, or even in hell. But she knew she didn't have the guts to kill herself, nor would she know how. *Such foolish thoughts.* And she was glad she never attempted such an irrational act.

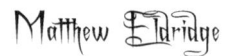

Much like the candle before her, the prince was a glowing flame—a shining light in the gloomy castle. He was illuminating. His presence alone sparked life into her again. He made her dream—and dream of him. Like so many lives he captured in battle, he captured her soul. He was more than a conqueror of kingdoms, he was a conqueror of hearts. Maybe not literally, but he gave her the ability to hope in love and life again. That was worth something. She hadn't felt warm like this since the night she kissed Jack…and even that didn't give her the tingly feelings now consuming her.

Jack's love was young, teenage, puppy love. She couldn't quite describe what this was…but it was different. This may not be love at all, but it was something that heated her insides in a way every girl desires.

She watched the wind blow the drapes, making them dance in the window. It was a fresh wind. *Yes*, that's what the prince was, she thought. He was a fresh wind, breathing life into her. He brought color to this colorless, graying castle.

Who would have ever thought that living with royalty inside a beautiful castle could be such a miserable experience? Who would've imagined that behind these monumental stone walls was a dungeon with an evil ruler—a ruler so physically beautiful, and yet, so ominous and ugly at the same time? Reality struck the girl deep in her soul, and she became homesick.

The queen was ugly, wasn't she? From the outside, Margarete envied the woman: her beauty, her castle, her easy life. But now that she was on the inside of it all, the child had a new perspective on things. The sight of the woman made Margarete nauseous. She would avoid eye contact at all costs from the hideous beast from now on. Yes, a beast. That's what Margarete swore she saw as she looked into the wicked woman's eyes.

She was a queen alright—the queen of deception... Margarete didn't know where that thought came from, except by discernment from God alone. She knew it to be true. She quickly dismissed the thoughts of the vile woman from her mind and focused again on the handsome prince from Spain.

The young girl twirled around the room as she changed into her bed clothes, and imagined she was a princess, trapped in a dark, medieval castle by an evil witch, and that her hero, Prince Charming, was coming to rescue her through the open window! She smiled with delight. *Oh, silly girl!* She thought to herself, almost giggling as she fell into her bed. *Such a dreamer!*

The handle on her door shifted and startled her. She pulled the covers up over her.

"Who is it?" she called out.

She saw the arm—a crushed velvet sleeve. *Could it be?* But why would he be coming in her room?

"Who is it?" she called again, the covers almost to her chin, her beautiful black hair draping over her shoulders as she sat up in her bed.

The prince walked in slowly, his finger over his lips in a hushed manner. He closed the door slowly behind him as not to make a sound. He walked leisurely to the bed and propped a knee up on it.

She was getting panicky. "What are you doing here? What do you want?"

"You," the gorgeous prince said with a grin.

"Me?" she answered timidly.

"I'm headed to England in the morning. I'd like you to come with me."

Margarete tried to hide the smile that forced its way to the corners of her mouth. Was this really happening? The prince was attempting to rescue her!

"For your services, of course. I need a servant for my travels."

She snapped out of her daydream. "Oh...of course!" The smile fell from her face. "How do you expect me to come with you? The king's not going to just let me go."

"The king knows that I can take whatever I want of his. He is subject to my father."

"Is that so?"

"Yes, that's so."

"And who said I belong to the king?"

Prince Philip smirked in response to her question.

"It's the *queen* I'm more worried about…" Margarete continued.

He put his finger over her lips and she stopped speaking.

"I am Prince Philip," he said slowly with confidence.

The couple heard a sound in the hallway. Prince Philip quickly stood, moved to the door and listened through it. After assuring himself that no one was in the hallway, he slowly opened the door and snuck out the other side…disappearing from Margarete's vision.

The girl was beaming. She pulled the covers over her head like any teenage girl would and tried to contain her excitement.

"Good night, my prince," she said softly, making sure he couldn't hear.

The evil queen hid behind the statue that guarded the hallway and watched the young prince make his way out of the servant girl's room and down the hall to his own.

Hours had passed. He felt the warm body next to him, awakening him from his slumber. He felt her hot, nervous breath against the back of his head. Her hand glided across his waist as she managed to slip in between the covers with him. He stretched his leg and felt hers. He slowly turned around, smiling at the thought of Margarete's bravery, but was startled at the face before him, just inches away.

"What? What are you doing here? Have you gone mad, woman?"

It was Queen Viktoria. She couldn't resist helping herself to the prince's bed.

"Crazy? Yes! Mad? No...come on, I know of your reputation and your inability to resist beautiful women."

"Women who aren't married to a king."

"He won't know."

"Even so, I know."

"Don't you find me beautiful?" She tried kissing him.

He squirmed in the covers and jumped off the bed to avert the touch of her lips.

"That's not the point. You're married... and... well... older."

"Older?" She questioned, offended. "I like to call it more experienced," she said playfully.

"You're not my type..." he pleaded, hoping she would stop this madness.

She could tell he wasn't giving in, and her tone changed as she crawled out of bed and stood beside it. "No, your type is pathetic, little servant girls who don't know any better. You can use them as you wish and you know there's no risk involved. You're only half a man."

"Choose your words carefully, queen. I have the power to destroy this kingdom, and take your husband's life."

"Go ahead. Then you can marry me and you'll have a beautiful queen who understands your lust for power."

"You are mad."

Whiter Than Snow

The queen darted for the door, spun around and said, "This never happened," as she exited the room. Her face offered a wicked grin as she softly commented, "And you're hardly your father."

Matthew Eldridge

Chapter 14

The cool mist morning showed promise of a beautiful day for traveling. Prince Philip held his hand out to help Margarete into the horse-drawn carriage. Although she was a servant, she was dressed beautifully for the journey—as the queen suggested while serving in the presence of royal guests. Even her hair was pinned up—to keep her cool in warmer afternoon hours, she told herself.

"Beautiful necklace," he said.

She sighed, excusing her nervousness. "It belonged to my mother."

With a flip of the reins, the twin Lipizzaner stallions kicked, bucked, and trotted out of the castle courtyard, following the prince's other carriage with his mighty men and his belongings. Margarete peeked out of the curtain and glanced back to the castle as they rode through the lower bailey, past the curtain wall, under the iron gate, and over the moat on the fixed bridge. The commoners waved as the carriages continued on to Main Street. In her heart, Margarete pretended she was a princess, going to a wonderful ball. She was going to a ball, perhaps, after all. But she was going to serve. She wouldn't remind herself of that until she got there. Let dreams be dreams.

The journey was long, but Margarete hardly noticed the hour. It was time well served—better than cleaning the castle or serving the demanding queen. No, instead, she spent her time allowing the prince to admire her. Every time she glanced in his direction, he was staring at her. She would blush and turn the other way. She pretended it made her uncomfortable, and perhaps it did, just a little. But honestly, she was enjoying it. She was attracting the desires of a prince—a handsome, wealthy prince at that.

Out of embarrassment or respect, Margarete didn't know which, Prince Philip would look away when they'd make eye contact, and then she'd catch him gazing at her again a moment later.

The repetitive nature of the whole flirting game caused her to laugh nervously. It had been over a two hour ride thus far, and he hadn't spoken to her. She knew better than to start a conversation with a prince—she was just a servant.

"What?" he asked.

"What, what?" she answered.

"Why are you giggling?"

"I don't know," she said nervously as she started giggling again.

"You find me funny?"

"I find you intriguing."

He blushed. "I find you intriguing as well. So what a pair we'll make."

Awkward pause.

"Your hair... it's beautiful."

Whiter Than Snow

She touched it, making sure the pins were holding. "Thank you."

"I mean when it's down."

"Oh…"

Awkward. What a way to sweep a girl off her feet.

"So…" she started to ask a question, but remembered who she was talking to. She shied back into her seat.

"Yes? Go ahead and ask. No one is here to stop you."

"Do you live in a castle, far away?" she asked, realizing the stupidity of the question. "That's not what I meant. I…"

He chuckled while interrupting. "I live in a huge castle, and sometimes I think it's not far enough away." He glanced out the window, and then returned her stare with his piercing eyes. "Some of these castles are nothing more than enlarged peasant homes. Not mine! You would love it!"

"I doubt I would love cleaning it."

"I didn't mean to clean it…I…you… are you hungry?"

That earned him a smile. "I'm starved."

The prince and his servant, Margarete, sat on the grand blanket after enjoying a meal together. She made him a royal lunch that she knew would be unforgettable. And enjoying it with him made it all the more special. She lay on her back staring up at the sky. The wind blew over her and rustled the leaves in the trees surrounding them. She prayed it was the winds of change. *Perhaps.*

She smiled, glanced over to Prince Philip, who was on his side—watching her as if she was the only interesting thing to look at in this beautiful meadow.

"You're beautiful…I don't even know your name."

Her heart fluttered, but she didn't answer. It amazed her how he didn't even seem embarrassed by giving such a compliment, or by her lack of response, or that his men surrounded them near the carriages looking on. Who was this overly confident man that executed compliments to helpless, young maidens the way he executed his enemies during war?

"Tell me, what are your thoughts on marriage?" he asked.

She answered nervously, "Why does the prince want to know? Why do my thoughts on marriage matter to you?"

"Because they do." He shifted, his eyes flirtatiously smiling at her. "Every girl thinks about it."

She laughed. "Oh do we, now? And how would you know that?"

"Little girls play a princess who marries a prince, do they not? That's what happens every time I watch a little girl during play time."

"Ah, yes, every girl wants to be a princess. They don't necessarily want to marry. It's just that as a girl you automatically assume that you *have* to marry a prince to be a princess. Trust me. A girl would rather not marry."

"Not marry at all? Or just not marry a prince?" he asked.

She laughed again.

"What if I could make you a princess?"

Whiter Than Snow

He was toying with her and it angered her. He could no more marry a servant and turn her into a princess than a girl could kiss a frog and turn it into a prince.

Silence. Yes, she was going to give him the silent treatment, at least for the next half hour, which bothered her because she really did want to talk to him. But he chose this punishment upon himself for treating her so unfairly.

"I can see you aren't going to answer. At least answer me this: would you ever marry a man because you knew that it's what you were supposed to do?"

"No." She shook her head and laughed. "That's absurd. Who's to tell me I'm supposed to marry anyone but the man that I choose?"

"Why would you marry, then?"

Was he really this naïve, she thought? "For love..."

"Love?"

"What, you've never heard of it? Or never experienced it?" She said sarcastically. Yes, it was her turn to flirt. She batted her eyelashes at him and smiled. A small dimple formed in her cheek and he took notice.

He smiled. She was talking to him again, and that's all that mattered at the moment.

It was the greatest day of her life, she told herself. They ate, relaxed, and bathed in the sun before continuing on their journey. She pretended to still be angry with him and excused herself from talking too much. The quietness caused quite a stir as most of their communication became non-verbal flirtatious gestures from their faces. She enjoyed every fleeting look he made, depositing it in her heart like a child depositing coins in a piggy bank.

There was chemistry. She nearly forgot she was a servant, and he nearly forgot he was a prince. In one small journey the world between royalty and peasant collided, erasing social class momentarily. They were becoming friends; good friends. She was unlike any woman he had ever met.

Evening had fallen, and the continuous sounds of horse hooves hitting the road lulled Margarete into a deep sleep. But the jerking motion of the carriage coming to a halt awoke her.

"We're here?" she asked through parched vocal cords.

"No. We have to cross the English Channel," said the prince. "We're in Calais."

She opened her eyes slowly to find herself propped up against Prince Philip, her head on his shoulder. He didn't seem to mind. She sat up quickly. "We're on the coast? I've never seen it before!"

"It's hard to see at night."

Margarete exited the carriage, followed by Prince Philip, and looked around to find the water. Total blackness filled the space before them. The darkness reminded her of the forest. She moved in close to him.

Whiter Than Snow

"That way," the prince said, turning her body to the northwest.

The smell of the salty air infiltrated her nostrils and lungs. It was a welcoming smell, however unpleasant it was. The breeze blowing off the coast pierced her clothes and she shivered.

"Allow me," said the prince as he retrieved his cloak and placed it around her.

She accepted, but hesitantly. He put his fingers to his lips. It wasn't acceptable for a servant to wear clothes belonging to royalty. But they were in the middle of nowhere. It would remain their little secret. Margarete took in the beauty of the scenery as they waited for the boat to arrive. The dim moonlight danced upon the waters with enough light to illuminate a few of the cliffs nearby.

"It's so beautiful."

"You should see it in the daytime."

"I hope to."

He smiled in response. "Do you know what a beautiful accent you have?"

"Are you jesting? You're the Spaniard. You're the one with the nice accent."

"My prince, my lady," the captain said as he bowed and welcomed the couple aboard, along with several of the prince's men.

A lady? Margarete's face delighted in amusement. She had never been called that before. The two boarded the boat and watched as the carriage and driver rode away in the opposite direction.

"Have you had many cross for tournament this season?" the prince asked.

"All but those who are still at war," answered the captain.

The novelty of the journey was short lived as Margarete could see nothing past the mist hovering over the black waters. The lantern on the boat gave little light for sightseers. She found herself weary in the late night hours and quickly fell asleep.

The English carriage the couple transferred to was a little smaller than the Spanish designs, and Margarete awoke in the early morning hours to find Prince Philip leaned up against her. She rested her head on his face. Her hand slid down his arm and she pushed her fingers through his. He responded by clutching her hand. She looked at their hands—her heart tingled as much as her fingers. She closed her eyes and fell back to sleep.

Whiter Than Snow

Chapter 15

It was nearly morning when Prince Philip, Margarete, and the Spanish guards arrived at Whitehall Castle in London, England—the home and creation of the late King Henry the VIII. The sun played peek-a-boo with the travelers, hiding behind beautiful cherry blossoms which lined the street.

"Oh my, those flowers are gorgeous. I've never seen them before."

"They're from Japan," the prince offered.

"How do you know?"

"Because my father brought them to King Henry as a gift."

"Wow." Margarete gazed at the majestic castle before her, almost ten times the size of the one she worked in Brussels.

"You've never seen one like it, have you?"

"No, I haven't."

"My father's is bigger," the prince bragged, a cocky smile on his face.

She ignored him, her eyes glued to the scenery around her. At first, they traveled through what would soon be the marketplace, but it was still too early for the people to be stirring. There was a small city of tents set up to the right and left along the clay street. Empty stands stood to the left. By noon, they promised to be filled by nobles and peasants alike.

"What is that?"

"Tournament. It's jousting season! We'll enjoy some wonderful entertainment while we are here. England is booming this time of year!"

She was still ignoring him, her faced glued to the window of the carriage. Since when did servants enjoy entertainment events?

"I would compete myself, but my father would never go for it. Risking my life for a game is not kingly-like, he says. Still, watching my general compete is almost as exciting as jousting myself. He is the best! He will win this tournament!"

She was unimpressed.

The carriage turned onto the brick road and approached the castle from the right. The bridge itself was at least a hundred yards long, and the moat looked like a giant lake. They passed through the barbican, which was large enough to house a community, and through the inner gate. To the right, in the lower bailey, a lush green lawn hosted beautiful marble balls the size of cannon balls.

"What is that?"

"Oh, that's called lawn bowling. You've never seen it before?"

"No. How could I?"

"Maybe I'll have to show you sometime…"

"Sure, take a servant to a sporting event," she said sarcastically.

Whiter Than Snow

He grinned sheepishly.

To the left was a large square court with a net in the middle. "And what's that?" she asked.

"That's a tennis court."

"What kind of court?"

"It's a game with a ball and two rackets… Why, you really don't know, do you?"

She was a smart girl, but knew little about entertainment or the modern games of English life. The kingdom in Brussels was more like an oversized village, and the royals who lived there were old-fashioned. Entertainment was an afterthought. Dancing and music were perhaps the only entertainment she encountered in Waldeck, before serving the king and queen. And she didn't mind it—music and dancing were her favorite!

"…We'll definitely have to bet on some cock fights later today. I'll tell you what, whatever I win is yours to keep. Spending money for your journey! I just love the sport of it."

"I've only heard of such brutality. People really watch roosters fight? For money? You don't find anything wrong with that?"

"Oh, how silly of me. I forgot, country folk keep roosters as pets. It would be like watching your pet fight to the death, now wouldn't it?"

She ignored him. His sarcasm was highly unappreciated. If he was trying to win her heart, this snobbery wouldn't work.

The carriage stopped in front of the great hall, where English soldiers greeted them. The prince lowered himself out of the carriage, and, this time, ignored Margarete, as one of the guards helped her out. Philip handed papers to the lead guard, and the two walked briskly out of sight.

"You must be the help," the woman said, as she approached the carriage. "Follow me. It's almost breakfast time."

"Great. I'm starved."

"Not for you; for the guests. There are lots of guests this time of year, and we need as much help as we can get. Do you know how to cook, or do you only clean? Or do you just stand around looking pretty?" the husky woman asked sarcastically.

"I can cook." Margarete was flattered by her comment, but realized it was an insult at the same time.

"Good. You have no idea how many peasant servants can't do a thing," the woman muttered while hurriedly walking Margarete to the kitchen. A number of eligible princes brought servants merely for companionship, and the head servant, Hannah, was simply addressing this.

Hannah walked Margarete through the back door of the kitchen, the heat of the ovens enveloping the two of them as they walked by. Hannah handed Margarete an apron and led her to a prep table where several other young servants worked. "Over there are the eggs, there's the stove. No time for introductions. Let's get to work. Put the eggs in there," the woman ordered, pointing to an odd dish.

Margarete took a cursory glance around the kitchen and saw the other servants hard at work. A young woman at the stove gave her a quick smile, then, returned to her work. She was a beautiful woman with dark hair, perhaps from Spain.

"In here?" Margarete questioned, looking at the odd glass that had a half-oval hole in it on the top end.

"Yes, in there." The woman seemed annoyed.

Margarete placed a raw egg in the cylindrical shaped dish. It was a rather odd contraption. She really didn't know what she was doing and it showed on her face.

"You country servants are pretty much useless, aren't you?" the woman said while taking the egg out of the contraption. "I meant after you've boiled it. Perhaps you'll make a better server."

The day was long and grueling. Eventually, Margarete was led to her sleeping quarters—which she shared with several other women servants. The Spanish woman with kind eyes occupied the cot beside her. Margarete plopped down on her own cot, weary from the day's work.

"Hola," the Spanish woman said.

"Hi," Margarete answered. Then, recalling some of the Spanish she learned as a girl from Jack, she said, "Hola. Comó estas?"

The woman looked relieved someone else spoke Spanish and began blurting her words at a rapid pace to Margarete.

"I…I'm sorry. Lo síento. No hablo mucho Español…I don't really know Spanish," Margarete answered sheepishly.

The woman's smile fell and she lied down in her cot.

Margarete whispered to herself, "I can only imagine how lonely it must feel to be in a strange environment with no one to talk to. I can relate."

The woman must've understood some of what she said, because she sighed and smiled at the young girl, and then closed her eyes to sleep. Margarete followed the woman's lead and was dreaming within minutes.

Chapter 16

The blistering sun made the day's work arduous. Margarete made herself comfortable in the stables to produce the early-morning milk, and then the kitchen to help serve breakfast. Before breakfast even finished, they were preparing the afternoon meal. She ate simply by testing what she cooked while she was cooking. She shared with the Spanish woman, who returned the favor. No time for herself. During lunch she served over a hundred castle guests, none of them Prince Philip. In fact, she didn't see him at all.

Evening fell and she found herself longing for sleep. She had been on her feet, serving, all day. She was lonely and exhausted. Other than the occasional smile from the Spanish woman, she had no communication with anyone. She wondered about the Prince. And it was while she was wondering that he appeared.

"Might I steal her away a bit?" the handsome prince said to the head servant.

The woman nodded in approval. It's not like she could have stopped him from taking Margarete. He was a prince, and although she was the head servant, she was still just a servant, after all.

Margarete felt self conscious. She'd been in the kitchen all day, working with greasy, hot, smelly food. She tried to fix her hair as they walked.

"How are you doing so far?" the prince asked.

"Fine…"

"Fine? You sure?"

She nodded as she walked absently.

"You don't seem too happy to see me," he said.

"I'm tired. I haven't been so tired in all my life," she said, half-heartedly laughing.

"I'm, I'm sorry about that…"

"And I've been in the kitchen all day. I smell."

He sniffed. "I think you smell delicious."

"Oh, please," she answered.

"You do. Like some kind of pie!"

That earned him a giggle. "Blackberry."

"I think I'd like to eat you up."

She continued walking, ignoring the comment. He was definitely toying with her.

The night was illuminated by torches aligning the castle walls and streets. Hundreds of tourists abound. The prince stopped walking and forced her to look at him. For a moment, he seemed vulnerable and transparent.

"I…thought of you…a lot today."

She was quick to answer. "Then why didn't you rescue me? They worked me to death in there."

"I'm sorry. I can't."

"I thought I came to serve *you*," she said softly.

"I am a guest in the king's home…"

"He's dead…" she interrupted.

"Alright, the queen's home. When you are a guest of the king or queen, your servant automatically serves in the host's home. There are hundreds of guests here. And all servants are needed to take care of those guests."

"You should have told me about this before you brought me."

"I thought you'd be delighted to get away from Brussels."

"Not to work four times as hard."

She was difficult. He found it attractive and amusing. They walked past a crowd of people, eyes following them.

"I'd suggest you don't address me in such a manner when people are present. You *are* just a servant," he scolded, his voice deep and quiet.

"Just?" she said softly, as she walked. She wanted to cry. She wanted to see Jack. She wanted to go home to Lucinda.

He glanced to her and saw her demeanor change. He took a hold of her elbow to stop her. "I will try to steal you away one day, I promise."

She tried to force a smile, but it wasn't working.

The prince let go of her arm and they started walking again. Margarete looked down the cobblestone road before them. She saw a young man in the distance. Her heart leaped. He glanced her way and she hid behind the prince, for fear it was, in fact, Jack.

"What are you doing?" asked the prince.

She stumbled, quickly glancing down at the road beneath her feet. "This pathway—I've never seen it before. What is it?"

"Cobblestones. A good waste of material and man hours if you want to know what I think."

"It's intriguing. But hard to walk on. Do you have them in Spain?"

"No. Our streets are beautiful the way they are. But I hear the French are creating many roads with them. My father detests them."

He held her arm again and helped her walk. As soon as he let go, she wrapped her arm around his. He unwrapped her arm as quickly as she wrapped it. He could not afford to be seen linking arms with a servant in England. Not like this.

Margarete looked up the road in the young man's direction. He was gone. It was nothing but a wish. She missed Jack and was seeing what she wanted to see. Her face fell as she yawned.

Prince Philip led her off the cobblestones and to a dirt path.

"Where are we going?"

"Getting you off this rocky street."

"I'm fine, really."

The thin dirt trail darkened and the woods stood tall before them. She hesitated.

"I really don't want to leave the cobbles."

"How can I kiss you, a servant, if we aren't hidden by the darkness?"

"Oh, is that why you stole me away? To use me for a kiss?"

He laughed. "No. I wouldn't be using you."

"It *would* be using me. If you can't declare your desire to kiss me in public and if you have to hide me away—and if it's only a kiss you want."

He chuckled. "It's time we stop resisting what we both want." He took her hand and kissed it. "I haven't been able to stop thinking about you from the moment I met you."

She pulled her hand away and wrapped her arms around herself. She was shivering. Whether it was from the cold, or from his words trying to pierce her heart, she didn't know. But she did know he was a professional heart-stealer. Perhaps he said this to all the girls. In fact, she was sure of it. As badly as she wanted to kiss him, she simply turned back towards the cobblestones.

"Please don't…"

"It's not you," she said.

"Then what?"

"I…I don't like the dark."

"You can't be serious. You encounter the dark every night of your life from birth."

"Yes, I do. But not in strange woods."

"I'll protect you." He moved in closer.

She could practically taste his breath. A moment passed and she turned away. Not here. Not now.

He could tell she wasn't going to change her mind. He was a lover who found a real kiss wasn't a kiss that was forced or stolen. No. A true kiss was given. And earning her kiss would become his mission. He was up for the challenge.

"I guess I should get you back. You'll need your sleep for tomorrow. In two days the jousting begins. I'll steal you away for that. You can watch General Luís destroy his competitors."

The prince walked the young woman back to the castle and to the entrance of her sleeping quarters. The Spanish servant was sitting by the entry.

"Hola, chica. They look for you," she said with broken English.

Before Margarete could respond, the prince and the young woman were speaking in Spanish fluently to one another. After a few minutes of quick dialogue, Margarete was feeling rather left out.

"What are you two talking about?"

"I'm wondering why she doesn't work for me. She is a Spaniard, after all," the prince answered, offering up a smile and a wink. He ended his conversation with the woman, who told him her name was Maria.

Maria smiled at Margarete with a twinkle in her eye and softly laughed.

"Comprende?" he asked.

"Sí," she said, giggling.

"Buenos noches," the prince commented as he walked away, ignoring Margarete.

Maria stared at Margarete, grinning.

"What? What did he say?"

Whiter Than Snow

"He said for me to keep an eye on you," Maria answered in her strong accent.

Matthew Eldridge

Chapter 17

It was the first day of the jousting tournament. Eagerness filled the streets by both spectators and competitors. And although Margarete wasn't into the sport, the enthusiasm was contagious. She walked with a guard in the early morning air. The streets were crowded with fans, vendors, and tents. She inhaled the sensuous smells of grilled foods being prepared for the afternoon. And although the tournament wouldn't start for hours, the streets overflowed with anticipation.

The guard led her past the tilt field towards the tournament stables. She looked back at the spectator's stands, confused. The guard directed her to General Luís.

"You must be Margarete," the general said. "You're more beautiful than the prince mentioned."

She blushed.

"Forgive me. I am General Luís. You know how to brush a horse?"

"Brush a horse?" she repeated.

"Yes. You do know horses, don't you?"

She didn't answer. He handed her the curry brush and expected her to begin. She looked down at it. She didn't know how to brush a horse, much less how to hold the brush.

"He needs to be curried," the general said.

Margarete walked slowly to the horse and adjusted the odd brush in her hand. She pushed the bristles against the horse's head. The horse looked at her wide-eyed and snorted. She started at the neck and made long, hard strokes downward. The horse's ears pushed back and he bucked slightly.

"Whoa, whoa," said the general. He looked to Margarete, who tried repeating her task. "Listen to the horse. He'll tell you what he likes. Round strokes. Softer. You're going to set him off before the battle!"

She tried again, clueless.

The general watched, shaking his head. "Cecil, come curry the horse!"

Just then, the warm blood charger relieved himself with a hefty warm pile of dung on the stable floor. The general handed Margarete a shovel. "Here. You can do this job right, I'm sure."

Margarete swallowed. At this point, she wished she was serving food again—or at least wished she knew how to curry a horse. She stared down at the waste. "And what do I do with it?" Her question earned a chuckle from the horse groomer and the general.

"And put this on!" General Luís commented as he tossed her a caparison. Of course, she missed and the cloth landed in the dung. She would still be forced to wear it, and she knew it. Perhaps they had another one available.

Whiter Than Snow

The crowds swelled to maximum capacity. Prince Philip was seated next to Queen Mary, the new ruler of England since her father's passing and brother's absence. Other royalty from all over Europe surrounded them. The final tournament brought guests from all over the world. It was the biggest sporting event of the year. Excited peasants watched from all angles under the canopy of the glaring sun, segregated from the royals, nobles, and aristocrats who enjoyed cushioned seats beneath cool shade.

Margarete watched from the floor. In her opinion, it was the greatest seat in the house. Maybe she had to shovel horse dung for it. And perhaps the horse did, in fact, scare her. But cheering the general on as he left from her side, racing to meet his challenger, was one of the most exhilarating experiences she ever had. She loved this sport. The adrenaline alone was enough to take her breath away.

The grounds thundered as the horses drove their riders towards one another. Each wooden lance aimed at the other man's heart. Ah, this was definitely a game of love and hate. Aim at the heart! If you hit the heart just right, you throw the man off his horse. They learned this move from a woman, she was sure of it!

At the same time, her heart stopped at every hit the general took by his opponent. And she couldn't help but notice him noticing her. He looked more like a prince than a general. His long, dark hair waved in the wind. His olive skin contrasted hers.

After each hit by his opponent, he would return to Margarete and hand her the broken lance—his eyes never leaving hers. And at the end of each match, he would gallop up to

Margarete, raise his helmet, smile at the young woman, and ask, "Did you have as much fun as me?" in his Spanish accent.

She would giggle each time, never answering. But she was having fun. She was consumed with emotion. Whoever thought that a sport could make a person feel so much? And flirting with a general, well...that was just the icing on the cake. Of course, she hoped Prince Philip was watching. At first she was angry with him, but now she was thankful. She peered toward the spectators for a possible glimpse.

There, in the center, under the cloth overhang and next to the queen, her *Prince Charming* sat, eyes fixed on the woman beside him—the Queen of England. They were laughing together, engaged in some kind of meaningless conversation. And honestly, although it stung a little, Margarete didn't seem to care. And when she realized she didn't care, at that moment she felt free.

The general dismounted after his third victory of the day. He walked closely to Margarete and leaned into her. "I look forward to seeing you at the ball tomorrow night."

The Royal Ball? Tomorrow? If only. If only she was going as a guest and not to serve. She didn't answer, and she didn't need to. While she was lost in thought, the general walked away. She lost sight of him in the crowd. She continued to watch, shading her eyes with her hand above them.

"Margarete!"

She turned around quickly.

"Did you enjoy it?" the prince said, a smile on his face.

"Oh yes, it was amazing!"

Whiter Than Snow

"And I see General Luís took care of you?"

She blushed and Prince Philip took notice. He inhaled, and if she wasn't mistaken, he seemed a bit jealous.

"Where did he go? I need to speak with him," he said.

She glanced toward the crowded marketplace—a sweet smile rested on her lips. He followed her gaze.

He held on to her arm a little long. "I'll try to see you later tonight." He seemed frazzled and disappeared into the same direction as the general.

All the while, Queen Mary watched the interchange between Prince Philip and his youthful servant, curiously eyeing them from her chair.

Matthew Eldridge

Chapter 18

The Ball. The Grand Ball. Everyone was getting ready for the Royal Ball. The anticipation swelled inside the hearts of young women, even servant women. It was a glorious moment, watching the world's elite in expensive beautiful gowns from the world's best dress makers. The aristocratic, noble, and royal women would pamper and prep themselves all day for the four hour event, starting with a massage.

Margarete, Maria, and a few of the other servants finished the preparations for guests in the main hall. Beautiful fountains of wine adorned the corners of the room. A seven tiered cake centered the room. A feast of fruits, salads, and meats covered the entire west wall. A stage was set to the north. It was going to be an incredible evening.

And the men; while Margarete and her friends were only servants, there was something vulnerable and stimulating about seeing men dressed for a Royal Ball, preparing to dance with a lovely lady. It was believed that the way a man danced signified his ability to love. If he was awkward and stiff, he would not be a very good husband. If a man was suave and could move with his partner and lead her in the dance, he was said to be a great catch as a husband. A man who can sweep a woman off her feet and make her forget she's dancing will make a woman forget all her troubles during harsh years of marriage. And so, there they were, ready to judge the dancing of each male in the room.

The sun slid beneath the castle wall. Torches lit the way as musicians filled the outer court. It was the grandest event Margarete had ever witnessed. She longed to be outside as the couples arrived in horse and carriage, but she was stationed to serve the ballroom and northern hallway. At least she would be able to witness the dances. This intrigued her most of all. Out of a hundred servants, the head servant picked her, Maria, and a handful of others to serve the ballroom. They were picked by looks alone. Homely people weren't welcome to serve in the beautiful ballroom, she was told. It hurt Margarete's heart when she heard the head servant say it, and felt ashamed when she was thankful that her beauty allowed her to stay in the room. People should not be judged on looks...*perhaps dancing abilities*, yes, but not looks, she thought.

Several of the musicians made their way into the room and began to play up on the stage. Margarete was too busy bringing out silverware to notice.

Two by two, guests entered into the grand ballroom. Margarete watched out of the corner of her eye while working. She stayed by the buffet, which worked in her favor, as the guests retreated to it as they entered the room. She replaced plates and added cheese and watched for the door, curious to see both the general and the prince. Who could dance? The general already proved he could fight. Could he be vulnerable, smooth, and cunning on the dance floor as well? A few more guests poured in. They were all so attractive.

"Who's that?" Maria whispered to Margarete, pointing to a gorgeous man who entered the room.

"Oh, that's Sir Thomas Wyatt, the Younger. He was the knight who won most of the tournament yesterday."

"He speak Spanish?" she asked impishly in broken English.

Margarete giggled. "I don't know. Go ask him!" she teased.

Maria playfully put her hand over her heart and frowned.

And then Margarete saw him. Her prince. He was radiant. He walked with the confidence, yet coolness that said he was secure in himself, and that this place was his, even though it wasn't. He was the master of charm.

Her heart jumped in her chest and tickled her throat. She could barely breathe. She longed for just a simple glance—a single look in her direction where their eyes would meet...for it was in his eyes that told all. They were the windows to the soul. By one look she could see his love for her. By one look she could be satisfied, though she would not dance with him tonight. It was to a woman's advantage to catch a man's eye. And while many women have caught his eye over time, she hoped that tonight, dressed as a servant, while so many were in beautiful gowns, he would still look her way and give her the connection she so desperately needed right now. Why? Because she felt worthless. She felt ashamed for what she was—a slave basically—and needed to catch the eye of a beautiful prince to make her feel something; anything.

He skirted around the room making small talk with the nobles. She continued to watch, waiting, hoping for a single gesture he noticed her; perhaps even a smile or even a fleeting glance. She held her breath as he approached.

The prince walked briskly past Margarete with his guards. She smiled, but he pretended he didn't even notice her. She followed him with her eyes, which brought more heartache. He met Queen Mary of England halfway across the dance floor, and bowed. She held out her hand and the young prince kissed it. The musicians began to play a new ballad and Margarete watched as the prince pulled the queen close to him.

Margarete couldn't help but be jealous. The queen's dress was gorgeous. It shimmered of gold, lace, and pearls. Her breasts practically burst out of the top of the dress, weighed down with a hefty broach. The servant girl looked at her own chest in comparison…it appeared almost non-existent in her servant clothes.

The queen was beautiful, Margarete admitted, but she wondered how much of her beauty was the dress she was wearing, and of course, the fashioning of her strawberry blonde hair, which was up and pinned with a lace of pearls.

The queen's eyes were no match for the servant at all. Charming maybe, but a softness found in so many beauties eluded the woman. She was hard. Perhaps that's why she was the queen.

Whiter Than Snow

Out of all of her siblings, she was the least favored, but the most vocal. She inherited the throne as the eldest after her father passed away and her brother, Edward, died at a young age. Some believed she was responsible for his death.

Still, it appeared her caramel eyes captured the gaze of the prince this evening.

Prince Philip II and Queen Mary of England began their dance on the floor as the nobles joined in. It was a beautiful dance, and the queen executed it without thought, as if she'd been conditioned to dance like that all her life. However, the dance itself was a new dance, originating in France a few years back. It was a very romantic dance. How appropriate that it originated in the city of love: Paris. Of course, she was sure that Prince Philip encouraged it, which made her more jealous. But she did have to remind herself that the queen traveled quite a bit. What made this dance so unique for the 16th Century was that the dance partners were so close their faces practically touched, not to mention their bodies were less than an inch apart. Philip pulled the queen closer, and the nobles followed with their own dance partners. King Henry would surely have a fit if he were alive today, she thought.

The queen leaned in and whispered in the prince's ear. His hand lowered on her back and he looked into her eyes and gave her his signature smile. Margarete's heart ached that it wasn't for her. The queen glanced to Margarete over the prince's shoulder. As they made eye contact, the teen stepped back and her rear bumped into the table behind her. She clumsily tried to catch herself, expelled a short scream, and knocked over a tray of cheese onto the floor, which sent her stumbling to catch it. She caught her hand on the table cloth by accident, and another tray of food followed her lead and fell to the floor as well.

The guests all turned in her direction to find the commotion. Maria ran to her aid and helped her up off the floor. The queen smirked. She then looked to the prince, who seemed concerned at the affair.

"Who is that girl?" Queen Mary addressed Prince Philip.

He ignored her question and stared at the servant as she fled into the other room, tears covering her face.

His hand loosened on the queen and he stopped dancing.

The queen looked angrily at him. "I asked you a question, Prince!"

He turned to her, his jaw set straight. Their eyes met, and she searched his.

"She's...she's no one. Just a servant."

"*Your* servant?" she asked, eyebrows raised.

"Yes, for now. She's actually the servant of the king and queen in Brussels."

"And you brought her here?"

"What?"

"You don't think I know? I can see right through you." Her words slithered from between her teeth as she forced a smile for anyone watching.

"I'll marry you on one condition." She took a breath and stared at him hard, her voice demanding. "Get rid of the servant girl."

Whiter Than Snow

"How?"

"I don't care. Kill her for all I care. Just get her out of my sight, out of my kingdom. Out of England."

"You can't be serious." The prince assumed she was joking. Her shocking silence and stiff jaw told him otherwise.

"You have a reputation, and so do I," she answered.

He looked stunned.

"Wait a minute, is this Prince Philip, the brave warrior who knocked out a third of all of the Eastern World?"

"That was different. That was war."

"Love is war."

"So they say," he returned.

"Kill the girl. I want her head on a platter. I want her eyes cut from her face so she never looks at you again."

He stood motionless. The music continued, but he refused to dance.

The queen, on the other hand, started swaying to the music. "Fine. Then leave her here with me," she said, pulling him into the dance again.

"She's not mine to leave."

"You are the Prince of Spain, and I am the Queen of England. We can do as we wish. Some petty king is not going to fret over the loss of a useless servant girl."

They continued to dance in silence for a moment.

"Why does she bother you so?"

The queen took him by the hand and guided him onto the terrace. They stood, overlooking the beautiful lawn below. "Look, you don't think I know about Prince Philip, the heartbreaker, and all his petty little girlfriends? Once we are married, this will stop. You will have no more girlfriends. Your play time is over, and so is mine. It's not good for our image, and certainly not good for our marriage. And I don't want to ever see that tramp again!"

"She's not a tramp."

"Oh, please. They all are. They all can't resist the magically charming Prince Philip. They're all nothing but toys to you. And they come willingly."

"She's not a toy or a tramp. And nothing has ever happened between us," he said, refusing to face her.

She laughed. "You think I really believe that? She hasn't taken her eyes off of you. If your father knew, you would be kicked out of the family. And she would be beheaded. You've disappointed your father enough, don't you think?"

She grabbed his face and lifted his eyes to hers. They were beautiful, he thought, but pale in comparison to Margarete's sapphire eyes.

"This stops when you marry me. No more girlfriends. Understand?" she commanded.

"Who said I'm going to marry you?" he said firmly.

She chuckled. "You can't be serious."

"And what if I am?"

"Are you a fool?"

"Perhaps," he answered.

Whiter Than Snow

She stopped dancing. "We are two of the most powerful dynasties in the world. United, we become the world's greatest super power!"

"What about love?"

"Oh, you'll love it."

"I meant, what about marrying for love?" he questioned.

She laughed hysterically. "Since when does anyone marry for love anymore?"

His face fell.

"Besides, don't you find me attractive? Trust me; you will learn to love me." She moved in to kiss his lips and he turned. Her lips brushed his cheek. Out of the corner of her eye she could see Margarete watching them from the next room. The queen leaned into him like they were enjoying an intimate moment, and smiled mischievously at the poor servant girl.

Margarete's heart retreated. She felt her pulse beat heavily in her neck. What was she thinking? Who did she think she was? She was no match for the Queen of England, especially as a servant girl. This woman could take her life for even looking at the prince. This woman would take this man, this handsome prince, and Margarete would be left with a broken heart. Better she turn her heart off now, before it gets crushed more than it already has, she thought.

Still, something inside of her wanted to compete. It was a womanly instinct. She wanted the prince, and he made it clear he wanted her too. No, she was no match for the queen, but from what she understood of the prince, the queen could never own his heart.

Margarete's heart was wild and it wanted what it wanted. She didn't realize she could feel something like this. Perhaps she was becoming a woman, after all.

The band began to play again, and the guests took their partners by the hand and danced around the room. Margarete had only dreamed of something so wonderful or magical. It was in fact, the most glorious dancing she had ever dreamed of, and she was here to watch it, even if she was a servant. And the music—she swore she knew it, but could not see the band from her post. Perhaps she dreamed of it. The ladies looked as if they were gliding on air as they danced. Their dresses were bowed out and barely touched the ground, hiding their feet. The men were dressed to match many of their ladies. They were all so handsome, well-groomed, and well-mannered.

She didn't see Hannah, the head servant, approaching from behind.

"Make yourself useful child or I'll put you in the service of something a lot less glamorous. Understand?"

"Yes," Margarete answered as she nodded.

"You know, if you don't let him go, you will find yourself in a whole heap of trouble. Let him use you for what he will, and leave him alone. Nothing more. And while you are here, you don't exist. Try to remember that, or off with your head! The queen will be sure to it! If he cared about you at all, he would have never brought you here!"

Whiter Than Snow

Margarete tried to contain the waterfalls that forced themselves out from behind her aqua colored eyes, but she couldn't.

The head servant had pity on her and placed a hand on her shoulder. "Go, child... go wash up," she said.

Queen Mary continued to watch Margarete, smiling at the obvious pain eating at the young servant. She may not take her life tonight, but she would wound her heart purposely.

Margarete ran out of the room with her face in her hands and bumped into someone...a handsome man...not just any handsome man...

"General Luís," she said, as she wiped her face in front of him and then ran around him into the hallway.

"What's wrong, child?" he asked, following her with his eyes.

She was too far away and too upset to answer. He looked in the direction of the ballroom and saw the prince dancing with the queen. The queen stared at him with a sly grin on her face, and the Spaniard quickly understood.

Matthew Eldridge

Chapter 19

The maidservants were all sleeping—exhausted from cleaning up after the ball. However, Margarete's wrecked heart wouldn't let her sleep. It ached. Why did she come on such a trip? Sure, the Queen of Brussels was cruel to her, but at least her heart would still be intact. *Foolish girl! Stop believing in fairy tales.*

She crept out of bed and made her way quietly out of the great hall and into the courtyard. She walked with her head down, staring at her feet…lost. She didn't know where she was going, and it didn't matter. She turned the corner and…

"Pardon me," said the handsome young musician as he bumped into her, carrying his instrument in a brown, wooden case.

The impact knocked her over. She was so consumed by her thoughts that the face in front of her didn't register. The musician reached down to help her up. It was then she looked at him and recognized the comforting face before her.

"Jack?" she whimpered.

"I think I would remember a face as beautiful as yours, but forgive me. How do I know you?" he joked.

She burst into tears and embraced the boy.

He dropped his instrument and held her tightly, her face smothered in his neck and shoulder. It was a full minute before she let go. She glanced up at him with desperate eyes.

"What are you doing here in London?" he asked.

"I came with…" she thought carefully about her words… *why was she here*?

"I'm just serving here for a few days while passing through."

"Passing through?"

"Uh…" She was flustered. She didn't want to tell him she came with the prince. For one, she felt dumb enough for coming with him, after everything that had happened. For two, the prince had a reputation, and she didn't want her fiancé to think she was unfaithful. "…the tournament," she answered, hesitantly.

"The jousting tournament?" he asked.

"Yes! That's the one! What are you doing here?"

"You know what I'm doing here! This is the greatest city in the world. I'm playing music everywhere I'm needed. Tonight a ball, tomorrow I'm playing at the tournament! I'll make a fortune this week alone. I'll make more money this week than I normally would in a month!

"Congratulations," she said half-heartedly. Her lack of enthusiasm troubled him.

"I'll hit France after this and be home by Christmas! And then we can get married!"

She didn't respond, but instead, turned away and sobbed.

Whiter Than Snow

Jack chased after her. "Margarete! What's wrong?" He wrapped his warm arms around her and held her as she cried. "What's wrong?" he asked again, wiping her tears with his hand.

"Nothing. I'm just homesick is all."

A voice echoed through the hallway and spilled into the open—a voice she recognized. That tone used to melt her, but she felt nauseated upon hearing it this time. The prince came around the corner with his entourage and saw her, then quickly glanced away, as if he didn't notice her. *Two times*, she stated mentally.

"Just take me somewhere, Jack. Somewhere away from here."

Jack took her arm and the two escaped the courtyard, into the bailey, and towards the castle's gate. She looked back at the prince and caught him watching her. *Mission accomplished.* She wanted him jealous. She wanted him hurt—the way that she felt hurt. She wanted him to suffer. The worst part was she was using Jack to stir the prince's jealousy.

This was Jack, the love of her life! Or was he? Confusion swept over her like a wave and slammed her into the sandbar of reality. Here she was with Jack, her fiancé once again, all the while, feeling incredible feelings aroused in her by this beautiful prince, this lover, this heart thief. When she was with Jack, she felt like a girl playing grown-up. But some things changed over the past few months. She no longer saw herself as a child. She was a young woman—a woman ready for a grown man's love.

The couple made small talk as they walked the dusty streets, through the desolate night market place and past the tents.

She looked to Jack again, catching a glimpse of his perfect profile. They walked to a tree and stood beneath it—hidden from the moonlight, just off the cobblestone path.

She forced herself to think rationally. Here was Jack, her childhood love, standing before her, ready to take her, cherish her, and make her a satisfied wife and lover. He would hold her as long as she wanted, when she wanted. He would make her feel safe and warm. She stared into his eyes. She evaded fear with Jack.

It was strange. It had been only a few months since they saw each other last, and yet, it seemed like a lifetime ago. The girl Jack loved was gone. She was a young woman now who had experienced so much. He was beautiful. Not a word she would usually use on a guy, but he was. He had shaggy brown hair, with golden highlights from the sun. His olive skin went well with his blue-green eyes. His high cheek bones were nicely rounded out with a small goatee on his chin. He wore a really cool beret with a feather in it. Typical musician. He had always been the artsy type.

As a boy he was lanky and tall. Now he was fit, but still thin—just perfect. He was not the manly war hero Prince Philip, but instead, he was the handsome young man, almost still a boy, creative, smart, and sensitive. How a girl could like so many different things in a guy confused her. Warrior or artist? Muscular or thin? Commanding or sensitive? It made her head spin. Of course, every girl wants a warrior. But to find a guy who is sensitive, gentle, and genuine is just as much desired.

He stopped and forced her to look into his eyes again, taking both her hands in his. "Do you still love me, Margarete?"

Whiter Than Snow

His heart ached. Why? Because she hesitated in her answer. He could see it in her eyes that she didn't. And while his heart swelled from the sting, he told himself he would win her heart once again.

He bent down and forced her lips against his. She became weak-kneed, and yet, she didn't kiss him back. Perhaps she was too distracted by her thoughts. Or perhaps by the open space surrounding them. He backed off, took her hand, and they walked again.

The two talked for hours under the moonlight. She told him about serving the queen and king, but skipped the part about the prince. He told her about his musical adventures throughout Europe. It was well past midnight when Margarete suggested she make her way back to the castle. She didn't want to go back. She was falling for Jack all over again.

When they arrived at the drawbridge, Margarete refused to allow him to walk her further. Jack turned to her and hugged her. "Ok, I guess this is goodbye until tomorrow?"

She smiled at him and sighed. "Tomorrow."

He kissed her on the cheek and quickly ran away.

She was in a dreamland as she skipped towards the gate. *Prince who?* She laughed to herself. Yes, she was already forgetting the heartbreaker. The old embers of her youth were rekindled—aged feelings towards Jack were coming alive again. Philip was just an ideology anyway. He was an out of reach dream: the magical prince. But she was a servant. And although he was handsome, his reputation betrayed him, exposing his inability to truly love, even if a prince could or would express his love for a servant publicly.

Prince Philip was really a contradiction. He felt strongly towards his faith as a Catholic, but lived a very liberal lifestyle when it came to women and alcohol. He was Spain's most elusive bachelor—stealing hearts and loving none, she was led to believe. And yet, he showed her a side of him she felt very few people saw. He had a soft, romantic side. Or perhaps that was all a show just to woo her.

Jack, she thought and grinned. She had a thing about music. His instrument alone made him attractive to her—especially the way he played it. However, even without the guitar or the violin (whichever he chose to play that night), he was more than delightful to look at, talk to, and be with. And he was a Protestant Christian. It's not like she was now magically back in love with Jack, but the fact that she could have feelings for another guy so quickly after feeling that she was falling in love with the prince was a good sign. Perhaps she would get over this after all. Still, the thought of marrying Jack frightened her. She would have to make him understand.

"Halt!" the voice yelled to her.

Margarete turned around, and before she could react, two guards grabbed her arms, one on each side of her.

Whiter Than Snow

Chapter 20

Margarete slumped against the cold, stone wall. The smell of moist dirt filled her nostrils. She placed her head in her hands and tried to cry silently, but a few sobs escaped between her deep breaths. A beautiful young woman approached the teen and sat beside her, lovingly playing with the girl's silky black hair, separating it and beginning a braid, trying to comfort her.

"What's your name, dear?" the young woman asked softly.

"Margarete," the child answered timorously.

The beautiful blonde woman smiled warmly. "Lovely name."

Margarete fell into the young woman's embrace.

"I know those tears. You are crying from a broken heart, are you not?"

Margarete didn't respond, but the woman knew, alright. Just hearing the pretty lady acknowledge the source of her pain brought almost instant relief. The woman was medicine: a soft, beautiful, kindred soul with a gift of discernment; a woman who understood.

"Would you like something to eat?" the kind woman asked, handing Margarete a piece of bread.

Margarete sat up against the young lady. It had been a while since she felt a motherly touch, although the young woman was close to her age, perhaps a year or two older. After she took a few bites of the bread, the woman gave her a sip of wine. Upon drinking it, Margarete smacked her lips and belched.

"Wine? In prison?"

"In a place like this, you'll need it!" the woman answered.

Margarete took another gulp.

"Easy, girl. Besides, we're not in the actual prison. We're in the tower—where they keep people who aren't really criminals. So I know your crime is an innocent one. Perhaps a crime of love?"

Margarete finished the wine. Realizing it, she looked up to the woman and said, "Oh, oh, I'm so sorry. I didn't mean to…"

"It's okay, I can get us more," the young woman interrupted.

Margarete wiped her mouth with the back of her hand and asked, "So why are you in here?"

"Same reason you are. I'm sure."

"I don't know why I'm in here," Margarete responded.

"My sister," the woman interrupted.

Margarete stared in confusion.

"My name's Elizabeth," the young woman added.

"Oh dear God. The queen is your sister?" Margarete realized.

"Yes."

Whiter Than Snow

Margarete sat up and moved herself off the woman, embarrassed that she didn't recognize the princess, Elizabeth, daughter of King Henry.

"No worries, child. I'm still the same woman you thought I was a moment ago." Elizabeth pulled her down again and continued braiding Margarete's soft, beautiful hair. "So I want to ask you a question." She paused, finished the braid and asked, "Are you the daughter of a king?"

Margarete giggled, but marveled at the thought. "No, I'm a servant."

"Are you sure?"

"Yes, I'm sure."

"We assumed you were the missing daughter of the King of Brussels, pretending to be a maidservant to avoid the wrath of my sister."

"Why would anyone do that?"

"Like Abraham pretending Sarah was his sister in the Bible—to save his own life?"

Margarete cherished the thought in her heart. She loved the king like a father, and how she wished it were true. "That's absurd. And why would I be trying to avoid your sister?"

"She's to be married to Prince Philip, you know?"

Silence.

"Did you know the king and his first wife?"

"I wasn't born yet when she died."

"Oh…" she continued to play with her hair. "He's just using you, you know. You're worth more than that."

"The king?"

"No," Elizabeth laughed. "Prince Philip."

"I'm worth more than what?"

The queen's sister sighed. "You are worth more than giving your body to some handsome prince for his moment's pleasure."

"I know."

Elizabeth smiled and placed her hands on Margarete's shoulders. She was at least half a foot taller than the teenager. She forced Margarete to look into her eyes. The servant found her eyes warm and inviting, consumed with sincerity. "Even a servant should protect her chastity, regardless of whom comes knocking at her door. Prince Philip has a reputation."

"Nothing has happened between us."

"Seriously, child?"

"Yes."

"Thank God. The prince hasn't corrupted you yet."

"Yet?" she laughed. "I don't intend on giving anything away to him."

"Does he know that?"

"I think I've made it clear."

"He will continue pursuing you unless you do. I've seen the way he looks at you… and so has my sister."

Margarete gave her a faint smile and said, "Thank you."

Elizabeth looked around and whispered in her ear. "Can I tell you a secret?"

"Sure."

Whiter Than Snow

"I'm a virgin."

Margarete's eyes widened. "Really? I've heard stories about this castle…"

"Well, not everybody gets around. Just because my father had issues… well… and my sister… and my brother…" she laughed. "Let's just say I'm not like them."

The women sat in silence for a minute.

"May I ask…," Margarete started.

"Go ahead, dear."

"Why did your sister put you in prison?"

"Well…several reasons. For one, she didn't want me at the Royal Ball. For two, she wants to kill me, but she can't exactly kill her royal sister without an uproar." She looked at the young girl to see if her response was satisfactory.

"Kill you? Why?"

"She fears I'll take the throne…and more than that, I'm not Catholic.

"You're not?"

"No…I'm a Protestant Christian," she said hesitantly.

"Me too."

"Really?" Elizabeth's eyes lit up.

"Yes."

"Let Prince Philip know and he'll probably leave you alone, either that or try to convert you."

"What do you mean?"

"You haven't heard?"

"Heard what?"

"My sister…and she's trying to pull in Prince Philip…the Christians…"

"What?"

"They are planning on murdering the Protestants in all of Europe. My sister has already murdered hundreds of pastors and their followers in England and the surrounding territories. She's moving abroad, and convincing the prince it's the right thing to do—that it's what God wants from them as Catholics. And the prince will listen. His father persecuted the Protestants before him. Once they join forces, they'll eradicate all of Europe of the faith. It will be the biggest massacre this world has ever seen."

"I don't understand. I thought your father was a Protestant. He fought to be free from Catholicism, Jack said."

"Jack?"

"Oh, a friend of mine from back home."

"Yes, he was…as I am. But my sister hated him, and she hates me as well. She wants nothing to do with us. Besides, my father's reasons for turning Protestant was nothing admirable." Elizabeth paused, looking at Margarete as if she should share the family secret, which really wasn't a secret after all. "My father simply became a Protestant because the Pope refused to allow him to divorce Catherine and marry my mother—which is another reason my sister hates me so. He replaced her mother for mine."

Margarete's stomach turned sour. "I still don't understand your sister. Why would she put you in prison? Why not send you away?"

Whiter Than Snow

"Because she can. I bring out the worst in her. And now I've given her an excuse."

"But you're sisters!"

"Half sisters. Mary was always jealous of me because I was the younger one. I got more attention. It was my mom who raised us both until her early death—and then we were separated. I didn't see her for years. And now that I'm a Protestant, she hates me all the more."

"I think you are much prettier, too," Margarete said softly, as if it mattered.

"I think she plans on having me murdered quietly," Elizabeth said, her eyes shifting nervously as she fidgeted with the wrinkles in her dress.

Margarete didn't know how to respond. The woman looked scared for the first time since meeting her.

"I'm a threat to her," Elizabeth continued. "If anything happens to her, then the throne becomes mine. The pressure is too much for her. There are people who would give their life to take her out of power, just to put me in it."

"And why don't they?"

"Because I refuse to let them. I am a Christian, child. Remember what that means. No revenge. Let God handle our battles. He is in control."

"Aren't you scared?"

"Maybe a little. Here's another secret," she whispered. "God gave me dreams of being the queen one day. Unlike my sister, I will serve the people, and I will serve as if I'm serving

God himself. If it never happens and my life is taken, then so be it. I'll be in Heaven, where I long to be anyway."

The guard returned with a plate of cheese and crackers and slid them to Elizabeth underneath the bars.

"…and I'd stop the bloody persecution of Protestant Christians. I'd stop Bloody Mary from her massacre of the innocent."

"This is horrible," Margarete responded, deep in thought.

"Yes, and by the time my sister and Prince Philip marry, all of Europe will be forced into Catholicism or die by the sword. We are talking about hundreds of thousands of wrongful deaths. Fathers, mothers, brothers and sisters. Abandoned babies will fill the orphanages. And I'm afraid my sister won't stop there. She's declaring a Catholic—Protestant war. And with the power she and the prince hold, there is no hope for the Protestants."

"What about your family?"

"I'm the only family she has. She terrifies us all. And she wants to secure the throne for her future children.

By now, Margarete's beautiful, shiny black hair was in two braids.

"Your hair is beautiful. It goes well with your face. I can see what Prince Philip sees in you."

"I'm surprised he isn't after you!" Margarete teased.

"Well, I've made it very clear I'm not for sale." Elizabeth turned away. "I'm sorry dear—I didn't mean it like that." She sat back down in the cold cell, trying to make herself comfortable against the hard wall, feeling uneasy about her last statement.

Whiter Than Snow

"I heard your father created the Book of Prayer?" asked Margarete. "My friend, Jack, had one."

"Thomas Cramner wrote it. My father simply hired him to do it. You know an awful lot for a servant girl. Are you sure you aren't the king's daughter?"

Margarete laughed. "I'm sure. I didn't grow up a servant. The serving thing is very new to me."

"Interesting. That explains a few things," Elizabeth said with a cock-eyed glance, half kidding.

"What's that supposed to mean?"

"It means I like you!"

The two girls giggled. There was camaraderie. In any other circumstance, they would probably be the best of friends.

"Thomas?"

"Oh, yes," Elizabeth answered, remembering the conversation. "Well, Cramner, the ex-Arch Bishop, was nothing but a pawn to my dad. He might have written the book, but he had not the heart to go with it."

"Really?"

"You'd be surprised what you can learn on the inside... The people who pretend to be the most religious or legalistic are usually the ones who prove to have the darkest hearts."

"Your sister?"

"Precisely...But there are a few amazing people of God as well. Have you ever heard of John Foxe?"

"Yes, I have actually," answered Margarete, proudly.

"I helped him escape," Elizabeth bragged, a smile on her face.

"Really? I met his cousin!"

"Cousin? He doesn't have a cousin."

"She said she was…and her son…"

Elizabeth interrupted, "That was his wife! Protecting herself and her boy, I'm sure. Anyways, that's why I'm in here this time, according to my sister. She's put a huge price on his head!"

"This time? So this isn't your first time in jail? Why is he so valuable to her?" Margarete asked.

"Haven't you heard of his book? He's making a book about all the Christians who were martyred by my sister and her partnering kingdoms. He's describing the horrible detail of these horrific events. She wants him dead. He's making her out to be Satan himself, in the flesh."

Elizabeth took a sip of her wine. "And I want the world to know, too. I want them to see what an animal she is. I will help every Protestant escape her horrible fate for them as I can—God willing."

"Oh dear. You've helped others?"

"Oh…lots of people. "John Knox, John Calvin…"

"John Knox? The radical preacher from Scotland? We've heard of him all the way to Waldeck. Jack thinks he's wonderful."

"The one and the same… He worked for my dad for a short time."

"Where is he now?"

"After my sister put him in prison, I helped him escape, and I don't quite know. I think he was headed to Geneva…"

The two women heard a commotion and turned to see new prisoners being brought in from the main entrance. Margarete watched as the guards marched Jack, his dad, his mother, and his brother down a solemn hallway.

"Jack!" she whimpered to herself as she ran to the cell door. He didn't see her.

"Hush!" Elizabeth ordered. "You don't want to draw attention to yourself. You need to disassociate yourself from your friends if you want to get out alive."

She heard Elizabeth, but her eyes bulged forward, her fingers wrapped around and through the metal bars. Her face was stricken with panic. "Jack," she moaned softly. "Where are they taking him?"

Elizabeth lowered her head. "To a cell less suitable."

"They're good people. They're musicians! Why would they arrest them?"

"These friends of yours…are they Protestants?"

"Yes…That was Jack…"

Elizabeth interrupted, "No one is safe within a hundred miles. This castle has eyes and ears. All will be told."

Margerete cried. "It's my fault."

"Shhhhh," Elizabeth hushed as she put her finger to her lips.

Margarete walked backwards to the cell's far wall and leaned against it. She slumped to the ground and placed her head between her legs as she started to cry.

The guard walked by and Elizabeth put a hand out. "Larry, I believe I'll need more wine tonight. And get a bottle for yourself."

"Yes, my lady," the guard answered.

Strangely, he was bid to serve her, save opening the cell. She treated him well by offering portions to him of everything she received. He, in return, treated her like the princess he knew her for before her arrest. It was a fair exchange. Both played their roles well with an unspoken assumption that one day Elizabeth may be queen. Perhaps she would remember Larry's kindness and offer him a higher rank to serve her. And perhaps he was just saving his head. Either way, she ate the best foods while hidden away in the tower of London, the abandoned centuries-old mildewing castle that became her prison.

Margarete awoke with her head in Elizabeth's lap. The young woman mothered her until she fell asleep the night before. Still in a slumbering daze, she sat up as Prince Philip and a guard stopped at her cell and opened the gate. The guard stepped inside quickly and jerked Margarete up by the arm. The prince refused to acknowledge her.

As they exited the cell, Elizabeth awoke by the clanging of her metal cage.

Whiter Than Snow

"God be with you, Margarete," Elizabeth whispered to herself.

Matthew Eldridge

Chapter 21

The guard accompanied the prince and Margarete to the carriage in the early morning moonlight. Once she was aboard, the guard nodded and stepped away. Prince Philip climbed inside and the driver snapped the reins, signaling the horses. What started as a beautiful journey just a week before was now a shameful reminder of the dangers of falling in love with a prince. Margarete gazed out the window at the naked market. It wasn't so grand, stripped from all the people. Her heart was sagging with disappointment and regret. It occurred to her that she hated this place and vowed to never return.

Through thick silence she watched the wind blow the cherry blossoms, the petals being torn from their trees and littering the streets. After that, she saw nothing but green, so she sat back in the carriage and rested.

She awoke at the crossing of the English Channel. It was still daytime, and she could see everything. The views at Dover were breathtaking. She looked back to see a majestic, historic castle to her right, one of the few still standing from the 1100's. As the road continued to the coast, she witnessed the magnificent views of the white cliffs. Prince Philip was right. It was very different in the day, and she had a million questions to ask him.

But they still weren't talking, so she kept to herself and let the scenery take her breath away.

As they crossed the English Channel, the wind blew hard against them in the autumn air. Without a word, the Prince stood close to her to block the wind until the boat reached the other side. She leaned back to be closer to him.

"Are you hungry?" the prince finally asked, breaking the silence.

Her eyes were glossy as she choked back her tears, still coming to terms with Jack's arrest and her possible involvement. "No."

"Well, I am. We'll stop soon for food." The prince waited a moment, then added, "You know, I didn't bring you all this way to see you with another man. No wonder you wanted to come."

"Why did you bring me?"

"Hold your tongue, servant, before you lose it."

She wanted to tell him she didn't come all this way to watch him rip her heart out by dancing and whoring with the queen, but that would earn her a hard slap across the face for sure.

The prince stopped brooding by dinnertime. It was obvious he was lonely for companionship.

"I'm sorry," he said. "Let's forget about what happened back there."

Whiter Than Snow

She didn't answer.

"Hello?" He touched her face and pulled her eyes towards his.

"I'm holding my tongue, as you requested," she answered.

"Please," he said gently. He was softening to her, once again.

The tone of his tender voice melted her. She wanted to cry.

"I was in a jail cell. How can I forget what happened?"

"I assure you—that was not my doing."

As much as she wanted to believe him, she didn't.

The sun was setting behind them shortly after the carriage exchange at the English Channel. Barely into France, the smell of burnt lumber lingered in the air. Remembering the smoky scent from her journey to Brussels, Margarete quickly jumped to the carriage window and peered out. Smoke billowed from the windows and doors of houses and barns.

"Oh no!" she cried out.

"What is it?" the prince asked, pushing her aside and looking out the window himself.

"You have to help them!" she pleaded.

"How?"

"Just go!"

"I am the Prince of Spain. These are not my people."

She gave him a stern look. "So they are worth nothing because they aren't part of your kingdom?"

He seethed. "Driver, stop the coach!"

The driver and the guard dismounted. The prince stepped out and together they surveyed the fire several hundred yards away. The small village was set ablaze. Even from this distance they could feel the heat on their faces. The second carriage carrying all of their belongings and a couple of guards caught up to the prince and stopped behind him.

Prince Philip pulled out his sword and addressed one of his guards. "Manuel, dismount your horses. You and I will ride to the village." He pointed to the driver of the first carriage and to the guard with him and commanded, "Continue the journey in case of danger. We'll catch up."

"Danger? I want to stay here," Margarete interjected.

He ignored her plea and addressed the driver again. "Go now!"

Margarete watched as the prince and his guard, Manuel, climbed bareback onto the horses and sped towards the smoldering village.

As they arrived, several soldiers from another kingdom were riding away from the scene.

"What is going on here?" the prince asked.

"None of your concern," the soldier answered snidely.

"This isn't my jurisdiction, but I assure you, it is my concern."

"Do you want us to leave you with the same fate as these people? I suggest you move on!" the soldier mocked.

Whiter Than Snow

Manuel blurted, "How dare you talk to the Prince of Spain that way!"

The two soldiers looked at each other and back to the prince. Then, one of them answered in a single word, "Witchcraft," and spit on the ground, as if the word was detestable to his lips.

Prince Philip looked to the villagers running frantically towards the dark woods. They hardly looked like witches. He glanced to the soldiers again and noticed one of them holding a strongbox under his arm. "And what is that? Evidence?"

The soldiers eyed each other nervously. The one without the box pulled out his sword and struck it towards the prince, slicing into the air. Manuel deflected it with his own sword. The soldier with the strongbox fled on his horse, the prince followed, and Manuel and the remaining soldier dueled.

The prince caught up to the rider and slashed at him with his sword. The soldier dodged. Prince Philip was at a disadvantage. His horse was hardly that of a warrior. The soldier outran him, but dropped the strongbox in the process. The prince gave up the chase, but galloped to the strongbox and cracked it open with a blow by the butt of his sword. Inside the box lay a rare Protestant Bible and enough coins to rebuild the village—money that was stolen from the villagers. He tossed the Bible in the woods to remove the speculated evidence and galloped back to the village, desperately searching for survivors.

A man covered in ash worked furiously to save his livestock from the burning inferno that was quickly spreading. The animals seemed confused by the blazes surrounding them and refused to exit through the gate's entrance. The prince dismounted and cut some of the fence down with his sword, helping the animals escape.

As the last of the swine ran from the engulfing cage of sure death into the black night, Philip shouted to the man, "Are there any more people?"

"My lord, they've all escaped into the woods, save one." He pointed to an elderly man who was slain a few feet from the door of the house. He died protecting it.

Prince Philip handed the man the strongbox and rode away.

Manuel met with him on the road. "Did you get what you were after?"

"Yes."

"What was in it?"

"Coins. Lots of coins."

Margarete leaned back in the carriage, the black night suffocating her. She hoped for a little moonlight, but a thick fog mingled with smoke engulfed the sky and everything surrounding them. The driver's lantern was barely visible, causing him to drive even slower than usual. One small branch in the road or even a dip in the ground could break the carriage wheel, leaving them stranded in the middle of nowhere. She shivered in fear. She wrapped her quaking arms around her body and lied down on the seat, hoping the squeaking wheels of the carriage would lull her to sleep. She was terrified to be alone. But she wasn't alone, really. She had the guard and the driver protecting her, she reminded herself quite often.

Before she realized what was happening, she found herself in a vision at the tender age of twelve, walking through the forest in the darkness of night. She was so innocent, and so naïve. Before that horrible night, she would spend time walking through the woods talking to God or picking flowers or berries. She was often home before dark, but this very eve, darkness fell fast—and she had a mission to find food.

She heard sounds following her and thought it was an animal—a bear perhaps. She held her breath, walking slowly so that the animal wouldn't give chase, and out of the corner of her eye she could see the shape of a dark figure moving towards her. Perhaps it was her adoptive brother. He was known for playing tricks in the forest. But then again, she remembered he was at home, ill.

Without warning, the beast stood before her. A man, a horrible, dirty man grabbed her and threw her on the forest floor. It was that day that her innocence was robbed. It was that day that she learned the forest had eyes full of evil, and she vowed to never be in the forest at night ever again.

She screamed in her sleep as she remembered the horror, awaking from the dream.

"Shhhh. It's okay," a voice whispered, as a finger brushed her cheek.

Realizing she wasn't alone, she immediately awoke and sat up. It was still too dark to see, but she knew his smell. It was Prince Philip. He had caught up with them and rejoined her in the carriage as she slept. She wrapped her arms around him in the darkness and hugged his neck tightly, her face pressed against his, her tears wetting his neck.

"It was just a bad dream. You're okay now. Go back to sleep."

And she did. With the presence of the prince, peace washed over her and she quickly fell back to sleep—in his arms, nonetheless.

She didn't wake again until the sun invaded the carriage window hours later.

"We're here," the prince said softly, stroking her hair.

Dread encompassed the servant girl as she and Prince Philip approached the castle in his carriage. It was a beautiful, quaint castle, and it was her home for now, but it was empty and cold.

"You will stay the night won't you—in the castle?"

"Yes, one night. I have to get back to Spain," the prince answered. "I've enjoyed your company."

"As I have yours." She was being polite, yet, sincere, savoring the tiny morsels of alone time they shared.

The carriage stopped, and the driver escorted Margarete out.

Whiter Than Snow

As she entered the threshold of the castle, heaviness draped over her. She walked the gloomy grey halls to her room. She just left one prison cell in England and felt she was entering another.

Matthew Eldridge

Chapter 22

Hours had passed since Margarete set her eyes upon the handsome Prince of Spain. She pampered herself in the few spare moments she had before serving dinner to the royal couple and their special guest.

"Oh, no!" she said to herself, staring in the mirror. She touched the small blemish that protruded from the outside of her right temple. To anyone else, it was hardly noticeable. To her, it might as well have been a mountain. "The prince can't see me like this!" she cried to her reflection. She wanted to make a lasting impression. She feared his last memory of her would be of the blemish on the side of her face. The funny thoughts of a teenage girl in love.

She tried several ways to cover it up, but nothing worked. Alas, she placed the kerchief on her head to cover her hair, but then, pulled wisps of hair from the sides of it to cover the blemish. "This will have to do," she remarked in humility. Part of her hoped he wasn't there. Another part of her hated herself for being so shallow and vain.

Margarete walked with the grace of a ballerina, carrying cups of soup for the king, queen, and their guest, before bringing out the evening meal. Prince Philip's eyes were transfixed on the beautiful servant as she glided across the floor. And after their trip to England together, their growing chemistry was evident to the queen.

Watching the eyes of the prince follow the young girl, the queen stretched her leg under the table and rubbed her foot against the prince's leg to get his attention. He pulled his gaze from Margarete and looked at the queen, dismissed her advances by pushing her foot away with his hand, and returned his eyes for a longer piece of eye candy from the gorgeous, dark haired servant.

The queen fumed at his rejection. She had to be the most beautiful, the most desired, the most powerful woman in the room! Beauty is power. She wouldn't have this. There would be no competition!

"There is a hair in my soup! There is a hair in my soup!" the queen shouted at the top of her lungs, before slamming her fist down on the table, hard enough that the dishes rattled.

The king and the prince just stared at Queen Viktoria, amused.

Exasperated, the queen turned to Margarete and spoke through clenched teeth. "Don't just stand there you stupid girl! Do something!"

But before the teen could answer, the queen picked up her cup of soup and threw it at her. The porcelain cup flew across the room and slammed into a stone wall. The soup fell in a wet trail

Whiter Than Snow

across the floor, some of it painting Margarete's clothes. The young woman held her face in her hands and shook.

"And clean up this mess!"

After cleaning the floor and walls in the dining hall, Margarete was brushing her hair in her room while the queen barged in. She marched towards her and the teen saw something sharp in the queen's hand, hidden behind her back. Margarete gasped as the woman grabbed her by the back of the hair, jerked her over the bed, pulled out the sharp instrument—scissors—and thrust them in the back of the stunning mane and began chopping away.

Margarete screamed as the bitter queen chopped and chopped until clumps of black hair fell onto the bed.

"No! No!" the girl cried.

"I will not have hair in my soup! And I will not have the royal Prince of Spain ogling over a servant girl!"

The king heard her cries and entered her room, witnessing his wife cutting the child's hair. "What on earth are you doing?"

The crazed woman threw the scissors down and marched out of the room, mumbling angrily to herself, leaving the king and his servant alone.

Margarete picked up the pieces of hair that lay on her bed and wailed bitterly.

"Oh my dear, I'm so sorry," said the king.

Without thinking, Margarete buried her head in his chest and wrapped her arms around him. He slowly reciprocated the affection, holding her in his arms, glancing to the door occasionally, knowing the consequences of the queen if she caught him in such a position. He wasn't worried so much for himself, as he was for the child—and what the queen would do to her. It wasn't a romantic hug, but more of a fatherly hug, affectionately embracing a daughter-like figure. He had never known his daughter, and, while he remembered her horrible death that night almost eighteen years earlier, something inside of him wished that Margarete was, in fact, his child.

The king wanted to cry. Where were these emotions coming from? He wanted to protect Margarete. He affectionately kissed her on the top of the head. "I'm sorry. I think you are a wonderful girl. You remind me so much of your mother."

"My mother?"

He snapped out of his daydream—his memories of the first queen, beloved mother of his only child. His face softened at the memory.

"Lucinda! She served me many years at the summer estate."

"Oh." Her face fell. "Lucinda raised me, but…"

Footsteps echoed in the hallway. The king quickly let go of the girl and backed away.

"The queen doesn't mean to be so cruel. I think she's going through the change."

Whiter Than Snow

Margarete nodded, choked with emotion. The king turned and exited the room, leaving the young girl alone to pick up the strands of chopped hair.

A candle flickered at Margarete's bedside, casting shadows on the wall. She rested on her pillow, watching the shadows as if they were creating an artistic dance. She tried to rest her mind from the recent events of London, and of course, the queen chopping off her hair. She had the seamstress fix it into a bob. While not her desired cut, the cute style accentuated her sea blue eyes. She was still just as beautiful.

She recalled the gentle words of the sweet prince, and of the breathtaking views of the white cliffs of Dover. "Where is my darling love tonight?" she said out loud, quietly to herself.

And at that moment, she heard footsteps outside her door. She quieted herself and hoped it wasn't the queen. The footsteps subsided and then started down the hallway again, growing faint with each step. "If I could but hold you tonight, dear prince," she said softly to herself.

Moments later, the footsteps returned, this time followed by the opening of the door. Her heart leaped at the sight of the prince. She bit her cheeks to hide her smile. He slowly closed the door behind him and climbed onto her bed, his finger to his lips.

"What are you doing here?" she said in a half-whisper.

"I can't get you out of my mind," he answered. He leaned forward and pressed his lips against hers, pushing her head deep into her pillow.

She pushed him off.

"Stop it!" she insisted.

He continued to kiss her.

"Stop it!" she said louder, her voice muffled by his kiss.

He pulled back, put a finger to his lips again and looked deep into her eyes, searching for a pleasurable response. "Shhhhhh. Do you really want the queen to hear you?"

"What do you want from me?" she said desperately. Her heart wanted to be with the handsome man, but her mind knew that it would result in nothing but severe heartache and guilt. She was already suffering from his kiss.

"I want you," he said boldly.

"You're engaged," she accused, searching his face for a true answer, hoping it wasn't so.

"Not yet."

She turned cold. "Leave, please."

He backed away and slid off the bed.

"Do you realize I can take your life?" he said half jokingly.

"For not giving into you? You'd take my life for that?"

He was startled. He had never heard such backtalk from any woman, much less a servant. But her boldness made him want her all the more.

"I don't want to take your life… I want your heart."

Whiter Than Snow

"My heart you may have. My heart you may already have. But that is all you may have," she answered in a whisper.

"Don't you want me?" he asked.

She refused to answer.

He smiled. "That is enough, Margarete. I will let you sleep."

With that, he shied away out the door and into the hallway.

Her body was still tingling from his sweet kiss and touch. She covered her mouth with her own hand to suffocate her exuberance. "Sweet dreams, beautiful prince," she whispered into the quiet air and blew out her candle.

The smells of a scrumptious morning meal filled the dining hall. Margarete worked diligently, making a special meal for the king, the queen, and of course, their delicious castle guest she called Prince Charming.

The king and queen took their royal seats, waiting to be served. Naturally, Margarete waited for the arrival of the guest. She was in a delightful mood and dressed herself accordingly with bright colors. She awoke an extra twenty minutes before sunrise just to fix her new hair. She placed a pretty blue ribbon in it, with a bow on top. She pulled the newly formed bangs out of the way.

"Breakfast!" the queen ordered.

Margarete entered the dining hall. "Your majesty...," she stammered.

The queen tilted her head and raised an eyebrow.

She averted the gaze of the queen and turned to the king. "If I may address you, Your Majesty?"

"You may," he answered.

"Should I not wait for the castle guest?" Margarete continued.

"Your friends left early this morning," the queen answered.

Her face fell.

"What are you waiting for? If I don't have a hard boiled egg, lightly salted, on my plate in thirty seconds, I'll consider putting you in the dungeon!" said the queen.

"We still have one of those?" the king joked, as it hadn't been used in half a century.

"Blame your father," the queen answered, snidely.

"You know, it takes longer than thirty seconds to boil an egg," the king commented to his wife.

The queen smirked.

Luckily for the girl, she had prepared a dozen hard boiled eggs earlier in the morning. She had one in front of the queen in less than twenty-five seconds.

"It better not be cold!" the queen warned.

After placing a second egg in front of the king, Margarete exited the dining hall and returned again with a special plate of French bread, dipped and fried in egg.

"What is that?" the queen asked.

"It's a delicacy from England, not really from England, but I learned about it in England… It's…," she was rambling.

Whiter Than Snow

"No. Not the food...*that*!" the queen interrupted, pointing at Margarete's face as she leaned over the table, placing French toast in the center.

Margarete stood and turned, facing the queen directly.

"That! Dangling on your neck. Come here," the queen ordered.

Margarete grasped the charm on her necklace. She had forgotten about it. She wore it for the prince the night before. She approached the queen and the woman gazed at it oddly.

"Where did you get it?"

"It belonged to my mother."

"I hardly believe Lucinda would own something like that." The queen faced her husband and addressed him. "Take a look at this."

"Come here, child," he said.

Margarete walked slowly, as if she was walking on the very eggs she just cooked. The king lifted his head and peered down at her necklace, curiously.

"Where did you say you got it?"

"It was my mother's."

"Thief!" the king yelled from the top of his lungs, so loud, Margarete held her ears and squinted. His face turned a raging red and his voice boomed like thunder, "Guards!"

Margarete's life flashed before her eyes. She was spinning, her face hot with fear. Her ears burned. The king ripped the necklace off of her.

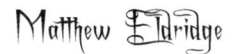

"No!" she cried. "It was my mother's! It was my mother's! It's all I have from her!"

Two guards grabbed her.

"Take her to the dungeon!" the king ordered.

"Your Majesty, we haven't had a key for some time," one of the guards commented.

"Good, then we won't be tempted to release her," the queen interjected.

Margarete looked back and forth between the royal couple, terror gripping her like tiny demons tearing at her thoughts. This was it. This was the end of her life. The guillotine was hungry for her neck. Her worst nightmare was coming true...she would die by the hands of the king and queen.

"Fine. Lock her in her room!" the king commanded.

The guards took her away as the king gazed at the necklace, rubbing it endearingly with his fingers.

"Is there something you want to tell me?" the queen addressed him, watching him.

"It belonged to my wife."

"You mean your *dead* wife?" she reminded him.

"Yes," he agreed. It wasn't time for arguments.

Chapter 23

The lone figure approached the solemn town. It had been years since his return. He stopped at a well and drew water for a drink.

"Excuse me. That's not your well."

The lone man turned around to see a handsome teen standing boldly before him. He smiled at the young man.

"There's been a draught," the boy explained. "Not much left."

"The days of the draught are almost over, my friend," the man said peacefully. He watched the boy in wonder. He was a handsome young lad, full of spunk and fire.

"What are you, some kind of prophet?" the boy joked.

"You must be Lucinda's boy."

"Do I know you?" the boy answered.

The door opened slowly.

"Mother?" the teen said as he pushed on it from the outside.

Lucinda was standing there, already noticing the tall man.

"Samuel?" she said. Her heart leaped. She was stunned. She dropped her belongings and embraced him tightly.

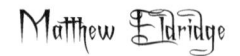

"Hello, Lucy."

It was at that moment all of her youthful feelings returned. Sure, she was happy to see the man of God. He was needed now more than ever. The country was falling apart at the seams. Protestant Christians were being charged with witchcraft and burned at the stake. The remaining Protestants needed an encourager.

But it was more than that. Samuel once fancied her in their youth. But he chose God. Out of what she assumed was obedience to God she ignored her heart and let it die the first time he left Waldeck to study under the Bishop as a teen. It was the very same Bishop that strayed away from the Catholic faith and led Samuel to a new way of thinking: a new type of Christianity called Protestantism. It was forward thinking. It was a faith based on love, not guilt or rules. Samuel embraced the new teachings and came back a different man.

Lucinda went on to marry another and Samuel remained a close friend. Their relationship only strengthened after the sudden death of her husband.

She let her heart die a second time the night Samuel left almost eighteen years earlier. But seeing him now, standing in her doorway, hearing his voice—her heart was alive! She didn't want to let go. She *couldn't* let go. She buried her face in his chest.

The teenager stared oddly at the couple. There was an undeniable chemistry between them. He could sense it. Lucinda's eyes kept turning to the handsome teen, whose eyes and face very much resembled the man of God's face and eyes. He was Samuel's son. She was sure of it. Her husband's death occurred ten months before the teen was born. In a night of emotional pain and heartache, she found solace in Samuel's arms. And he offered her more than that.

Hiding the princess was a perfect alibi to run away. Samuel wasn't just hiding from the king, he was running away from his sins. He was running from guilt and shame. He was running from forbidden love. He prayed a thousand times she'd forgive him. His fear of her rejection kept him away.

Lucinda reached out and pulled the boy to them, embracing them both as tears fell from her face. She would have to tell the boy that this was his father, but not now.

Margarete lay in her bed, her face soaked with tears. She heard a key enter the lock and turn. She stood, still shaking, albeit the event occurred two days prior.

The king entered the room slowly, moving calmly to the girl. His guard walked behind him.

"Do you like living here?" the king asked softly.

Margarete wanted to tell him the truth; that living in this castle was next to living with Satan himself; that darkness consumed the hallways. Gloom was the mildew that clung to the walls. Death…yes, death could be tasted in the bedrooms. The king and queen, they live…but not really. She wished she could tell him how the queen's blackened soul blocked all light from entering in, how the queen was a wicked vessel where evil resided, and how she sucked the life out of her king, and those that serve the two of them. She wanted to tell him that many who serve the queen pray for an early death. And she wanted to ask him, why? Why would he marry such a wretched soul? Perhaps she put a spell on him. Perhaps she intrigued him with her beauty and promises of tricks in exchange for their union? Perhaps he wanted a trophy on his arm. He was a good man, and this evil beast he called queen was sucking life out of him. He had become a shell of a man.

But she had to give him the answer he preferred. "Yes, Your Majesty."

"I've been good to you, haven't I?"

She looked down, unable to look into his face. He had been good to her. Although he never protected her from that witch he called a wife. "Yes, Your Majesty," she answered.

He lifted up the necklace in his hand. "Tell me the truth. Are you a thief?"

She shook her head, her chin trembling as tears leaked from her eyes. "Never, never in a thousand years."

"This was my wife's; my first wife's. It was her favorite necklace." He looked around nervously. "I don't know how it got in your possession, but I remembered it missing during her pregnancy. It became too tight around her neck. She used to rub it between her fingers whenever the baby would kick her too hard—to keep her distracted. She said she was saving it for our daughter."

"I'm sorry. It was a gift to me, I promise."

Whiter Than Snow

"Anyways, it's back in my possession, and that's what matters. But what can I do with it? It looked..." he hesitated. "It looked beautiful on you."

The king took a few steps towards her and she froze.

"I want you to have it."

She felt an ache in her heart, not out of sadness or fear, but from anxious joy.

"Just do me a favor, don't wear it around the queen. You understand, I'm sure."

"Yes, Your Majesty," she answered with a head bow.

"May I?" he asked, as he held the necklace up to put it on her.

"Yes," she answered softly, and turned around as he placed it around her neck and latched it.

She turned around to face him again and caught his eye. He coughed and turned to the side, eluding eye contact, trying to hide his emotions—covering his mouth with his hand.

"Are you alright, Your Majesty?"

"Yes... I.. uh...uh...," unable to speak, he coughed a few more times. "I've been staring at the sun too long on my travels," he excused himself. It was a lousy cover-up for the sensation he was feeling. "I must go." He turned a few feet from the door and looked at the young woman once again. "I know this sounds crazy, but, I know my wife would have wanted you to wear it. No one possessed her beauty. No one was worthy to wear such a gem, but child, you are..." he searched for the right words to say, "...you are glorious! Such a radiant beauty. You remind me so much of her."

"Really?" she smiled. It was the compliment of a lifetime.

"Yes. Except your black hair; she would have loved it." The king walked to the door. "Margarete, I'm going away on business for a few weeks. Things may be a little different when I return. I wanted to thank you for serving us."

"Am I being let go?" She was both fearful and hopeful at the same time.

"No. I just wanted you to know that you have made a difference in our lives..." He reflected on his words, "...in *my* life."

"Thank you, but your servant has done nothing but her job."

"Sometimes it's what you don't do that speaks the most. And sometimes it's what you do when you think no one is watching or listening. God bless," he said as his guards shut the door behind him.

God bless, she thought, as his words echoed in her ears. She smiled, acknowledging that the words came from the very man who denied God months earlier.

And the queen crept away from her hiding place around the corner with bitter jealousy eating her soul, sour from every word that came from the king's lips. Most of all, from his compliments of Margarete's beauty, and of course, her comparison to his first wife. She wanted this girl dead—as dead as the king's first wife. She wanted the child buried six feet under with worms consuming her dead flesh. The imagery of it gave her satisfactory chills. She would have her dead once he was gone, and she would make it appear an accident.

"And in telling the king, I risk my life. He'll put me in chains, or worse, take my life," Micah answered his old mentor as they met in the thick of the woods at Samuel's request.

"He'll be so delighted that his daughter is alive, he'll reward you."

"I was there. I'm partly responsible."

Samuel leaned forward, his face glowing in the small fire between them. "No, none of it was your doing. You were just a teen. I did it. I take full responsibility. The time has come. The king needs to know. It can save us all from that horrible bloody Mary."

"He'll take your life if he asks me any questions," said the young prophet. "I cannot lie." He took a deep breath, bowed his head, mustering the courage to address his friend. "What a terrible burden you've placed on me all these years."

"And if I must die to save our brothers in the Lord, so be it. To live is Christ, to die is gain. I will go before you into England and share the news with the prince. He'll be shocked to see me, but happy at the news none-the-less. Perhaps he'll even give me a pardon."

"But England? A reverent Protestant going to England is like a fish jumping into a frying pan. Are you mad?"

"Not mad; simply and passionately inspired. The prince needs to know. His true love awaits—and she is more than just a servant."

"And you are willing to die for this news?"

"We live in exciting times, my friend. Could this be the very purpose we were created for? Do you think it was by accident that we found the princess in the woods on the night of her very birth? An angel led us there. Do you remember?"

"If only we had an angel now," Micah answered.

She's our only hope. If the prince marries Queen Mary instead, that murderous snake will purge the world until no Protestant Christians remain," reminded Samuel.

"Very well. To God be the glory."

"To life and to death in the name of Jesus Christ."

The two men grasped arms.

"It is so good to see you again, brother."

"You, too, Micah."

Chapter 24

"Servant! Greta!" the queen yelled from the bottom of the stairs, ringing her bell. "Servant girl!"

"Here I am!" Margarete descended the stairs quickly, holding her skirt from brushing the steps.

"It took you long enough! Greta, I need you to do me a favor today, darling."

"My name is Margarete," she answered in a soft, timid tone, reminding the queen—the very reason she didn't realize the queen was calling to her. Greta was her replacement while she served the Prince of Spain in England.

The queen slapped her across the face. "How dare you correct me! I will call you what I want. I'll call you Snow White if it suits me! You're so pale, it's sickening. You need to get some sun! Some fresh air will do you good."

Margarete held her face in her hands. She sobbed silently—no sounds, but obviously crying from the movement in her shoulders.

The queen relaxed, lifted her boney fingers, the only sign that she was, in fact, aging, and pulled Margarete's hands from her face. Her voice softened. "I wonder if you could pick some fresh flowers for me today. It's looking rather gloomy in the castle."

Matthew Eldridge

The teenager nodded and quickly exited the castle door.

"And no begonias!" the queen yelled. "Or off with your head," she half-joked, laughing to herself.

It wasn't often that Margarete was free to leave the palace. And although the forest often frightened her, she welcomed this adventure with open arms. For one, it was daytime. For two, she longed to be out of the presence of the queen, and she knew where the prettiest flowers were to be found. Without looking, she made her way through the courtyard and to the forest. She ran through the trees to the east. She fled into the meadow where an array of wildflowers grew, perfect for her choosing. Her jog became a sprint as she continued to run through them, her face still in her hands. Through the cracks in her fingers she could see swirls of purple, yellow, violet, and white. She began to sob uncontrollably until she finally fell into a bed of lavender flowers. She was lost.

She rested on the forest floor for what seemed to be an eternity, tears streaming down her face. A small chipmunk warily crawled up to her and began sniffing around. She opened her water-logged eyes to see the little creature.

"Hello there… Are you lost, too?"

A bee buzzed by her, stealing pollen from the flowers that surrounded her. She listened to the sounds of the forest. She heard the crickets calling one another to her left. She heard the bubbling brook a few yards away. She listened to the leaves tickled by the wind. She looked up to see the tips of the trees swaying, dancing to a beautiful tune sung by the birds of the forest. For once, she wasn't afraid.

Margarete, or as the queen just called her, *Snow White*, looked around to witness a sea of flowers encircling her. She sighed deeply, picked a lavender flower from its stem, placed it up to her nose, and sniffed. Yes. It was an Opium Poppy.

Her eyes were filled with sorrow. Her heart was heavy. She thought about her life, oh, just for a moment! Like a child in a candy shop she began picking the potent flowers one by one, faster and faster until she held at least fifteen.

This should do it! She thought to herself. Just to be sure, she picked a few more. She took a bite of the first one and started to chew. It was bitter. She could barely manage the taste, but continued by biting into another. "I shall fall asleep, and never wake up!" she whimpered as she chewed. She hadn't the guts or the strength to swallow, not just yet… and by the third flower, realized that she couldn't.

"Pppfffffffttt!" she spit the flowers from her dry mouth.

More crying. She wanted to die. But she couldn't do this. She had nothing to live for, she thought. But then she remembered the prince, the wonderful, charming, ruggedly handsome prince.

But it was too late. She was suffering the effects of the plant.

The queen turned abruptly in her chair. "Are you sure?"

"Yes," said the man of God. "As God as my witness, Margarete is the princess—the king's very daughter."

The queen stood up and walked over to him, stopping inches from his face—so close he could taste her foul breath. It was such a contrast to her beauty.

"And does anyone else know?"

"No one else."

"No one?" She stared him down, extracting truth from his eyes. "Perhaps Lucinda?"

He stood speechless.

"I thought so," the queen replied. "You can't lie to me, man of God. It isn't in your character."

"Your Majesty, I would never lie to the queen, nor even a peasant. It is true. I am telling you because the princess can stop the royal wedding. If Queen Mary has access to this land, you can kiss your kingdom—*our freedom*, goodbye. You know it to be true. And anyone but Catholics shall die by the sword."

"Anyone?" she questioned. "Do you really think the prince will choose a small town princess over a powerful queen?"

"Yes," he said. "For love. He loves her, my queen. Servant or not, the chemistry is evident. And she loves him. And until now, it has been a forbidden love." He stepped back as if he was preparing to leave.

"You know, marriage has never been about love." She walked to him, putting her finger on his chest in a seducing kind of way. "Love is love, lust is lust, and power…what man doesn't want power?"

Whiter Than Snow

"He already has more power than any king would ever want. His father owns more land than…"

"His father could be the very one encouraging this marriage!" the queen snapped, interrupting him.

He looked down and folded his hands. "Perhaps you are correct."

"Perhaps?" she mocked. "I *am* correct."

"And perhaps the prince will follow his heart. Power is nothing to him. His past shows us that. He has it all. But the love of a beautiful princess—that is what he longs for."

"How did you become so well-versed on what the prince needs and wants?" Queen Viktoria stated, not really asking a question or expecting an answer.

"True love…it's what we all want. It's God's design," he answered, taking a few steps towards the door again. "When men go to war, they do so for love—believing they are fighting for a loved one. If not for love, they fight heartless."

The queen rolled her head back and chuckled. She walked towards him like a lioness, one foot in front of the other, her hips swaying, eyes engaged, targeting her prey. "Love is misery. Love is pain. It's jumping into the darkness of the abyss and expecting to survive. Love is the suffocating fragrance that smells sweet but ends in death. Love is an intoxicating killer, taking willing victims whose heads aren't on straight. Love is a murderer. Those who love commit suicide." She stopped at the end of her statement, standing just a foot from Micah.

"Love is a sacrifice," he answered, quietly.

She moved into him again, her face just inches from his. "Yes, and the end result is pain and death. Love is a welcomed poison." With that, she turned her head to the side and sneered. "Have you ever tasted poison, prophet?" She picked up a golden apple from a bowl that rested on the table beside her. She took a slow bite, her teeth sinking deep into the skin, while her eyes stayed on the prophet. She was flirting and it made him nervous.

"Christ died for love. And his death was sacrificial. And then he rose to life again from that death. That, my queen, is the power of love."

"That's to be disputed," she said. She placed her hand on his shoulder and traced his curves down his toned arm with her fingers. She looked into his eyes.

"Yes, it was love which brought him death, but it was also love—pure love—that allowed him to rise from that death," he said again, trying to make his point, his lips quivering, his mind and words distracted by her sensual touch.

She moved in closer, so close he could feel the heat from her body. Micah tried looking away, but his eyes refused. She was mesmerizingly beautiful. Her deep eyes pulled him into her. Her face; the face of an angel fallen from Heaven. Her moist lips were begging to be touched.

She spoke softly, "And what do you know about love, prophet? Have you ever loved?" Her hand moved down his arm and grasped his hand. She pulled his arm to her and placed his hand over her heart. "Feel my heart beating. Don't you want to love me? Does God love me? Does God want you to love me?"

Whiter Than Snow

His heart raced. Other than the child, Margarete, he had never seen such a strikingly beautiful woman. If he were to ever give into sin, this would be the moment, and she would be the woman.

With her other hand, she placed her fingers over his swollen lips and rubbed them. "You are a beautiful creature, man of God."

His lips trembled.

"Are you nervous? It's okay. I won't bite. Or maybe I will," she grinned devilishly.

And her smile almost unfolded him. Her smile was marvelous, probably her best feature.

"I can't…"

"Can't?"

She leaned forward, closed her eyes and kissed his cheek, brazing the corner of his lip.

Anxiety ate at him. He wanted this. He wanted her. He wanted to taste the venomous lips that pressed against his face. He knew she was poison and yet he was still willing to drink from her hazardous well. The power of beauty was a funny thing. Like a preying mantis, he would give in and she would devour him. He understood this and yet he couldn't resist.

She leaned against his ear and whispered, "My husband is away for a few weeks. Love can be ours tonight."

Her hot breath tickled his ear. Her words echoed in his soul, fighting the very words of God he planted there so long ago. Reason and morality eroded quickly. She leaned up to him and kissed his lips. He didn't kiss back. Her sour breath was a reminder of the grossness inside of her soul.

"Don't you find me beautiful?" she begged, searching his eyes, her own eyes like deep oceans pulling him in and wanting him to drown.

He pushed her hands off of him and took a breath. "You're the most beautiful..." He stopped.

"Go ahead and say it," she whispered, playfully.

He stood there, not another word from his lips.

She became angry and stern. "Finish it! Say it! Tell me I'm the most beautiful woman you've ever met!"

"I'm sorry, I can't defy my God or the king," he said, sobering up to the truth. "Will you please, help me stop this wedding? For the sake of our country? For the sake of your kingdom? For the sake of our faith?"

The queen exhaled, obviously vexed by the rejection. "I was testing you," she commented. "Well done, faithful man of God."

He nodded.

"Perhaps you are right. We shall introduce Margarete for the princess she may be, and end this massacre madness. Are you sure no one else knows?"

The sounds of wings fluttered from up high. At this point, Margarete didn't know if she was dreaming, hallucinating, or if this was real. Maybe she was dead. The glowing winged figures floated down from the tall, swaying trees. Perhaps it was their song that the forest sang.

"Fairies?" she giggled to herself, knowing that fairies weren't real. But every girl dreams of fairies. She rubbed her eyes and looked again. The beautiful, translucent figures came closer. These weren't fairies at all. No, they were the size of a human; maybe bigger.

"Hello, child," the angel called out.

Margarete stared in wonder.

"God has a purpose for your life."

"I am nothing but a poor servant, a slave to the queen. What could God want with me?"

"You're the daughter of a king!"

"I know, I know, I'm a child of God. I wish you would take me to him. My desire to be with him now is greater than ever. I am nothing but a slave living in a dungeon…"

The angel interrupted, "No, you're the daughter of…"

Ppppppppppppffffffffffftttttttt!

The arrow flew right by Margarete's ear and pierced the tree beside her.

The angels were gone.

Startled, Margarete awoke to see the king's hunter standing twenty yards away.

"I didn't have to miss."

"What are you doing?"

"Choosing my fate: Let the girl I love live, but in doing so, I will be sacrificing my very own life; or, serve the orders of the queen."

"What do you mean?" she asked.

He pulled out another arrow and pressed it against his bow.

"Greater love has no man, than to sacrifice his life for his friends," she mumbled, quoting the Bible.

"Are you telling me to kill myself, Margarete?"

"No, but you can take my life, if it will save yours."

"Always such a sweet girl." He lifted the bow, squinted an eye, and placed the bow down again. "The queen has commanded me to kill you and bring her your heart. But how can I shoot something so beautiful, so rare, so innocent?" He lifted the bow again and pointed it at her. "And how can I give her something that I want for myself?" he said softly.

She was flustered. "But you shoot deer. Aren't they beautiful and innocent?"

"Ah, but I don't love a deer."

She ignored him and began picking flowers, not knowing how to handle the situation.

He lowered the bow again. "Run away with me!" he pleaded. "Run away with me, marry me, and I'll take us both far away from here. It's our only escape."

"Marry you?" She was caught off guard.

"Yes, marry me." The brave hunter got down on one knee and stuck his hand out towards the fair-skinned beauty. She looked at the beautiful silver ring on his finger. He obviously had money and could provide for her.

"Marriage is not supposed to be out of convenience. Marriage is for love."

"And I love you. I have loved you since the first moment I laid eyes on you. Surely you knew that," he responded.

She quickly turned away, blushing. He was very handsome. He had the chiseled face of a statue, and the body of a warrior. She had noticed him on many occasions, of course. When she first arrived at the castle, he had taken her breath away at their first greeting. His shirt was off, his toned muscles glistening in sweat, and his long brown hair hung in his face. He had green eyes that captured her. He had asked her to skin a bear that he had caught, showing off, of course. She was so taken by him, she didn't respond, but just kept staring at him and the bear on that first day. She was so embarrassed after that moment that the two rarely talked. She remembered him making efforts, but she ignored them all.

He would make a perfect husband, she thought. He was attractive, he was a hunter, and he would keep his promise to take care of her. If anyone could help her escape, it would be him. Nonetheless, she hesitated.

"The heart can be deceiving," she said, her back facing him.

"What?"

"Nothing."

"Whether it's deception or not, I'm in love with you. Marry me."

She burst into tears. How could she resist. She was a fool after all. She abandoned her first love. Then, she gave away her heart to a man, a powerful prince, no doubt, a man who could never marry her because she was but a servant. True love could never exist between her and the prince. Only a secret love, a deceptive love, which was not something her integrity would allow her to do.

She turned around. "I cannot marry you. My heart belongs to another."

The hunter looked as if the arrow pierced his own heart. His head fell. "You could learn to love me."

She wanted to hug him. She wanted to wrap her arms around his big neck and tell him how wonderful he was, but that her heart belonged to the Prince of Spain…and she was also already engaged to another man. However, offering that information would make her look even more foolish—oh what a mess she was. She should leave with the Hunter. He was her escape—her way out. She wanted to love him. But she couldn't. She knew that it would only confuse him all the more, and her wayward heart would beg her to run away, always questioning, always dreaming of the Prince, or even of Jack. And if the Hunter still wanted to kill her, it would be welcome, because being in love with a man whom she could never marry was torturing her. She would be better off dead.

"I cannot. I'm sorry."

Whiter Than Snow

Bitterness stirred in his soul. His eyes squinted and he lifted his bow. She turned her back to him to make the shot easy. She closed her eyes. She could hear the bow flex.

Pppppppppppffffffffffttttttt!

The arrow sailed at alarming speed and pierced deep into flesh. The thud from the impact echoed through the forest. She heard the hit. She even thought she felt its impact. Still, she felt no pain. Perhaps it was the affects of the opium poppies.

She opened her eyes to see a beautiful doe fall on the forest floor, just a few feet behind her. His arrow pierced the delicate creature, not her. Margarete screamed. She looked to the innocent deer, its large eyes desperate for death.

"Run! Run away from here! Never come back!" the hunter yelled to Margarete.

Margarete burst into tears and started running, stumbling warily through the forest. She ran for what seemed to be forever, and with the advice of the hunter, she didn't look back. She ran past the meadows into a myriad of trees. And once that forest cleared, she ran down a valley, up a hill and into another forest. She glanced back but only for a moment. The castle was nowhere in sight. She was lost again.

Matthew Eldridge

Chapter 25

Margarete's body quaked as a blanket of evil swept over her. She was enveloped by the wicked forest. So many ancient trees stood against one another that the diminishing red sun was blocked from ever touching anything below their limbs, making the sky appear black day and night. She held herself—arms folded, and nervously looked around. Eyes followed her from the trees.

Red.

Glowing.

She heard a sound from behind. She inhaled a short, quick breath and turned around. There was squawking. Then a rustling in the woods…barking, howling. Wolves or coyotes! She didn't know which. Margarete continued to creep along, almost in tears.

"God, help me, please!" she cried.

Then it flew at her. She followed the red, glowing eyes as the black creature descended from the trees and swooped down towards her head. The high shrill the beast produced was more intense than the actual attack. It was a battle cry. The black-winged, hairless bat grabbed at Margarete's hair with its claws before retreating into the woods again. Other bats followed. She screamed, falling to the forest floor. The bats retreated into the bloody night.

The sun fell below the earth and the moon was cradled by the tall, thin, dead tree branches that extended to the fast moving dark clouds, finding its place in the mystic sky. Darkness and fog consumed the forest like a disease. The queen made her way through the castle and to the far south room on the western wall, and stepped inside the secret passage behind the fireplace. She took a torch off the wall and continued her journey into the dark winding underground walkway, which would eventually end deep into the second forest. The passageway was built in the 1100's as an escape route for royalty if the castle was under siege.

Margarete cried softly, paralyzed by fear. She hushed as she heard the sounds of voices in the distance. She listened carefully. A woman's voice! Now two voices! Two women, possibly more—assembling in the black forest! Now she could see a dim light. They were carrying a torch!

"Thank you, God! I'm saved," she whispered.

Margarete forced herself up off the ground and started running towards the light. "Hello?" she called out.

At first they didn't hear her. Margarete pushed back leaves, ducked under limbs, stepped over dead branches, trying to force a straight path to the strangers in this dark place. She couldn't quite make it through the brush and had to take another lengthy route around the outside of a direct path, all the while keeping her eyes on the torch.

The women stopped walking and Margarete watched through the trees as the torch touched the ground, and then a larger fire started under a pot. She was hungry. This could be a perfect rescue, she assumed.

"Hello!" she called out again. This time, heads turned. There were more women than she originally thought. They all appeared to be dressed in dark-colored cloaks.

"Hell-mmph!" she yelled a third time as a hand grabbed her from behind and covered her mouth. Before she had a chance to scream or even see who it was muffling her, she heard a very recognizable voice in the forest coming from the pack of dark clothed women—a voice which made her stomach turn.

"What was that?" the woman's voice commanded.

"Just the leaves," another answered.

"No, that was a voice."

"Probably coyotes," said another.

"Don't worry. We're safe out here, my queen."

Margarete watched in horror. She had almost forgotten about the hand that held her mouth. It wasn't very forceful. The hand loosened, but she was so frightened by the sight of the queen and her coven of witches in the distance, she didn't scream.

"Shhhhh," the man's voice whispered in her ear as he removed his hand from her mouth. "Don't let them see you."

She recognized the voice, although she hadn't heard it in years. She quickly turned around and wrapped her arms around his neck.

"Micah!" she whispered excitedly.

It was Samuel's apprentice, the prophet of Waldeck. He placed his fingers over his lips to hush her again, then, directed her attention to the queen and her co-conspirators.

"Silence!" the queen yelled. The witches quieted. The queen held up a wooden keepsake box. All the witches looked on with anticipation. She lifted the box high and brought it low.

"The heart of the righteous!"

"The heart of the pure!" another one cackled.

"The heart of a virgin!" crowed another.

At that comment, the group laughed, amused. It was no secret that Margarete had a crush on Prince Philip, and he came with a nasty reputation. Still, the queen knew it to be true. The girl was in fact, innocent.

"The heart of my enemy," the queen finished as she opened the box.

"It's not very big," one of the witches protested as she stared at the bloodied heart inside the wooden case.

The queen rolled her eyes. "It's the heart of the girl, I swear it!"

"Looks like the heart of an animal to me," another witch answered.

The queen ignored her, lifted up the opened box, and poured its contents into the boiling pot.

Whiter Than Snow

Another witch stirred the contents.

"Are you sure she's the one?" asked Peg. She was a discerning, homely, dark haired wench who claimed to hear directly from the spirits without invoking them.

"Has our magic ever failed us? The spirits tell me it's her," the queen rebutted. "Besides, I've seen it in her eyes. She's the king's daughter, I swear it. Stupid fool—he can't see it himself. He has affections for the child and doesn't know why."

"What if he finds out?"

"How would he? She's dead. If he hadn't figured it by now, he never will."

The queen poked the heart with a stick and tore through it.

"And now, freedom from the curse. Freedom from the prophesies. Freedom to reign. And along with the princess's death—her true identity to never unfold."

The witches laughed and several danced around the pot.

The queen inspected the heart closely.

"You're really going to eat that?" Rhonda, the young witch, asked.

The queen placed the heart in the fire and watched it sizzle as she twisted the stick, watching the small flame lick the sides of the meat. She pulled it out, let it cool for a second and shoved it into Rhonda's mouth and answered, "No, you are!"

The young witch gagged on the heart, her eyes bulging in fear.

"Chew it!" the queen ordered, thrusting it further into Rhonda's mouth with the stick.

"Let's get out of here," Micah whispered.

"She's a witch?" Margarete appeared shocked.

"What do you think?"

"I think my heart has known all along."

"I think she thinks they're eating your heart; witchcraft in its darkest form."

"Why would she do that?"

"Witches believe that by eating an enemy's heart, they gain all of their best attributes, and add years to their life."

"What would she want of mine?"

"Your beauty…" he answered, "Your youth and your innocence."

"Then why did she make the young woman eat it?"

"Good question. Come on," Micah answered, tugging her wrist.

Chapter 26

"Where are we going?" Margarete inquired.

They had traveled most of the night. The young woman followed Micah deep into the forest, then, into a clearing which led to a small mountain. They stopped halfway up the trail and Micah let out a caw, much like a bird. He waited a few seconds, and then cawed again.

"What are we…"

"Shhhh…" he silenced her.

The sound finally returned. He followed the direction of the caw until he was lost again. So he cawed, and less than thirty yards away, someone else cawed.

He quickly followed the voice until they reached a small cave in the face of the mountain, hidden by brush. A young boy sat out front on a tree stump.

"Micah!" the boy exclaimed, getting up from his seat and running to the man of God, arms open wide, embracing the man's waist and burying his head in the man's stomach.

"How are you tonight? You're on watch duty, huh?"

"Yes! They finally said I was big enough!" The boy was proud of himself—as if protecting the camp was an honor.

Margarete's heart sank. The boy couldn't have been older than seven or eight. "Where is his…"

"No questions. I'll explain tomorrow. Tonight, you'll need sleep. We have a longer journey ahead of us." Micah pushed his way into the door of the cave, where a dozen small children greeted him with hugs.

"What did you bring us this time?" One of the children asked.

"Well…I brought you something…or…*someone* very special."

Margarete entered the room and watched the playful children climb all over Micah. She giggled.

"Who's she?" a little red-headed child asked.

"Is she your girlfriend?" questioned another.

"She's a friend. And she's going to stay the night with you!"

"Yeah!" they yelled, almost in unison.

Except for one, who yelled, "No girls allowed!"

Margarete found him humorous.

"Can you all protect her?" Micah asked solemnly.

"I can," answered Timothy, the oldest in the group. One look at the boy and Margarete could tell he had been there for quite some time. His pants were too short, tattered and torn. With his height, he wouldn't be there much longer. He would be banished from the makeshift orphanage and thrust into society, where more than likely he'd become a street rat, eventually arrested for stealing to survive.

Whiter Than Snow

Micah placed his hand on the boy and affirmed him. "Timothy, I know you can. I'll be back in the early morning."

Timothy had become like a son to Micah—one of the original orphans in the mines. Micah made it his mission to minister to the boys, teaching them right from wrong, before they were removed as a ward of the town.

"Wait! Where are you going?" questioned Margarete.

Micah ducked to exit through the doorway. "I won't be far. I need to make sure we weren't followed."

"Who would follow us?"

"The queen's men," he answered, and with the mention of the queen, all of the orphans made a hissing sound and spit on the ground. They hated her. She was the reason they were part of this children's camp devoid of adult supervision. Most were orphaned because the queen killed their parents for one reason or another, and some were orphaned to pay back a family debt. In either case, she had a specific job for these orphans in the middle of the mountain—a job only a small person could do. She prided herself on the genius of her plan, however unsuccessful it was. Unsuccessful because, regardless of how many days or weeks the children spent mining deep into the core of the mountainside, few had found gold or precious stones. Or if they had, they hid it well from her and the soldiers. It wasn't uncommon for soldiers to appear and plunder the place while looking for hidden gold.

Just a few years earlier, the mines were created and manned by midgets—dwarves who were exiled from civilization for their differences. The Queen of Brussels conned them into mining labor because of their small size. After finding their first pieces of gold, she didn't compensate them as she promised. In fact, she forced them to work twice as hard, treating them as slaves, so they left—vanished into the night, never to be seen or heard from again, except one—the one they called Brannon. But even he only came near the town at night, and was nearly impossible to spot. He distrusted and hated people, and yet, was drawn to watch them from the forest's edge several nights a week.

When Queen Viktoria couldn't find any more dwarves to dig for her, she replaced the midget men with small children—and when she couldn't find enough orphans in the town to run the mining operation, she created more any way she could, all without the king's knowledge.

Micah awoke the sleeping princess early in the morning just before sunrise. The boys were scattered around her, sleeping soundly. Margarete looked them over, quietly listening to the soft breathing of innocent children robbed of their youth; children who were probably dreaming sweetly about a mom and a dad who loved them, who would rescue them from their hellish environment.

Little Peter, the youngest and smallest of the orphans, nuzzled up against Margarete as she tried to get up from the floor. He opened his weary eyes and rubbed them, yawned, then stretched. "Are you leaving?" the boy asked, clinging to her.

Whiter Than Snow

Margarete's heart sank as she saw the sadness in his eyes. She rubbed his head gently.

"We need to leave before sunrise. We can't chance being seen," Micah answered, whispering.

She gazed at the children sweetly and suggested, "I could stay here. I could be a mom to all of these boys."

Micah let out a tender sigh. "I know you could. But you would be found."

She looked at their kind, sleeping faces once more, memorizing the minute detail of each one. Her heart ached. She fought back tears and begged, "Please. They need someone…"

Micah shook his head. She would have to let go, and it was breaking her heart from the inside out. She kissed Peter's head and rubbed it one last time.

He grabbed her delicate hand and tugged at her. "Don't leave," the little boy pleaded.

She turned around, reached down and hugged him tightly. Tears seeped from her eyes. She let go of the boy and quickly exited the room.

Margarete and Micah traveled the dirt trail through the cold morning mountain air and into the midday sun—although it provided little warmth. Fall was upon them, and today was a sure reminder of it.

The terrain proved difficult, if not impossible at times. Still, they climbed. Her calves ached. She was lost for sure, but trusted Micah's sense of direction. He knew where they were going and when they would get there; in the evening, he promised. How he knew where they were she had no idea. There was no clear path anymore after the first mountain…but they continued on as if he could see one, going up and up, and then down, down, down….several times… several mountains, she presumed.

They had crossed six of them to be exact and wearily climbed the seventh.

"I can't keep going…" Margarete whined, out of breath.

"Not much further."

They continued to climb in silent dusk for the next twenty minutes, following a narrow man-made trail.

"I can't do this…"

"Shhhhhh," Micah whispered as they climbed the last few feet, escaping the forest and into the clearing near the mountaintop. "Turn around," Micah whispered while putting his finger to his lips. He took her shoulders and twisted her slowly to face the east as they reached the peak of the seventh mountain. They were just above the timberline.

The sight took her breath away. She looked below to the seven small mountains she crossed, watching them in awe as the blue moon reflected off the swaying trees beneath her. She lifted her eyes to the sky as a brown hawk flew overhead calling to the night, the moonlight silhouetting the bird's beautiful wings. Afterwards, she heard nothing but the whisper of the wind.

"It's beautiful!" she gasped.

"You can feel God up here," he offered.

Whiter Than Snow

God? Where was he? She was quite certain he abandoned her.

"Let's hurry," Micah said, taking her by the arm.

"Where to?"

"Just the other side of the mountain!"

"I'm hungry and exhausted. I don't think I can make it any further. My legs burn," she cried as she followed him, too frightened to stop on the obscure trail as they started the descent.

"We're almost…"

Micah's sentence was interrupted by the sound of twine snapping—a trip wire—which triggered a snapping branch, which released a net that fell on the couple. Margarete screamed as she struggled to remove it, unsuccessfully—her arms flapping uncontrollably.

"Relax or you'll get us stuck even more," Micah ordered.

They heard more twigs snapping and then the altered ground beneath them crumbled. The impact of the fall knocked Margarete's breath out of her, so much, that after a few gasps, she passed out in the prison pit they fell in.

Matthew Eldridge

Chapter 27

"She endangers us all," the voice said.

"She's the one who can save us," Micah answered, simply.

"I know who she is," the little man returned. "But they'll come looking for her, and when they find her, they'll accuse us of kidnapping her."

"It's only for a few days…until I can arrange her safe travels."

She warily opened her eyes. Four little men—midgets—stood around her bed examining her. Micah towered over them as he reached down to her and touched her hand. She jumped, startled.

"Easy now. You've had a nasty spill," said Winter, one of the little men, as he placed a cold cloth on her forehead.

"Where am I?"

"You're safe. That's all that matters," another little man answered her.

She tried to sit up but felt light-headed and lost her vision, causing her to pass out again.

Margarete awoke a day later in an odd, small cottage-style house nestled in the woods near the top of the seventh mountain. She was lost and in a strange environment, but still questioned if the little men were just a dream.

"Hello?" She said in a soft whisper, timidly awaiting an answer.

But no one answered.

"Hello?" she said again, this time more audibly.

She peered around the room and the makeshift home left much to be desired. It was pretty evident that no woman had ever entered the house. The corners of the room were cluttered with pine needles and leaves, and enough sand covered the floor to mimic the beach. And the smell; the musty pungent smell of sweaty, dirty men suffocated the room. She rubbed her nose, shuddered and quickly opened the front door to let the tiny cabin breathe.

The sunlight spilled into the doorway and kissed Margarete on the cheek. The high mountain breeze chilled her but she didn't mind. She warmed herself with a hug as she wrapped her arms around her body. Once again, she breathed in the pine air and enjoyed the view, this time lit by the colossal orange sky.

"Good morning, beautiful view," she said to the scenery around her as she noticed the trinkets of light reflecting on the leaves of the trees.

A bird responded with a beautiful song.

"Good morning, sweet bird. Did you come to sing me a song?"

Whiter Than Snow

Once again, the little creature chirped and then flew along the man-made path.

Margarete followed it with her eyes and ventured out of the house towards the path, only stopping for a quick glance back to the door. She took a short breath and descended the mountain to see if the trail would lead to a river, perhaps. She didn't see any cisterns of water in the cottage and was thirsty. Surely, there had to be water nearby.

She walked briskly down the mountain path and within seconds she was smothered by the mammoth trees that hid her from the sunlight. She became uneasy as the sun disappeared from sight and she slowed her pace. It wasn't long before the knife of fear stabbed her in the chest, causing her to wheeze from anxiety, stopping her in her steps. Two things she hated: the darkness of the forest, and being lost. To make matters worse, in her anxiety, she assumed someone was following her.

She heard the rustling sound of feet beside her and quickly glanced to the left. She saw nothing…but then a shadow of a man protruded from behind a tree, or at least it appeared to be. Someone was watching her, she was sure of it.

She took a few minute steps and looked again. The shadow was gone. She calmed herself, studied her surroundings, and challenged herself to move.

"One, two, three," she whispered to herself. Her feet broke free from the earth and she walked briskly in the opposite direction, regretting her move now that the shadow reappeared and stood between her and the path back to the open space and the cabin. She would have to loop around through the thick of the forest and try to find the house again if she was to get away.

Her walk turned into a jog as she desperately looked up through the towering trees, her eyes begging for rays of light to cut through the thick limbs and leaves.

She heard the sounds of something coming toward her with haste and she ran deeper into the darkness of the woods, her mind racing with fear. She had only traveled about thirty yards when she noticed a small make-shift cabin to her right. Several dead animals hung in the front of it, their skins stripped and hanging off their bodies. The sight terrified her and almost made her vomit. She shoved her hand over her mouth and nose to stop the reek of rotten flesh from invading her nostrils.

Without a thought, she sprinted to the door of the home and thrust it open. She turned around once more and thought she saw a shadow quickly moving behind a big oak less than five yards away. Either she was delirious, or she truly was being followed. She ran inside the cabin and saw the walls dressed with trophy heads of animals and a plentiful display of weapons; some for hunting, some not. Dried blood stains marked portions of the floor. The stench of this slaughter room was nauseating. It was at that moment she realized the home probably belonged to the shadow following her. She choked on the smoke that filled the room from a badly ventilated fire in the fireplace, covered by a boiling pot with animal parts hanging out of the top of it. By the time she caught her breath, it was too late. She heard footsteps on the porch. She yanked at a sickle hanging on the wall, but it wouldn't give.

Whiter Than Snow

She saw a blood-stained knife on the kitchen counter and ran for it as the door squeaked open. Clinging to the knife, she turned back around to the door and saw...

Nothing.

But then she heard the sinister laugh. She looked down and saw feet; small feet. And then she followed the feet to the legs and the body and finally saw the face. It was another little person, the size of a six-year old, but stocky and grizzly-like. He had a thick beard and brown teeth. He growled at her as he blocked the exit. He looked more like a troll than a dwarf, if trolls truly did exist.

He saw the knife in her hand and gave her a sly grin, spreading his feet to widen his stance. She didn't dare move or speak. The little man kept his eyes on her and waddled to the wall of weapons and pulled down the sickle with a hard yank. He took a few steps towards her, enough that he could smell the fear expelling from the pores in her skin.

"I've killed bears bigger than you," he said, as an evil grin formed on his lips. He lunged forward to frighten her.

Margarete's fear erupted into a blood curdling scream so loud that she sent every bird to flight within a hundred yard radius.

The man dropped the sickle, grabbed her wrist and squeezed tight with his rough, dirty fingers, removing the knife from her grasp with his other hand. He tossed it at the wall and it stuck into the wood about an inch deep. Margarete wanted to faint.

"You belong to me now, my dear," he said with a growl.

The front door burst open and several of the little men stood in the doorway, holding their picks for mining.

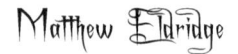

The grizzly man glared at them. "Stay out of this! She's mine!"

"She belongs to the king."

"I reckon I'll get a reward for her then," he said. Then, winking at the scared beauty, he said softly, "What's left of her when I'm through."

The men looked back and forth: the grizzly beast and the other little men of the forest. There would be a duel. That would be the only way to save her and they knew it. But they knew what fighting would bring. He was an animal, and he would take several of them down. But he was also their brother.

The grizzly beast of a midget also knew that he was outnumbered. And she was the king's property, after all. If she was harmed in any way, his death would be imminent. Instead, he would use her as a bargaining chip.

He let go of her wrist, his eyes surveying the other men and then his wall of weapons, just in case he had to use one. He steadily calculated what to use and how to use it, and they knew that he had it down to a science in his mind. He was no dwarf to mess with. He looked to the sickle at his feet, and the knife in the wall, just a few feet behind them.

"Just let her go, please," one of them said, kindly.

"How'd she get here? Not on her own, I can tell you that." He stepped back and grasped the knife and jerked it from the wall.

"Micah brought her."

He shook his head and squinted his eyes. Micah was no friend of his. Theirs, yes, but not to the wild man of the forest. If

Whiter Than Snow

Micah represented God, then he represented Satan. The little beast was a prophet of the earth, a friend of darkness. And yet, he feared Micah. At one time he vowed to take Micah's life only to face two giants with wings holding him down, threatening to remove him from the earth if he ever touched Micah. None of the other midgets knew about the angelic encounter, and he made sure to it that they would never find out.

"He has her hiding out with us for a few days. There's danger in the kingdom."

Brannon lifted the knife to her. His eyes changed to charcoal. It was as if something took over his body. "Leave now, or share in her fate," he said, his lips quivering, his eyes squinty. He breathed heavily, ready for a fight.

"We're not leaving without her."

Queen Viktoria, leader of *The Sisters* and Queen of Brussels, sat before her mirror staring attentively into it. She searched for something that could not be seen. She leaned in further, looking intently at the reflection of her own eyes. They were dark. Nonetheless, a glimmer of fire reflected in them. As she leaned back, the fire reflected in the upper corner of the mirror. The actual torch reflecting hung in the back of the room about thirty feet behind her. She glanced back at it, and back to the mirror. With vanity she blotted her skin with a cloth, admonishing her own beauty—the beauty that seemed to seep from her life with each new given day.

A dark shadow covered the mirror. Viktoria shut her eyes and inhaled deeply. A strong wind filled the room and silenced the light, the fire no longer burning from the small torch on the wall. The room was consumed with heavy darkness.

Viktoria opened her eyes and engaged the mirror. Her eyes were different—as if milky callouses covered her pupils. The ghost-like figure in the reflection stared back at her. Without words the creature communicated with the witch who called herself queen.

"What? What do you mean she lives?" the queen asked out loud, talking to the ghost in the mirror. "That's impossible!" She stood up and paced the room, the conversation continuing. "I did not fail you! The hunter failed!" she yelled. She paced a few more times. "No!" she shouted, holding her ears. "You will not talk to me this way!" she said angrily, shaking her head. She picked up a comb resting on a table beside her and hurled it at the mirror with all her strength.

The mirror shattered into a hundred minuscule pieces. Queen Viktoria walked slowly over to it, the realization of what she had done stinging her—a look of fear in her eyes. "Are you there?" she asked, trembling, but the voice was silent.

She knelt to the floor, rubbed her fingers across the broken cracks that resembled a spider's web or a diamond. Her fingertips caught the edge of the glass and it cut her. Thick, red blood covered the tops of her fingers. She held her hand to her face for a better glimpse, and then sucked the blood from her hand. She looked to the mirror again, gripping her chest and coughing

Whiter Than Snow

uncontrollably as if something was invading her body, or perhaps even exiting it. A sulfuric smell permeated the air. Perhaps she was free from the demonic spirits that controlled her. Or perhaps she just sealed her fate by destroying her communication with the ghosts; her guides and her protection since childhood. The spirits weren't known to let go so easily—a humble lesson she learned by watching the death of her own mother. And she was following in the woman's footsteps.

She regained her composure, her face taunt. She hastily looked at the mirror—what was left of it. "She will pay. They all will," she said quietly to herself. "Yes. I have the perfect plan for her," she cackled. "Why didn't I think of it before? She's going to wish she was dead after what I do to her…and to her beloved Prince Charming." The queen spun around, her cloak flying like a cape as she exited the room.

Matthew Eldridge

Chapter 28

The King of Brussels sat across from the Duke of Norfolk, and to the right of Thomas Wyatt, the lead conspirator in the effort to stop the royal wedding. Prince William, the Silent, sat across from Wyatt. A single candle in the center of the table illuminated the men's faces, but not enough to read each other's eyes.

"Who am I?" said the king, humbly. "I am nothing against the Queen of England."

"If you don't join our efforts, you *will* lose your kingdom. You know that. We're all in trouble," answered Wyatt.

"And if word spreads of my involvement, I would lose more than my kingdom. I will lose my head!"

"We're not asking you to go to war. We're simply asking you to help us stop this wedding. You are friends with the prince. We know for a fact he visits you," said Prince William.

The king sighed. "He won't listen to me. He merely uses us for a place to stay. We're under his father's control. Either way, my control over my kingdom is just an illusion. I wish we had some sort of leverage."

"Ah, but we do," the Duke of Norfolk responded.

The prophet Samuel entered the oak doors and walked cautiously to the king. "My king," he said as he nodded.

"Samuel? Samuel? Is that you?" said the king, searching the man of God's face, a hint of emotion in his voice.

"Yes, Your Majesty. It is."

"May God shine down on us this night!"

The man of God looked nervously at the other plotters sitting at the table.

"What's this all about?" asked the king. "Why is Samuel here?"

"It's time to regain your kingdom. It's time to end this wedding, before all Protestant Christians are slaughtered in our hemisphere of the world," answered Samuel.

The king addressed him, "So you…you are with them? You are conspiring against this marriage?"

"It's the only way, my king. Thomas knows what he's doing," answered Samuel.

Chapter 29

Time stood still. Brannon, the caveman of the forest, had control. Margarete quivered violently, harassed with fear while the cold, rusty blade touched her neck. Grey, the leader of the dwarfs, nodded to his boys, lifted his mattock and thrust it towards the ground in Brannon's direction. It sliced through Brannon's shoe and pinned his foot to the floor.

Brannon dropped his knife, grabbed at the handle of the pickax and pulled hard, ignoring the searing pain that ran up his leg from his pierced foot. He jerked free and was about to toss the tool back at Grey when the little man tackled him to the ground and pinned Brannon's arms down.

The other two dwarfs, Garrett and Josef, ran to Margarete, grabbed her by the arms, and yanked her through the door.

"I love you, brother, but I'm not about to let you hurt this child of God. Now we can do this the easy way and let it go, or we can do this the hard way."

"She's the one, isn't she?" Brannon argued.

Grey ignored his question, pleading ignorance, knowing that the information would be dangerous in Brannon's possession.

"Man of God," the voice called to Micah, as he watched the castle from his post in the dark woods, spying on the queen near the castle entrance. He knew little about the underground passages that escaped beneath him. The voice was faint and rumbled like thunder.

"Man of God," the voice called again.

This time, Micah stood and twirled around, unable to determine where the voice came from. A ghostly fog filled the space surrounding him, enveloping him until he could hardly see.

"Is she alive?" the voice questioned. "Where is she?"

He didn't answer.

"We will find her."

His skin started to sting as a swarm of small bugs the size of gnats infiltrated the fog. He could feel them in his mouth as he breathed in. He spit and coughed, holding his hand over his mouth and nose. He thought for sure the bugs would choke him to death.

"You can't save her," the voice whispered from all around him. It was as if the voice was coming from the wind or the leaves on the trees.

"Who are you?" he called out.

"Evil," the voice answered, overlapping itself as the word echoed in the forest, bouncing off the gloomy trees as the wind rustled through the dying leaves. Micah could have sworn they were shriveling right before his very eyes. The voice gave him chills as if a ghost were breathing cold air onto his neck, standing over him.

Whiter Than Snow

"In the name of Jesus Christ, I command evil to leave me alone!" he yelled, his voice tense with fear.

The voice laughed as the wind swirled around Micah like a miniature tornado, dead leaves encircling him, carried by the thick air. The bugs had vanished moments before. And it was in the sinister laugh he thought he heard the queen's voice. Then the winds subsided and Micah felt drained as if his strength was robbed from within. He rubbed his skin. It itched as if a thousand tiny ants were crawling all over him, but nothing was there.

The queen opened her eyes; pieces of the shattered mirror before her. The image of Micah faded and she saw the reflection of her guards entering behind her. She turned to them.

"Follow the prophet and find out what he knows. Then, take his life. Better yet. Keep him alive…for now."

The guards bowed in acknowledgement and exited the room.

She called out, "The girl is still alive. Keep her alive, and bring her to me!"

The king wept uncontrollably. "My daughter is alive? I should have known. I was so blind!"

"Your Majesty, there's no way you could have known," answered the man of God, Samuel.

"Yes, yes there was. God was showing me—telling me. But I wasn't listening. I stopped listening long ago. My heart was hardened and the poor servant girl kept trying to get in. I was drawn to her but I didn't know why. Can God forgive me? Do you think she will forgive me?"

"Your Majesty, I know you have every right to take my life—or to imprison me for a thousand years. Do to me as you will, but as God's servant, I am telling you he forgives, and I ask your forgiveness as well," Samuel responded. "Now, please…we can use this for good."

The king looked up at the broken man of God with tear stained eyes, the candlelight glistening in the wetness of the man's face. "Why did you leave me when I needed you the most?" the vulnerable king asked.

Samuel lowered his head, his lips trembling. "I lost my son that day, too. I was frightened…" He choked and turned away.

The king studied his face quizzically. "You have a son?"

"I have been reunited with my son. I was wrong for taking your daughter from you. It was not my job to play God. I was only thinking of our future—,"

"Help me find my daughter," the king asked in desperation. "That is all I ask of you."

Samuel sighed in relief. "If all is well, she's with Micah. He went to speak to you at the castle. I had no idea you would be here."

"We must return…"

Whiter Than Snow

"No, no…there isn't time. We must travel to England to stop this wedding," answered the Duke.

"My daughter…"

"If all goes well, Micah will arrange for her to meet us in England," answered Samuel. "There is one small matter."

The royals turned to Samuel, all eyes on him.

"Evil lurks in the land, fighting us with every bit of power she's been given."

"Witches?" questioned Thomas Wyatt.

"Precisely. And they're growing stronger. With all due respect," Samuel addressed the king, "the Lord has revealed there's a coven in your kingdom that is growing like weeds, inhabiting the land and purging it of anything godly. The spirit of God is suffocated there. Enough black magic controls the region that the princess is no longer safe there, if they discover who she is."

The king's eyes were filled with regret. "T'is my fault. I saw it happening, but I did nothing. I was so bitter at God that I did nothing to fight the darkness."

"You were ailing," said Prince William to the king. "We've all turned our backs on our kingdoms when we've suffered personal loss."

"And my fault, too, Your Majesty, for leaving the land God gave me to watch and pray over. I ran from God and from you, and our land is paying for it," answered Samuel.

"For eighteen years?" the king answered, looking at Prince William. "I was numb. There is no excuse. I've let my kingdom go to ruins."

"Then by God, let us help you get it back," said the Duke.

"You can start by fighting with us. Fight the Queen of England and her horrible oath against Protestant Christians. Fight to keep your land!" said Thomas. "Don't let the queen marry Prince Philip. Help us bring him his true love." He pushed the scroll towards the king. "Let's make this right."

The king signed his name on the treaty and exhaled. "My daughter…"

"We will find her, I promise," Prince William answered, placing his hand on the king's shoulder.

Thomas stood and addressed everyone. "We'll reconvene tomorrow night and go over the details. Make sure you aren't followed. May God be with us…and Elizabeth. Let's pray she's still alive."

Whiter Than Snow

Chapter 30

A sign reads: *Witches beware! Any persons assembling in these lands for the purpose of witchcraft or are caught participating in witching activities, whether alone or in the presence of others, will be hung by order of the king.*

"The king?" Madeline, the oldest witch in the coven said, turning to Queen Viktoria.

"My husband had nothing to do with this, I assure you," the queen confessed, the tone of her words tinged with anger.

"He *is* the king," another witch protested.

Queen Viktoria took a shaky breath and looked at the different faces of her sisters. They glared at her with long, cold stares, brooding at the very thought. Then again, she was their leader and queen, and she had her husband wrapped around her witching finger.

"Women of the forest, I assure you, this is preposterous!" Her lips thinned and her right eyebrow raised. "This, I'm afraid, is the work of our dear Prince Philip."

"Why would he care about witches in Brussels?"

She smirked. "It's a warning. He wanted me. He made a pass at me but couldn't have me."

The witches shrieked and cawed at the thought.

"So does he know you're a witch?" one of them asked.

She answered cautiously, her eyes twitching. "I don't think so, but he knows I'm not a good little Catholic girl, nor is he a good little Catholic boy. He's a dog in heat." She laughed at herself, taking a shallow breath, hoping the sisters bought her answer, whether it made sense or not. "Just like that bloody Queen of England, he'll accuse anyone and everyone of witchcraft to eradicate those he wants out of the way."

"And why would he care to do that in Brussels, my queen?"

"To flex his muscle. To emasculate my husband, the king. I wouldn't be surprised if we were targeted for sport. And perhaps I'm too irresistible."

"With all due respect, I thought the king and the Prince of Spain were on good terms," said Madeline.

"Are you not listening to me?" Queen Viktoria shouted defensively. "I said the prince wanted me, did I not?"

"Let's get out of here," said Angelina, the young witch who shadowed the queen. "This place has eyes even witches fear."

"There's a difference in the air, I swear it," answered Peggy.

"Foolish girls. Don't let a few signs run you off. We're witches! Wonders of the night! We hold the power of darkness in the palm of our hands. This land belongs to me! I am the Queen of Brussels! Since when have we feared?"

"They obviously know we convene here," said Angelina.

Whiter Than Snow

The queen walked slowly to Angelina and studied the young girl's face, purposely intimidating her. "These signs were posted here by men... and all men have a weakness. Weak, stupid, foolish creatures. Every man can be bought with a price—once you find his weakness. If it's his heart, steal it. If it's lust, you can feed it; trap him in it. If it's power, you can make him believe he has it, while sucking it from beneath him. No man can escape it. They were created that way. Dumb. The weaker sex," the queen said so arrogantly. "We're goddesses who can control any man we wish. You know this to be true."

"What of the prophet of God?"

"What of him?" the queen answered with a rush, thrusting her head around to see the witch who dare question her ability to carry out a plan. She calmed, her head still high in the air, filled with arrogance. "I told you, every man has a weaknessssssssss..." she carried out that last letter long enough that she sounded like a snake, giving the wickedest witch chills. The queen turned back around slowly and spoke through clenched teeth, "...even Prince Philip."

"And the spells?"

"Let me worry about the spells," the queen answered.

"Are you sure the girl is in fact, the princess?"

"Yes, of course. The prophet confirmed what we already knew."

"And she lives?" asked Madeline, already knowing the answer, but trying to make sense of it all to herself, while trying to control her anxiety.

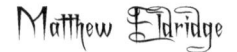

"So whose heart did Rhonda eat?" asked another.

The queen sat in silence for a moment. "Women, we were deceived, but the deceivers will pay. Never, never cross a witch."

They heard a rustling in the bushes.

"I told you, this forest has eyes. Let's leave," warned Angelina.

"Show yourself! I can smell you, dwarf!" demanded the queen, loudly.

The bushes rattled some more and Brannon appeared.

"And what has earned you the right to spy on us?" asked the queen.

"You're looking for the servant girl? I know where she is," answered Brannon.

"The king's daughter?" Peggy asked for confirmation.

"Your step-daughter?" Madeline said, addressing the queen.

The queen turned to the elderly witch with an icy stare. Madeline realized her comment may have been out of line and lowered her head, cowering in fear.

"And why would you offer us this information?" demanded the queen, speaking to the scruffy, little dwarf.

"She's the one, isn't she? The one prophesied about. I know you want her dead."

The queen smirked. "Not anymore."

Whiter Than Snow

Chapter 31

Margarete swept the cottage while singing an old tune she learned from Jack as a young teen. She had been a guest a day and a half, and already the place looked completely different. The sun poured into the room and danced through the dust clouds she made with the broom. She thought about her good days of cleaning—her days with Lucinda and adopted brother. She longed to see them again, and at that moment, decided she would find a way to escape and return to the village. However, she felt safe in the cottage on the seventh mountain, surrounded by tough little men who loved God. She was willing to accept this as her home, at least for a short while, until Micah came back for her.

She heard a quick knock on the door, and the princess made her way slowly over to it and opened it.

"Hello?"

But there was no one at the door. She surveyed the area, listening to the wind rustle through the trees, and returned to her work. She welcomed the fresh air entering the room.

She heard a thud as she swept and turned her eyes to the doorway. A black crow stood on a weathered package in the threshold. She could have sworn it was trying to communicate with her as it stared at her with frigid, red eyes. The bird gave her the creeps.

"Shooo!" she called as she swatted at it with the broom.

The crow flew off and she retrieved the package, assuming it was for the little men of the house. She carried it inside and placed it on the table.

An hour later, she noticed the package leaking onto the table and decided to open it. She tore at the outside wrapping, exposing a burlap bag underneath. She untied the strings around the burlap bag and let the bag flop open, the contents exposed which forced her to involuntarily vomit on the floor, followed by screaming; lots and lots of screaming.

The door burst open and two dwarves ran to the princess.

"What's wrong?" Grey asked. He followed the path of Margarete's eyes to the table. She didn't even acknowledge his presence, but stared in horror at the package, blood leaking through the cracks on the table and dripping to a puddle near Caleb's feet.

Two dirty, lifeless hands of a man lay on the burlap, severed at the wrists.

"Where did this come from?" Caleb asked.

"It was delivered." She shivered, holding her arms around her body.

"By whom?"

"I don't know, really... a crow, I think."

They gave her a quizzical look.

Whiter Than Snow

Margarete examined the severed hands a little closer, noticing the special silver ring on the index finger. "Oh, dear God," she whispered.

"What?" the dwarfs said in unison.

Her hands trembled at her face, muffling her mouth. "It's the hunter. He offered me his hand in marriage. I said no."

"But why?" asked Caleb.

"It's the queen, isn't it?" asked Grey.

"She must know you're here," Caleb responded.

Margarete couldn't stop crying as she ran out of the cottage, her face in her hands.

The young man of God, Micah, stood atop the third mountain, his arms lifted high to the heavens, his eyes closed. He heard the small army approaching and knew he was in trouble. Nonetheless, he continued to pray for the land below as the sun bowed beneath the earth, a thick fog of darkness climbing the eastern sky like a demon coming to swallow him whole. He prayed for God's spirit to move in Brussels. He prayed for the revival of God's people and for the princess to be safe. And it was with those last words of safety that the army reached him and tackled him to the ground, tying his arms and feet with a rope, much like a wild animal being roped for the slaughter.

Blackness consumed the sky. Margarete and the little men sat outside on wooden logs, their bodies warmed by the fire in front of them. The princess hugged herself, still trembling, deeply troubled by the day's events. She stood up and stared into the darkness, the silent sounds of the forest frightening her. Remembering the hunter, she shuddered. Anxiety choked her with invisible hands and she whimpered.

"Don't you worry, you're safe with us. We're beyond the queen's land here," Grey said, trying to comfort her.

"Shall we take communion?" Caleb asked.

Grey nodded in agreement. "Remembering the Lord's sacrifice will help us to acknowledge his protection as well. God's peace be with us."

Winter, the oldest of the dwarves, stepped inside the cottage and returned with bread and a cup of red wine. He tore a piece of the bread and passed it on. One by one they collected from it.

"This is the body of Christ, which was given for us," Grey said.

"Here, here!" they shouted in unison, then, stuffed the bread into their mouths.

Winter held up the silver cup, wine spilling down its sides.

Grey pointed at it and said, "The blood of the covenant! Let us remember the blood of our Savior, Jesus, the Christ, which was spilt out for us."

Winter added, "The purifying blood that covers our sin; the blood that makes us whiter than snow."

Whiter Than Snow

"Whiter than snow!" they repeated.

"The blood that protects us from darkness and evil," another little man shouted.

It was at that moment they heard voices in the distance. Caleb ran past the cottage to the top of the mountain that overlooked the other six. He could see a small army of men carrying torches through the forest.

"There's an army coming this way; men with torches!" Caleb yelled.

Margarete stood and walked to the edge of the mountain, her heart convulsing as she watched the torches moving swiftly below in the distance.

Grey hushed everyone, "We don't know what they want. Don't fear—not just yet. Caleb and I will go meet them and cut them off before they reach the seventh mountain."

"Don't leave me," Margarete cried.

"You'll be safe. You have strong men watching you," he said with a smile.

Matthew Eldridge

Chapter 32

The leaders of the alliance met once again in the hidden room of the aged, stone chapel. Thomas Wyatt enthusiastically delivered the plan to thwart the royal wedding, and then, of course, his suggestion to remove the Queen of England from power and restore the throne to her sister, Elizabeth, who just so happened to be a devout lover of God and a Protestant Christian.

The men reveled in their plan and prepared to leave and meet again in England for the royal wedding—the very wedding they planned to destroy. They were all invited, lending to the perfect excuse for their presence together, making sure their plan was executed correctly.

"We ride out separately and enter London far enough apart. If there's even a thought of our union, we'll all pay the price," said Thomas Wyatt. "And if we're caught, Elizabeth, the queen's sister, has no chance. They'll pin it on her."

"To the dethroning of Mary!" answered the Duke of Norfolk.

"To the queen to be, Elizabeth! May God be with us!"

"To true love," answered Margarete's father, King of Brussels.

"To God and his mighty favor on us!" the prophet Samuel added.

London would be surrounded if the men could gather a large enough army, from Northumberland in the north, to Norfolk, and Kent in the south. And across the channel, more territories were willing to join forces. It would take at least six months to plan such an attack and put the queen's sister on the throne, so sworn secrecy was a must. The only fear was that Philip's father reigned over the territories that the queen didn't already control, and he too supported her effort to spread Catholicism, so gaining the support of the kingdoms under the Emperor's control was almost impossible and a gamble. Many kingdoms wanted the merger. It was a matter of time that either the two kingdoms joined and became the strongest power in the world, or they would fight for control and destroy one another. Many feared that a war between the two would mean forced labor and soldiers, depleting the economy to build armies. It would be either starve to death or join the military. The previous century taught them that their fears could very well be realized.

However, under Queen Mary's reign, the economy was already waning, leaving country folk starved and hopeless, many entering the military just to feed their families, causing her army to be massive. Many moved to the city for hopes of a better life, or became outlaws and refused to pay taxes. And anyone who questioned her authority was tried for witchcraft and hung or burned at the stake. She ruled with an iron fist. While the territories under the Emperor had a little more freedom, both the

Whiter Than Snow

Queen of England and the Emperor of the European territories agreed that any Christian belief outside of Catholicism should be eradicated.

And if the men's plan to remove the queen from power didn't succeed, there was another plan at stake, one that threatened to take the life of the queen and put her spiritual advisor, John Dee, in power. And while both men wanted Mary out of power, Wyatt's purpose was nobler than the spiritually dark Dee who pretended to hear from angels and practiced Catholicism only in the presence of the queen. Behind closed doors he was nothing more than a mystic who dabbled in the occult and magic, while claiming to be the very mouthpiece of God himself. The queen was fooled for sure. He fed her what she wanted to hear, and in exchange, she fed him secrets he could one day use against her and gain power to the throne.

By spiritual forces, John Dee claimed to know of Thomas Wyatt's plan and wanted to join efforts. And although the man could expose Wyatt, Wyatt repetitively refused.

It took nearly thirty minutes for Caleb and Grey to reach the base of the mountain and begin to climb the next. The forest was thicker at the base, but they knew the path well, even with dense fog and little moonlight. The dwarves could hear the soldiers approaching, although they couldn't see them.

"Do we meet them head on?"

"Let's approach them as friends. Everything should be fine," Grey answered.

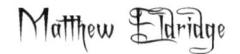

"Dogs! I hear dogs!"

And before Grey could respond, the dogs were just yards away, followed by small trails of light from the torches, shimmering through the tree limbs.

"The trees!" Grey whispered, as they both climbed a different tree, ten feet from one another.

The dogs followed the scent of the little men and reached the base of the trees. They barked and howled uncontrollably, jumping and clawing at the trunks.

"You! Come down from there!" yelled one of the queen's soldiers, lifting a torch to expose the little men.

"Gladly," answered Caleb. "Just call off your dogs!"

"What are you doing up there?" another soldier asked.

"Oh, you know…looking for honey," Caleb said sarcastically, staring at a beehive above him as he scooted down the branch, watching the soldier grab the collar of his dog.

"Who are you? And why are you in the queen's forest?"

"I'm Grey, and this is Caleb, and this is not the queen's land. Her land ends at the first mountain. But we're here to greet you in peace."

The rest of the small army caught up to the dogs and their owners.

"You're the outlaws protecting the queen's servant?" one of them asked.

Grey didn't know if he was asking a question or making a statement. Regardless, before he could get a word out, the butt of the man's sword slammed into his face, knocking Grey out.

Whiter Than Snow

Caleb pulled out his knife, and another soldier sliced his fingers that held the knife. As Caleb grabbed his bloodied hand and fell to his knees, the soldier kicked him in the head, knocking him out as well.

"We're almost there!" the soldier yelled, earning applause as they gained momentum, moving down the face of the sixth mountain and heading up the seventh.

Hearing Caleb scream, Winter and the other dwarves prepared for a fight as they talked by the fire, while Margarete paced inside the cottage. One of the dwarves, Josef, rushed in, tipped over his bed and exposed a hole in the floor. "If anything happens to us, this is for you."

Margarete stared in disbelief. The hole was filled with dirty gold nuggets. "Did you steal it?"

He laughed. "No, we're miners. This is what we do. We dug it up from the earth. This is why we protect this mountain from the queen and her wicked ways. We give the gold to the poor." The dwarf covered the hole and slammed the bed back down and ran out of the door, screaming, "To God be the glory!"

"Wait!" Margarete screamed, running after him, grabbing his arm, pleading desperately. "Don't leave me alone!"

"To God be the glory!" Winter repeated Josef, drinking the full contents of the silver cup.

"To God be the glory!" the little men shouted in unison.

Margarete tugged at Josef, tears in her eyes. "Please don't leave me. Please," she whimpered.

Winter said to Josef, "Stay here. Take care of her! We'll be fine! To God be the glory!" Then rushed down the face of the mountain, holding his hatchet as a weapon, with Garrett closely following him.

Inspired by adrenaline, it only took the queen's men and their mangy dogs an hour and a half to climb the face of the seventh mountain. Margarete could hear the slashing of swords and what she thought was men groaning in pain. This was her fault. The little men were dying and she was to blame, at least that's what she told herself as she and Josef slipped out of the cottage and ran down the dark path on the other side of the mountain, straight towards the home of Brannon.

Their run became a tormented walk as they crashed into barren limbs. The trees pulled at Margarete's clothes and ripped the flesh on her face and arms. She could see nothing, but still she moved forward, holding the back of Josef's shirt, and sometimes his hand.

After another twenty minutes of walking briskly in utter darkness, a light illuminated the path behind them. It wasn't a small light, but a great orange glow—the radiance of a fire. Josef stopped. Margarete stared at the fire and sank to her knees. Even a quarter of a mile away, they could tell the dwarf cottage was set ablaze. She used the distant light as an opportunity to run again.

"Wait for me!" Josef yelled, his tiny legs trying to keep up with her.

Whiter Than Snow

She picked up speed down the steeper face of the mountain, her eyes blurry from tears. She heard Josef slip down the face behind her. Black shadows hid the light occasionally, causing her to slow down.

And then one of the black shadows moved.

She squawked, darting in another direction. "Josef?" she yelled, but he didn't answer. She started running again guided by fear and adrenaline and slammed into a tree trunk, knocking herself down.

A small figure stood a few feet away.

"Hello, my pretty catch. I knew we'd meet again," said the voice.

"Brannon? Help me!" she said. "Your brothers…they're dying."

He laughed and growled at the same time. He tilted his head, admiring his prize, pulled out a club and swung it at her. She rolled on the ground, the club barely missing her head as it thudded into the earth.

"Help!" she screamed at the top of her lungs as she stumbled to her feet.

Brannon took another full swing, this time his club contacting a tree as she slid behind it.

"Cat and mouse. I'm good at this game, my precious little rat," he said. He followed her shadow in the dark to another tree, and tiptoed to the other side of it. Facing the dim moonlight, she didn't see him approaching her from behind. Brannon lifted the club to knock out his prize.

"Aaaaggghh!" yelled Josef as he tackled Brannon to the ground. "Run!"

Margarete ran further down the mountain path, listening as Brannon and Josef struggled on the ground in the distance. When the moonlight receded and her eyes were consumed with total darkness, she felt her way along a rocky cliff that appeared beside her to her left. And that's when she felt it—a hole in the midst of the rocks. She stopped, lost in the dark. At this point she lost all sense of direction: north, south, east, or west. She didn't know if she was walking up or down the mountain, or parallel to it. She hesitated, wanting to go into the crevice, but fearing what may await her inside. Perhaps a bear or some other wild animal.

And then she heard rustling in the woods coming towards her. Margarete felt for the opening again. She could have sworn she heard something touching the rocky face just ten yards away or so—and coming towards her. She leaned against the brittle rock, trying to breathe silently, but the nervousness inside of her expressed itself externally through wheezing and bodily shakes.

The figure moved closer. She could hear a hand gliding along the wall and leaves crunching beneath little feet. She wanted to run, but she couldn't move—her feet were swollen with imaginary lead inside of them, illumed by fear.

The person was closer.

And closer.

And closer still—walking gently, feeling along the stone. He was now so near that she could hear his shallow breathing.

Then the sounds of feet scurrying down the mountain to the left caught her off guard. As she focused on those little legs and the sound of crunching leaves, she forgot about the figure slowly coming towards her against the rocky terrain.

The small figure grabbed her from the side. "Shhhh. Follow me," Josef whispered.

She sighed in relief.

"Josef! Josef, I will find you!" screamed Brannon into the empty, dark space, less than twenty yards away.

Josef pulled Margarete into the hole in the rocky wall. "You'll have to slouch down," he said in a whisper, forcing her to bend over. He led her by the hand and they ascended deeper into the face of the mountain. It was a cave; a narrow, short, winding tunnel. He walked briskly with confidence. It was evident he knew where he was going.

"Aaaaaagghhh!" Brannon yelled into the mouth of the secret mine. "I know you're in there, and you know I'll find you! I created this mine!"

"Is that true?" Margarete whispered fearfully to Josef.

"We all created it, together. He went a little crazy after a small mining accident in here. He was trapped for days. It got to his head and he hasn't been the same since."

Matthew Eldridge

Chapter 33

Josef pulled Margarete deeper into the cave, which widened as they walked. She could feel tracks beneath her feet and stumbled on them a few times.

"Be careful," Josef said, offering her his hand, which was short and stubby, his finger tips calloused and coarse.

She placed her palm in his. He had never touched anything so delicate and soft. And although he couldn't see her hand, he could tell it was tiny and precious; flawless. It made his heart flutter.

"How big is this place?"

"Dunno. We've been digging for years."

"What are you digging for?"

"You'll see."

They heard a sound coming around the corner and Josef pulled the young woman against the wall and into a smaller, dead-end enclave. "Shhhhh! He's coming," he warned.

She could feel the damp earth against her. It was cold to touch. And the lack of ventilation caused the loose dirt to choke her.

And then light spilt into the room. Brannon walked the main tunnel clutching a small torch. Josef and Margarete leaned back in the small pocket of the cave they were in, trying to slow their breathing, hoping to blend into the wall.

"Come out, come out, dear brother. You know I will find you and your little rat too…if the flesh-eating bats don't get you first!"

"Really?" Margarete panicked.

"He's just trying to scare you. Shhhh," Joseph whispered back.

As Brannon passed the side-cave they were in, his torch illuminated the room, reflecting miniature stars that sparkled within the dirt and stone walls.

"What is this place?" Margarete mumbled softly, noticing the jewels as they shined in the firelight.

"Diamonds. This is what the queen is after. She'll kill anyone to get it. And if we get out of this alive…it's yours."

"Mine?"

"Yes. Yours. All of it. At least it will be yours."

"I don't understand," she asked, a puzzled expression on her face.

"You will."

"What would I do with it?"

"I don't know. God knows. The people in your kingdom are starving. Imagine the good you can do with it."

"But I'm just a servant…"

"The prophesies…you don't know, do you?"

Distracted by discussion, the two failed to see the walls illuminating again.

Whiter Than Snow

"Why hello, dear brother," the disturbing voice echoed off the smallness of the room.

Josef turned around and absorbed Brannon's club with his face. The tender-hearted dwarf fell to the ground, either knocked out cold, or dead. Most of the torch was extinguished by the blow.

Margarete's high-pitched shriek shocked Brannon enough to allow her to escape out of the enclave and run deeper into the main tunnel of the mine. Brannon chased after her, holding his ashy, flameless torch in front of him. The tip of the club burned red, casting a miniature light. He could see her thin frame, barely in reach of the dim glow cast upon the walls.

He grunted.

Margarete ran cautiously, wanting to put distance between her and the little beast of a man, while hoping not to trip on the tracks beside her.

The tracks...follow the tracks, she thought to herself. Eventually they would lead her to the exit of the cave, she believed. However, in her panic, she failed to realize she was running in the wrong direction.

As Brannon's torch cooled and the light from it diminished, he yelled, slamming it against the cave's wall, small burning embers ricocheting from the hit and flying around the space surrounding the little man. Margarete glanced back and saw the eyes of the little man one last time—the embers looking like burning red fireflies furiously dancing around the madman's angry eyes.

The young woman turned around and ran awkwardly down the blind tunnel, feeling the tracks beneath her feet until she slammed into something hard obstructing her path. She ignored the ache to her shin and felt the object vigorously with her hands.

Wood.

A wooden box. It was somewhat square, she assumed, and it felt empty.

Metal wheels.

A mining cart! She realized as she felt the brake with her hand.

Brannon drew closer.

She proceeded to walk past the mining cart and felt loose gravel beneath her feet.

"I wouldn't go any further if I was you," Brannon warned, walking slowly. "The mine drops off a good fifty feet or more here."

Perhaps he was bluffing. And even if he wasn't, she would rather die trying to escape than surrender to his control, which in her mind, could be much worse.

Her foot felt the loose gravel in front of her as she accidentally kicked small rocks forward and propelled them over the invisible cliff. She listened as the echo of them falling and hitting other rocks further below informed her that Brannon wasn't bluffing after all. She desperately felt for the mining cart again. Unsure of what to do, she climbed inside the wooden structure.

Whiter Than Snow

"You don't think I know the sound of a person climbing in a mining cart? Do you give up? Or do I have to beat you into submission?"

She heard the slap of the club against his hand.

She quickly felt for the handle—the metal brake that stuck up above the top right corner of the cart. She placed her hand on it just as Brannon grabbed it, too. She screamed and released the brake. Brannon grabbed her wrist, and with her other hand, she clawed across his face with her finger nails. She didn't know how bad she hurt him, but she knew that she had hurt him enough that he let go for a second. And in that second, as the brakes were released, the cart moved on its own towards the cliff, brought on by gravity.

Brannon grunted again, holding his stinging face. Through his teeth he seethed. "I'll pick up your bodily remains at the bottom of the ravine after you're DEAD!" he yelled hastily.

Margarete screamed. The cart descended down the track in the dark, picking up speed. She ducked low, waiting for the track to end or possibly falling to her death. She felt the twisting and turning which made her quite nauseous. It appeared the cart was following a trail circling a large hole in the bottom of the mine, and as it descended down and around the cave, the circle got tighter and the cart continued to accelerate.

As the cart propelled dangerously with speed in the steeper parts of the track, twisting and turning and almost out of control, nearly throwing Margarete, she couldn't help but scream. And her scream signaled Brannon to where she was on the track.

Finally, the cart reached the bottom of the ravine and the air felt heavier. The track straightened out and the cart slowed, yet, still traveled briskly enough to force Margarete to stay tucked. Suddenly, something grabbed at the wheels and the cart jerked to a halt, tilting over and spilling Margarete into the shallow, rocky water below. Her arms and hands stung as they slammed against the wet, gravel ground. The icy water forced her to her feet. Overcome by emotion, the princess couldn't resist crying for a solid minute or two.

A dim light reflected on the water. *But how?* She looked up to see a pinprick of light piercing the ceiling of the cave. *Moonlight.* There was an open top in this mine. Margarete allowed her eyes to adjust and saw sparkles reflected under the thin layer of water.

Diamonds.

She followed the light dancing off the water's current, which directed her into another cavern. Perhaps it would lead her out. She gasped in wonder as diamonds sparkled in the soil and rock crusted walls. As she walked the path, the moonlight retreated and the diamonds no longer reflected light for her to follow. Faithfully she moved forward, continuing into the bleak darkness, but it appeared to be the only option of escape. She gently felt the walls with her palms and fingertips as she continued to walk in the damp blackness. For quite some time she could hear nothing but the sound of her own breathing… and then she heard the sound of trickling water near her feet. The water had to flow from somewhere, she assumed. The cave became narrower as it escalated. Eventually, Margarete had to duck to keep going as the earth tightened around her. She rubbed her hands against the cave's walls which became heavy with moisture. Water was coming from somewhere above.

The smooth terrain below her feet turned to worn gravel and as the elevation increased, Margarete slipped a few times, falling to her knees. And it was while she was on her knees the third time, weary and out of breath, that she saw another pinprick of light coming from further up the tunnel. She crawled a few feet in moist gravel, desperate to reach the end, but eventually stood to her feet in a hunched over position as the rocks cut into her knees from crawling.

"God, please help me," she cried.

Margarete marched to the cave's open mouth with quickened steps as the moonlight poured in. By the time she reached the clearing outside of the cave's narrow entrance, she collapsed from exhaustion. She could see the silhouetted trees swaying in the mystic wind beneath the dying moon. She choked, frantic for clean air to fill her lungs. She flipped to her back and stared at the sky. And although the chilly air nipped at her exposed, damp skin, she found it welcoming after suffering fear in the windless mine.

Voices.

Margarete could hear the voices of men in the distance. She quickly rose to her feet and surveyed the dark woods to find a better hiding place. Gray clouds traveled quickly above her, covering the moon occasionally, limiting her vision.

The sounds appeared much closer than before. Margarete knelt behind a tree to listen as she heard twigs breaking near her.

Without warning, the tip of Brannon's club plunged into the back of Margarete's skull. The beautiful young woman fell to the cold, hard ground.

Margarete's father, the King of Brussels, left the quaint chapel in Kent, just seventy miles from his destination. However, to ensure their secrecy, he rode horseback with a few of his men towards Canterbury where his driver and carriage awaited. Once he was out of view, Prince William left the chapel, followed by the Duke of Norfolk.

Thomas Wyatt knelt on the floor of the secret room in the back of the chapel. His blonde hair hung over his face, hiding his bluer-than-blue eyes.

"Dear God," he cried, beginning what should have been a deep, sincere prayer that was quickly cut short by interruption.

The thick drapery to the room moved and a silver sword pushed the curtain back. Thomas felt his side for his own sword which wasn't there. He remembered leaving it at the door, a requirement by the church to use the room for their private meeting.

The road to London was cluttered with the queen's soldiers. However, with the wedding ceremony taking place in the next few days, many wealthy travelers would be wandering the path, lowering suspicions from the army. Still, it didn't ease the rebel's anxieties. Avoid all suspicion they agreed, and in doing so, they would remove any questioning of their secret alliance or even the fact that they were in communication with one another. The queen suspected a rebellion. It was just a matter of time. One by one, with the exception of Thomas Wyatt, the members of the alliance graciously passed Queen Mary's men, showing the wedding invitation when requested, which was more often than they expected.

"I assume you're looking for this?" the dark figure said, approaching Thomas Wyatt, holding out Thomas's sword.

Thomas didn't speak, but remained on one knee.

"Oh, don't bother getting up. That's where you'll stay—bowing to me once the merger is through and my plan executed."

"I told you, I'm not interested in your way of doing things," Thomas answered.

"Too bad. I can blow your cover and ruin your rebellion. And don't think I won't."

"You won't," answered Thomas as he got off his knees and walked around the figure. "You need me. You need my influence. No one will follow you and your dark ways, and you know it. You may have power, you may fool the queen, but the people don't trust you…and I don't trust you."

"Oh, I will make sure to it the merger will happen," answered John Dee, the creepy thin man who tugged on his long beard. "And then I will remove the queen and her new prince from power, with or without your help. Your timing is all wrong, and so is your method. Work with me on this. If you join me, you will have everything your heart desires. I'll make sure to it," the tempter spoke.

"What my heart desires is for an honest ruler, a Christ-centered ruler who will stop the bloody massacre of my brothers; a ruler who cares about the people more than they care about their own desires; a ruler who cares for the truth."

The slender figure let out a slow, rumble of a laugh and turned to Thomas. "Truth? You want truth? You're planning a secret rebellion to remove the queen from power, stealing men's hearts from right under her nose, and you are telling me you care about the truth?"

Thomas took his sword from the man and stepped out from behind the curtain to exit the room. "How did you find me here?" he asked, turning back around.

"I have eyes everywhere, Wyatt. I work for God, remember?"

Chapter 34

It was such an uncommon event for the market square. Wood beams supported thirteen dead bodies hanging from thick rope. All of the bodies were covered in black or brown cloaks and ranged from 17 to 70 years old. All were women except one. And all knew the queen and her identity as a witch. Every witch in the coven was hung, save the queen and her medicine woman, who walked freely through the market square with her guards.

She inspected each face of the dead, unattached emotionally. She stopped at the very last one and lifted the lifeless head of the man and looked at him with a sneer.

"This is him," the queen addressed the Captain of the Guard.

"Are you sure?" he answered.

"Yes, I'm sure. He's the leader. He's the warlock, the conspirator of evil in our forest, parading as a man of God. He makes me sick!" She looked into Micah's null eyes. "There are no more." She dropped Micah's lifeless head, which fell hard against his chest. The queen walked away, keeping her composure, her head held high. She muttered under her breath, "You should've chosen me, man of God."

She brushed away her conscience. She told herself it was necessary. She was the queen, after all. She betrayed the coven to protect herself—to protect her identity and her ability to influence the throne. Within a few days, all witches would be terminated in her husband's kingdom, from Waldeck to Brussels, and she would oversee the entire witch hunt. It was the only way to save herself. Besides, she didn't really need them anymore. She already gained the throne through her marriage, and she had better uses for the princess than what the witches had in mind.

Part of the prophesies were coming true, and Queen Viktoria was the main instrument to carry them out. A witch betraying other witches. How appropriate she thought. By the weekend, over a hundred witches would be dead, including Lucinda, Margarete's surrogate mother. No, Lucinda was not a witch, but she would have her tried as one for the secrets she kept.

And perhaps the queen's involvement in the movement would catch the attention of Prince Philip. Perhaps, she hoped.

Whiter Than Snow

Chapter 35

Margarete awoke in her bed, rubbing the back of her head which ached profoundly. She sat up, startled. How did she get here? Was it a dream?

And then the unthinkable.

"My darling, we've been so worried about you. Did you get lost?" the Queen of Brussels said, dripping with sympathy, as she sat down on the bed beside the girl.

It took Margarete a full minute to realize where she was and answer. "Yes. I guess I ventured too deep into the woods."

"I'm sure," the queen said snidely. "You know, you caused us a lot of trouble. It should be off with your head!"

The girl lowered her chin. It wouldn't be unlikely for the queen to order such a thing. The queen looked to the guard standing to her right—the guard that Margarete didn't even notice until that moment. His face stiffened. Margarete placed her head back on the pillow, her hands trembling. Her fate would soon be revealed. There was a long pause of silence between them.

"And just what did you do to your face and arms?" she yelled at the poor girl, seeing the red-stained scratches caused by the branches from the night before.

Margarete hardly noticed the pain of the cuts on her body compared to her throbbing headache from Brannon's club. She felt the back of her head and rubbed it. She could hardly touch it without wincing.

The queen addressed the guard, "Take her and have her washed up, and bring her back to me. We leave this evening." She then turned back to Margarete. "Pack a small suitcase and put on your best dress." She moved in closer, inspecting the fresh scars on Margarete's face. "Where *did* those scratches come from? You look like hell!" the woman moaned, disgusted. She stood up, turned for the door and said, "And make sure you pack nicely. We want to be presentable."

Margarete and the guard entered the queen's special vanity room. The child nervously glanced around—this room had always been forbidden.

"Come in," the elderly woman said softly, dressed in a brown cloak, sitting aside the queen's chaise. "Have a seat, please." She gestured with her hands.

Margarete slowly walked to the chaise and sat down, sitting straight.

"Lie down," the woman commanded.

The young princess was hesitant, but the queen entered the room, giving her approval to the old woman's direction.

Magarete surveyed the room from her horizontal position. To the left was incense burning—a trail of purple smoke spiraling up to the ceiling. Perhaps her eyes were playing tricks on her, but it appeared as if the smoke was alive, slithering around the ceiling like a smoky snake. To her right, the medicine woman rubbed a mixture of lotions and ointments in her hand. It smelled sweet and tart. Next to the woman was her walking cane. Further in the distance, she saw the queen's shattered mirror.

"Sit back and close your eyes," the woman instructed as she leaned over her.

Margarete leaned back and closed her eyes. She opened them one last time for reassurance, but didn't feel any calmer. She tried to rest but couldn't in this room. A queer heaviness lingered in it. She felt a rope pulled tightly around her wrist, attaching her to the chaise. She opened her eyes to see the guard assist the woman as she did the same to her other wrist.

"I said close your eyes. You don't want this ointment in it," the old woman said firmly.

Margarete could feel the cold lotion penetrating her cuts as the woman spread it over her face, followed by her arms. At first the ointment tingled and soothed her cuts. But after a few minutes, it burned—so badly, Margarete wanted to peel off her skin. She screamed and the woman shoved a cloth in her mouth to muffle her. The rag tasted sour and numbed her tongue. She opened her eyes wide, gasping for air, and swore she saw the devil in the eyes of the old witch standing over her, painting her face again with some smelly concoction that soothed the burning. She felt her skin tighten under the ointment.

Margarete didn't know if it was the ointment on her face, or a substance on the rag, or even something in the air itself, perhaps from the incense, but she felt dizzy. The room warped around her, moving in circular motions as a wave of nausea consumed her. She was turning green.

"Keep your eyes shut," the witch said again. "The dizziness will go away."

She glanced to the eyes of the woman again, and something seemed oddly familiar. She remembered seeing this old woman's face before—and strangely from this horizontal position. She remembered, in fact, looking up at the woman, the woman looking down at her, carrying her in the dark woods. She was just a baby. And although a baby knows no fear, somehow Margarete remembered it all—even the fear she felt. Perhaps it was all a dream. Perhaps it never really happened, but Margarete remembered it as real as the black wavy hair on her head. This was her kidnapper that helped give birth to her almost two decades earlier.

Perhaps it was just a delusion created by whatever ointment the witch was putting on her. Either way, Margarete wanted to cry. She closed her eyes and felt as if she was spinning again, her soul being stripped from her flesh. She saw herself floating, looking down at her physical body. She watched as her veins turned blue, starting with her finger tips and crawling up her arms to her heart and to her neck and face. As she screamed, she was back in her body, this time, lying in a coffin. The wooden box surrounded her and she screamed helplessly. And although her soul was screaming, she was pretty sure she was dead.

The snow gently fell from the pale sky, coating the dead trees that hid the entrance of the modest castle. Margarete watched in wonder. How the white contrasted the dark woods. How the snow smothered the gloomy tree limbs. The snow covered the sins of the woods, very soon making it all white and beautiful. Margarete was always less frightened when the woods were filled with white powder. She didn't know why. Perhaps it reflected off the moon and provided a natural blue glow that seemed warm and inviting? Or maybe just the beauty of it all gave her peace. Perhaps because it reminded her of her favorite time of year: Christmas.

I'm alive. The realization of it smacked her in the face as the cold wind blew against her flesh in the open air. The coffin was nothing but an illusion. Or a bad dream, perhaps.

Just before they entered the carriage, the queen grabbed Margarete's face and inspected it intently. "The scars are barely visible. It worked…*Good.* You won't fail me, do you understand?"

Still unable to talk from the witch's concoction, Margarete nodded her head. What she was agreeing to, she didn't know. Her mind wandered with a million thoughts at once, filled with a million possibilities. None of them were positive. Of course, the queen would plan her wicked revenge in the absence of the king. The young girl mumbled a prayer in her mind, then, sat in silence for the next twenty minutes while listening to the creaking of wagon wheels.

What was the queen doing? Was she taking her deep in the woods to execute her? Oh how she wished for the king. He would never approve. Was she trading her off to another country as a slave? The woman was mentally insane, and these minds games were a little more than Margarete could stomach at the moment. She thought of the sweet Spanish girl, Maria. She was being traded to another country. It had to be. That's why she had to look presentable. She would become a victim of trafficking. And Lucinda would never know.

"You cleaned up well. You must look your best," the queen said, inspecting the girl again as the carriage continued the long journey. "I brought a few of my own dresses I didn't want, if you want to try them on."

"Yes, Your Majesty," Margarete said out of politeness. She could talk again, which relieved her. She would rather wear rags than the queen's clothes, in all truthfulness. She quickly remembered the days she envied the queen's wardrobe. My, how time changes everything. Margerete knew the queen wanted her dead just days before. Perhaps the woman felt remorse. Perhaps she felt sorry for the young girl. The queen never had a daughter, and perhaps she realized Margarete was the closest she'd ever get to one. Then again, vain queens don't want to be associated with children, because it reminded them that their own youth is fleeting, and old age with all its wrinkles and aches is quickly approaching.

Whiter Than Snow

Perhaps that's why she forced so many children out of the city to work the mines on the mountain. Perhaps she was just plain evil.

And while she was thinking such thoughts, the queen leaned over and fixed a lock of Margarete's hair. By now, Margarete was quivering. The queen was not herself. Perhaps she knew of the betrayal? She felt as if the queen was toying with her, using her as a little experiment.

"Tell me about your mom," the queen said, her body swaying from an unsteady carriage ride.

Margarete thought hard for an appropriate answer. "She enjoyed serving the king and queen and knew I would, too."

The queen snickered. "I don't mean Lucinda. I mean your real mom; the woman who gave birth to you."

Here it comes, Margarete thought. This woman would torture her with words, playing games with her emotions. She took a breath and answered slowly, "She died."

"Oh really?" The queen seemed intrigued. "Tell me more."

"While giving birth…that's what I was told."

The queen sat forward. "I bet you miss her."

"I do. Very much. Although I never met her."

"Well, I can never be your mom, but…I can be someone you can confide in."

Margarete was speechless. But she was thinking how confiding in the queen would be as dangerous as confiding in Satan. Did the woman really think the innocent child would confide in her? Did she not realize that Margarete could see right through her, whatever game she played?

"Now tell me, dear child. How was your trip to England with the prince?" the queen asked, her eyebrow raised, a hint of a smile on her cold face.

"Don't you dare throw this away, son. With this marriage you become King of England," said his father, pressing into Philip. "You need to make something of yourself, without me always handing it to you."

Nonetheless, Philip's heart sagged heavy in grief. While he knew the marriage would be strictly political and would create a powerful dynasty, something in his gut told him to run, to leave and never come back. His father's plan dripped of trickery and usury. Oh, if but a moment, he thought what it would be like to truly have sanctity of marriage under God—marriage from love, marriage with the woman of his dreams. Once again, he was the dreamer in the presence of his disapproving father, still longing for healthy intimacy, a soulmate and best friend to share the rest of his life with. Oh how he wished he could choose the girl of his desires and run away and elope with her, and then hide in a country where no one knew who he was. How he wished they could start a family and enjoy each other as the commoners did—and it was at that moment he realized, he was in love.

The beautiful kids in his mind's eye were miniature versions of the breathtaking Margarete. The thought of her warmed him. He could spend an eternity with her and never be tempted to look at another woman. He could listen to her soft melodic voice

Whiter Than Snow

all day and night and never tire of it. And oh, how he would never sleep. No, sleep would waste precious moments with the girl...he would be so enamored he would stare at her as she slept. He would play with her thick, black hair as she counted sheep. His soul was aching to see her again.

But that was impossible. The world knew the young prince, and where they didn't know him, once they discovered who he was, they would tell the world or worse, behead him to send a message to his father. He was a prisoner to his title. He was the heir to something magnificent, yet, very imprisoning and cold at the same time. As great as he was or was to be, he was nothing but a pawn. His one heart's desire would never be attainable, not as long as his father was alive.

"This is for our family. With this union, you'll take over the world, don't you see?"

"I don't love her, father. She's annoying and controlling."

His father stared sternly at Philip and spoke through clenched teeth, "I didn't say anything about love. What do you expect? Of course she's controlling—she runs one of the greatest countries in the world! You don't do that by sitting back and taking life easy. Being sweet only gets you so far. Why do you think she's the one on the throne?" His father leaned back, his eyes steady, sternly staring into his son's eyes. He could see doubt, fear, and disillusionment. He sat forward again and spoke firmly, "Don't you dare do this, boy! Don't ruin this. Now quiet, the council will be here any minute to sign the treaty between the two of you."

Philip and his father went over it once again. He would be elevated to kingly status once they wed. From the day after the wedding and every day forth, currency would be made with both Mary and Philip's pictures on them—as a symbol of their union. All official and royal documents had to be signed by both parties, and they would co-reign with each other over all of their properties. As a wedding gift, his father conquered Naples and gave the control of it over to them—a sure sign of his strength and power still in the expanding southern part of the hemisphere. It was also a suggestion for the couple to continue conquering the lands between London and Naples, and not remain content with what they already reigned. Philip's father desired the protection and use of Queen Mary's armies in exchange, which would build him a super army, but she refused to agree to his military terms. He offered his men to her in return, but both parties knew that no army compared to the queen's heartless soldiers. How she trained them so well, or made them so ruthless, only God knew. She claimed it was the power of God, while her adversaries claimed they saw God's very adversary, the devil himself, riding with her men and reflecting in the eyes of her captain.

The doors opened and the council spilled in. In unison, they all took their seats.

"The queen regrets she will not be able to meet with us for the signing of the treaty," one of the men confirmed in the presence of the others.

"Then how do we know the queen will agree to the terms?" the prince asked.

Whiter Than Snow

"The terms have already been discussed. This is simply an official signing of the agreement. It will be bound the day after the royal couple weds. Besides, we are the council. We make the decisions in this kingdom." He looked sternly at Philip. "Remember that."

Something about this man bothered Philip. Whether it was his tone of voice, his statement, or just a hunch, Philip had a bad feeling. And of course, he had no idea that this man was in the presence of Thomas Wyatt a night earlier, holding a silver sword to his head in a Protestant-converted small chapel, making threats to take out the prince's life. Yes, it was none other than the queen's spiritual advisor, John Dee, who appointed himself as the voice of the council. He convinced the queen her absence was a sign of power over the prince, and she obliged.

By the end of the month, Thomas Wyatt would be a household name, and this man would make sure to it. He would protect the wedding, ensuring the quick marriage. Then, he would allow Thomas to carry out his plan, while sabotaging him along the way, sacrificing Thomas and then taking all the glory for rescuing the abandoned kingdom, after pinning the murder of the prince on Wyatt, first, of course. He assumed to be seen as a hero by the following winter, and ruling England would never come so easy. Unlike Thomas, he wanted Elizabeth to rule for one simple reason; she was so nice she'd practically give him control. And if she didn't, he didn't have a problem ending her life as well. In fact, he hoped she wouldn't. The kingdom needs a good suicide story, he thought. The compassion and confusion the loss would bring would create more instability, giving him greater influence under the guise of the need for control and order by a spiritual leader.

And assuring the marriage before the murder of the royal couple, he would have a much easier chance taking out the two love birds with one stone. In the couple's death, he would no longer fear the Emperor's men attacking the great nation—because they would be allies.

Whiter Than Snow

Chapter 36

The cold winds blew through the cracks in the carriage. Margarete shivered.

The queen snuggled under a wool blanket and held it out to Margarete to use as well.

"Get under this. It will keep you warm."

Margarete shook her head, denying the blanket, almost in shock by the queen's offer.

"I don't need you catching a cold. I need you in optimal performance," Queen Viktoria said as she placed the blanket over the girl's legs.

Optimal performance? Margarete was curious what the queen meant by that.

The carriage was silent for most of the journey, and although she didn't tell the girl where they were going, the queen told her they'd be there by midday, the next day. And Margarete would have been totally clueless to the journey except they awoke to cross the English Channel at daybreak. Margarete remembered the spot well and the memories warmed her soul.

They were returning to England, she assumed. She both longed for it and was haunted by it at the same time. While serving in the giant castle proved difficult, she felt connected to the wonderfully charming Prince Philip there. Or perhaps it was Jack; both men that stole a piece of her heart. No. Stealing isn't the correct word. She willingly gave pieces of her heart to both men. And if she were ever given the luxury of choosing either one, she didn't know what she'd do. Unfortunately, one was a royal prince and out of reach other than letting him use her as a toy, and the other was rotting away in prison, or perhaps even martyred by now. She felt so much guilt for his capture. Although the prince promised it wasn't her doing, she wished on a thousand stars a thousand times over that she didn't meet up with him that horrible night that led to his arrest.

After they crossed the channel, Margarete felt as if she could hear angels singing in the wind. She stared into the morning sun, letting the ocean air kiss her face. It stung a little, but she welcomed it, nonetheless.

"You need some more sleep. I want you to be presentable," said the queen. "We can't have bags under our eyes, now, can we?"

Presentable? Margarete's stomach tightened. Perhaps the queen was offering her as a gift to the Queen of England? Perhaps that's how she must perform? How twisted of a tale, and it was exactly something Queen Viktoria was capable of doing. At this point, she preferred death in Brussels. Torture would be worse than death, and serving the Queen of England would torment her, especially if she were to marry the only man who made Margarete weak in the knees. She would see right through the girl and kill her for sure. Perhaps boil her in hot oil, cover her in tar, or worse yet,

Whiter Than Snow

make Margarete serve her and Prince Philip every single day, cleaning the master bedroom, the very room the royal couple would spend as lovers and bedmates. It would be a constant reminder of her foolishness for falling in love with a prince. She could only imagine her gaping emotional wounds never healing—being torn wider and deeper with each passing day.

"The wedding is in a few days. But tonight we have the celebration for the bride."

"Wedding?"

The queen smirked. "Why yes, you didn't hear?"

Margarete's gut twisted a little more and she turned her head away from the queen. She knew who the bride was, but the queen said it anyway.

"Prince Philip and Queen Mary are to be wed in a few days. I brought you to accompany me. I assumed you would enjoy the experience, since you seemed to love England so much before."

The ache in Margarete's heart led her to believe she was having a heart attack. She gripped her chest and tried to resist the water that filled her blueberry eyes. Hope aborted her and dread covered her like a body bag for the dead. She was in so much of an emotional daze that she didn't even recognize their arrival in London. It wasn't until they reached the market place in front of Whitehall Castle that she realized where she was.

The queen took a few deep breaths and grabbed Margarete's hands. "Look at me. I want you to act like my traveling companion, not my servant, while we are here. I want you to enjoy the week."

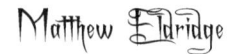

"I don't understand…"

"There are plenty of servants in this castle, and you aren't one of them. You are simply here to keep me company."

Margarete held her breath as they traveled through the lower bailey.

The black stallions stopped along with their carriage.

"My queen," one of the guards said, helping the queen out of the carriage.

Margarete trembled, observing the foggy scenery around her as if it was the last time she'd see the freedom of daylight.

"My princess," said the guard, offering his hand to help Margarete out of the carriage.

Margarete was so much in an emotional fog, she didn't even see the nice soldier approach the carriage, nor hear him call her a princess. She would have corrected his mistake had she been more aware.

One of the guards grabbed both bags from the back of the carriage and followed the queen as Margarete stepped down to the earth beneath.

The queen turned around and addressed the guard. "Take her bags to my room as well."

Margarete was flustered and confused. She wanted to tell the queen that the servant's quarters were in the opposite direction, but feared a face slap or another form of punishment for addressing the wicked woman. And then it hit her; the queen wanted her bags because she wanted to look through Margarete's things. Perhaps she would accuse her of stealing something else. Perhaps she had planned on selling or giving Margarete to Queen Mary this very evening, and she wouldn't need clothes after all. Perhaps Margarete's permanent service was the queen's wedding gift. Oh, the imagination of a nervous young woman!

Margarete lowered her head and trudged behind the queen and the guards as they walked the halls of the Whitehall Palace, her stomach in her throat. Finally, they reached a private room and the host opened the door as one of the queen's guards walked in, checking the corners of the room and under the bed for intruders or unwanted objects, and then nodded to the queen.

She entered.

"I requested two rooms," she said sternly to the host.

"Yes, my queen. This is the queen's quarters. I hope you find it satisfactory."

"It will do," she answered. "Margarete, please follow this man to the other room, and wait for me there."

"Yes, Your Highness."

Margarete entered the quaint room with the most exquisite furniture she'd ever seen. She rubbed her hand along the ornate wood on the dresser and then the bed frame. She sat on the bed and tried to enjoy the moment, for a moment was all she had, she assumed. Such exquisite beauty for a guest. Such a waste of money she thought to herself, thinking of the peasants who suffered greatly outside of the castle gates. And then she thought about all of the aristocracy that stayed there.

The queen entered Margarete's room holding a dress, and a beautiful one at that—beads hanging from the neck.

"I want you to try this on," she said.

Margarete was moved. "For me? I don't understand."

"We have an important dinner tonight, and I need you looking your best. You are coming as my guest, not my servant, remember?" The queen walked over to the girl. "I looked through your bags. I didn't see anything worthy for you to wear."

Margarete took the dress from the queen's hands and admired it. She had never worn anything so delicate and beautiful. "Are you sure, Your Highness?"

"I can't bring a guard to the dinner, now can I? It would be rather out of place—this is a bridal shower for the Queen of England."

Margarete slowly carried the scarlet dress to her bed and placed it down. She retrieved her smock and put it on.

"You're taking too long. Let me help you," the queen suggested.

While Margarete and the other servants dressed the queen on many occasions, this was the first time the queen helped anyone, much less a servant. The roles were reversed and it frightened the young woman. She slowly made her way to the queen and the woman pulled the laces that crossed her back as tightly as she could, so much that Margarete almost lost her breath.

Whiter Than Snow

And then, staring into Queen Viktoria's eyes, the change occurred. The queen's eyes became black with jealousy. She squeezed the strings harder, and the poor child gasped for air.

"I can't—," Margarete cried, the airy words barely escaping her lips, her lungs feeling punctured.

The queen spun her around and tilted her head, staring the young beauty in her fearful eyes. She spoke with much haste. "You listen to me. If you want to live and live long, you do everything I say. You don't screw this night up. You keep your mouth shut, and when you answer, you answer with my permission. And when you do, speak like one with authority. On this night, you will act like royalty. There's a lot riding on your performance tonight, your life included. Do you understand?"

Margarete was too frightened to answer but she nodded her head while wiping a tear that seeped from her eye.

The countenance on the queen changed and she turned Margarete around again. And then, with the queen's assistance, Margarete put on her dress. A mirror on an easel faced them, but Margarete dared not admire herself or the dress in front of the queen. The mirror wouldn't lie.

"Look at yourself," the queen ordered.

Margarete turned to the mirror and looked at herself in the scarlet wool dress decorated with lace and beads. She looked like royalty. She wanted to smile but was afraid.

"Beautiful," the queen said. Not because she wanted to, but felt she needed to—and saying the comment almost made the royal woman throw up. She felt as odd saying it as Margarete felt hearing it from the queen's lips. "I'm sure you can do something with your hair…"

"Yes, my queen."

The queen glanced at her own image in the mirror. "…After you do something with mine. You're not the only one who has to look perfect tonight."

"Yes, my queen."

And with that comment, the queen left the room, leaving Margarete to herself. The young woman waited a few seconds to let it settle in, then, twirled in front of the mirror like a young girl playing dress up.

"God, is the queen playing games with me?" she said into the open air. "Perhaps I will capture the eyes of the prince if I see him tonight," she said to herself. "No wait…I don't want that. I don't need the Queen of England taking my head for feeling beautiful."

But secretly, Margarete wished and wanted to see the handsome prince. The thought made her heart giddy.

Whiter Than Snow

Chapter 37

Fireflies lit the violet sky with tiny bursts of amber glows. Margarete caught one and stared at it in magical wonder as it crawled on her hand. Oh what a simple life a firefly must have. And what natural beauty they emitted.

"Child, no time for foolishness. Tonight, you are to behave as royalty, not a servant, remember? Do you understand me?"

"Yes, my queen."

The firefly flew from her hand and over the helmet of the English soldier guiding their way. The soldier swatted at it. It amazed Margarete how someone could swat at something so little, yet so amazing of a creature. How many creatures had a light that shown from its body? How many creatures illuminated the light inside of them for the world around to see? And how many ignore that light, swatting it away like an ordinary fly?

The trio reached the dining hall and entered. Mary, the Queen of England, along with other royals and nobles, sat around a table, talking girl talk. Queen Mary stopped mid-sentence as the help introduced Queen Viktoria.

"May I present to you, Queen Viktoria of Brussels," the man said, and exited the room.

"Congratulations on your engagement. He's quite a catch," said Queen Viktoria as she took a seat at the table.

"He's not a fish. But I am the Queen of hearts," Queen Mary answered with a crooked smile. She looked at Margarete, who was still standing in the dark corner, her eyes half-slit open. "Servants are not needed for the bridal shower. I'm sure you can make yourself useful in the kitchen."

"What about princesses?" asked Queen Viktoria.

"Excuse me?" answered the Queen of England.

"I'd like you to meet the king's daughter, Princess Margarete." She let that sink in for a moment and then continued, "My stepdaughter."

Queen Mary's lip quivered as Margarete stepped into the light, revealing the beautiful dress she was wearing.

"Is this some kind of joke? I saw her…"

"She's the lost child," Queen Viktoria interrupted with a smile. I'm sure you've heard of her. The king's daughter has been found, isn't that right, dear?" she said with a whimsical smile while looking to Margarete.

Margarete's eyes searched back and forth from queen to queen, her heart heavy with questions, fear, betrayal, and hurt.

"This better not be a game. You are in my kingdom now, Vikki," answered Queen Mary, sinisterly.

"No game. She is the king's missing daughter. She's been in hiding for some time," she said simply.

Whiter Than Snow

Drowning in a flood of emotions, Margarete ran out of the room and down the hallway. The torches which lit the walls blurred by like large fireflies as she ran. She covered her face with her hands as she forced her legs to move, her chest heaving as her throat choked in emotion.

She was lost somewhere in the palace. Falling to her knees, she called out, "Oh, God. What's she doing?" And she paused in that position for the next ten minutes, still before God, hiding her eyes from the stone walls that faced her, her voice mumbling unintelligible words to the world around her.

And then she heard a sound. Someone was near, watching her. But she was too embarrassed to look. She sniffed, wiped her nose with her sleeve, and through wet eyelashes, glimpsed at the man to her right. He had a kind look on his face. She slowly turned her head to face him.

"Are you alright, my dear?"

She didn't answer.

"Silly question," he said. He held his hands up in a square and squinted at her.

"What are you doing?" she asked.

He shook his head. "Beautiful."

"Excuse me?"

"I must paint you."

She exhaled and showed him a quick smile, then returned to her frown. "No," she said. And she got up to walk away.

"Please. I must." He walked over to her and offered his hand. "Forgive me, where are my manners? My name is Anthonis Mor. I'm a painter, at your service."

She was still lost in her own little world.

"And you are?" he asked.

"I don't know." For a moment, confusion stole her identity.

"Well, well, dear, whomever you are.... I paint beautiful things. And I want to paint you."

She rolled her eyes. "Why would you want to paint me?"

"Why does God create?" he questioned.

She sat in silence, waiting for more encouragement from the famous painter.

"I capture God's beauty with my brushes, please…"

She sighed at him as he reached to her face and wiped away her tear with his thumb.

"I'm going to get my brushes. Please don't leave," he said.

"What are you doing here?" she asked.

"I was hired by the prince to paint boring things. Tomorrow I'm painting an engagement picture for the royal couple," he joked with a smile. "But tonight, I'm free." He looked around to make sure they were alone. "And I want to paint something intriguing, and I found it in the crying doll in front of me…the most beautiful thing I've seen in this castle all day."

"My face…it's a mess," she complained, wiping her tear-infested eyes.

"You are beautiful just the way you are."

Whiter Than Snow

"You are very kind. Still, I can't."

"Are you here for the wedding?"

"Yes."

"We have plenty of time. People pay me lots of money to paint them. But I will pay *you*."

"That's not necessary," she answered. "But I'm not comfortable here."

"Wait! I know the place," he said. "In the garden, by the water. You'll love it."

Margarete questioned herself. She was afraid, but for some reason she trusted this gentle man. The lighting was perfect. Margarete sat on a stone bench in the garden, snow all around, the white reflecting the moonlight—a natural bounce—illuminating her face from below and beside her. Anthonis stared in wonder, lost in the moment. Everything was perfect for his painting. He took a deep breath, stepped back to his easel and picked up a brush.

She lowered her head.

"Don't."

"I'm sorry?" she asked.

"Don't lower your head. The lighting is perfect where you are. You'll cast a nasty shadow if you move." Without even looking at the easel, he outlined her face, his eyes never leaving the scenery before him. He carved out the shape of her heart-like face with imaginary tools coming from his eyes, and then translated that onto paper. His chest pressed in and out as his pulse raced. He worked furiously, trading brushes and mixing paints.

"I can't hold my head like this much longer."

"Oh, but you must, you must." He ignored her plea and continued to paint.

"May I see?"

"When I am through, my love." He stopped for a moment and stood straight. Eccentric didn't begin to describe his personality. "I'm sorry. That was highly inappropriate. You have to forgive me. I'm just a little excited. It's as if God himself sent me an angel, straight from Heaven, to paint. I can't let this moment slip away. I'm afraid this is all just a dream."

"I wish I could see what you see," she said, lowering her head once more, as shame crowded the forefront of her thoughts.

"Your head?" he suggested, reminding her gently.

"Oh, sorry," she answered, as she lifted it.

"With this painting, I will make you one of the most famous women in the world. Paint you I must, and everyone will wonder who this beautiful woman is for centuries to come."

"With a painting?"

"Yes. Sorry if I'm a bit arrogant, but I am one of the best, if not the best."

She smiled. "I guess so. You do work for the prince."

"Correction, I do not work for the prince. I simply paint the prince for money. I work for no one but myself."

"Sorry...I..."

"No need to apologize. Let's just hope the prince doesn't see this painting of you. You would wreck the royal wedding for sure."

Silence.

A tear formed in her eye.

"Oh dear," he said, standing up straight again. "That's why you were out here crying, wasn't it? I can see beauty in the dark, and yet, be so blind sometimes." Anthonis took a few steps, pacing in a circle. "That swine!" he shouted. "I should have known! He hurt you, didn't he?"

"No, no. It wasn't the prince at all."

"The queen?"

She closed her eyes.

"Beauty can be such a curse. You are royalty, I presume?"

She rose from her place on the bench and walked to the man. Her eyes darting back and forth behind forming tears, her mind in a foggy state of confusion. "I don't know."

More tears.

"Either you are or you aren't."

She looked back up at the man peering into his tender brown eyes. "I don't know who I am."

"What do you mean?"

"Everything I've ever thought was a lie." Her breathing stopped. She suffocated in the horror of her thoughts. Could it be? "I would rather kill myself than be subject to her as a stepdaughter." Tears streamed down her face. She thought back to her earliest days of serving. The only thing she truly longed for, was in fact, to be the daughter of the queen—as wicked as she was. She let go and tears poured down her face like water works.

"Shhhhh," the man hushed her. Anthonis traced her face with the back of his bare hand. "I have painted every royal family from Spain to England, and my paintings don't lie. You have more noble blood in your skin than anyone I've ever painted. You glow with an aura of angel dust. Even your tears are like holy water, blessed by God himself. I've never painted something, *someone*, so beautiful in all my life."

She looked to him, her eyes puddled like lakes, and gave him a hint of a smile.

"Trust me. You are royalty."

She hugged him tightly and whispered, "But that confuses things all the more. My heart is owned by the prince."

"And do you have his heart?"

"I thought so."

"Arranged marriages are such the destroyers of love and anything pure. Cursed be the man who marries for power. And cursed be his kingdom!"

He walked away from her and gaped at the full, blue moon.

Short sobs expelled from the troubled young woman.

"Extraordinary moon. Extraordinary. It's a sign!"

"A sign?"

He peeled his eyes from the moon and back to her. "You, my dear. If anyone could steal the heart of the dear prince, if anyone could stop this wedding, it would be you."

Whiter Than Snow

She whispered in a hurried rush, "Do not speak such things, please. I do not need to lose my head to the queen!"

He just smiled at her, calmly. "This can be done. Perhaps you are an angel in disguise, sent from Heaven for this very purpose."

"You do not wish the prince to marry the queen? And yet you paint them?"

"Let's just say I'm a free-thinker. I think little of powerful governments. Nonetheless, I enjoy painting royalty. It pays the bills and allows me to travel the world at their expense. Please…may I continue to paint you?"

She returned to her seat on the bench and re-entered her pose.

He dabbed his brush in the water and onto his cloth. He put his brush down again.

"Do you wish to see him again, tonight?"

"I cannot answer that."

"But I can arrange it," he said, raising his eyebrow.

"There you are!" a guard interrupted, speaking to Margarete.

Matthew Eldridge

Chapter 38

Princess Margarete entered the dining hall with the guard.

Queen Viktoria tilted her head and addressed the child, "I was afraid you were lost. Please, come eat."

The teen walked cautiously to her seat at the table. A plate of food awaited her. Queen Mary followed her with cold stone-like eyes, continuing her conversation with the other women.

"...If you want the blessings of God, my friends, then you will endorse this God-given mission."

"And your husband to be? He agrees that we force people into Catholicism by the sword?" Queen Viktoria questioned, the other royals nodding their approval of such an inquiry.

"My vision is right in line with Prince Philip's father's mission. Of course he agrees. And we aren't forcing anyone into Catholicism. We are simply removing the infidels; the devil-worshiping Protestants from spreading their witchcraft, trickery, and lies. God has put me on this mission. We're purifying the land for the better good. Why do you think we've been blessed with so much favor in my kingdom?"

Margarete held her tongue, although her soul moaned to speak the truth—or perhaps it was the Spirit of God—but at this moment, she knew that speaking her mind was not for a servant, or even a princess. This was the Queen of England, the most powerful woman in the new world, and she had an agenda to massacre anyone who disagreed with her religious beliefs. Margarete felt faint. Her head fell on the table as she nearly passed out.

"Are you not feeling well?" asked one of the royal guests.

"No... I..."

"I think you need to lie down. You're blue around the face," the guest said.

"I hope I'm not coming down with something. I'm feeling rather ill," answered Margarete.

"Must be from the long journey. Eat something," commanded Queen Viktoria.

"Guard, please help her to her room," Queen Mary demanded, trumping Queen Viktoria's request.

Margarete looked to Queen Viktoria for approval. The woman gave a quick nod and turned her gaze away from the child as the guard led her out of the room.

The newly claimed princess entered her room and discovered a note on her dresser.

Come to my quarters tonight so I may finish my painting of you. I have a small gift for you.
-Anthonis

She exhaled and was caught completely off guard by Queen Viktoria as she entered her room.

Whiter Than Snow

"I thought I'd come check on you," the queen said to Margarete.

"My queen, I do not mean any disrespect, but why did you say that?" Margarete asked while crumbling the note in her hand, hiding it from the queen.

"Say what?"

"That..." She took a breath. "...that I was a princess."

The queen hesitated. "Isn't that what you want? To be a princess? Don't tell me you haven't imagined it."

"You lied to the Queen of England."

"Did I?"

Margarete stilled herself. Was the King of Brussels, in fact, her father? "What are you saying?"

"You need your sleep. We have a wedding to eviscerate."

"I'm afraid I don't understand..."

"Goodnight," Queen Viktoria said, while exiting the room.

In her heart, Margarete knew what the queen was up to, but she didn't want to accept or believe it. Looking back to the note, Margarete battled within herself. What if this man, this painter, wanted to harm her? What if he led her into a trap? Who would protect her? Then again, he did paint her alone in the garden for over an hour. She hated this plague of fear that often seized her.

Beyond all reason, her feet found their way to Anthonis' room and the door was wide open. She steadied herself in the doorframe and peered inside.

"Hello? Anthonis?"

But there was no answer.

However, she did see the painting of her on the easel near the bed. And next to it, a wide painting of the prince with a sketch of the queen beside it, covered in the shadows of the room. She walked over to the paintings and admired them. More than twenty candles still burned around the paintings, so Anthonis couldn't have gone far, she assumed.

"Is that you?" Prince Philip asked from the doorway, seeing the painting of her.

She gasped, startled by his voice. She didn't answer, but slowly turned to face him.

The door shut behind him and he walked slowly to her, his eyes never leaving hers.

"I've thought about you every day." He moved in closer. "Have you thought about me?" he asked.

She hesitated. Her three second pause seemed to be an eternity. Dreaminess consumed her face as her guard fell. She turned around so she wouldn't have to say it while looking in his eyes. "When I watch the stars and moon at night, I can't help but to feel comforted, knowing we are both under that same moon, staring up at it perhaps at the very same time."

"You are my moon and stars. I can't stop—I won't stop thinking about you," he said as he touched her shoulders and turned her around to face him again.

"Why do you have to be so perfect?" she asked as a tear fell from her eye.

Whiter Than Snow

He lifted his right hand and wiped her tear, then, lifted her chin with his fingers. He leaned down and touched her warm lips with a soft, long kiss.

"Stop. Please," she cried. "How can you do this? How can you kiss me like this when you are engaged to her?"

He lowered his head in shame and backed away. "I'm sorry, I..."

"Wait...Don't go," she insisted.

"I need to go. I can't be in here with you and not feel something inside. My heart is overwhelmed. Your beauty alone has me spellbound. Goodbye, my love."

Margarete shook her head in frustration and confusion. "What do you want from me?" she yelled with a partial cry, the sound coming from the ache in her soul.

"I want...you," he answered. "All of you." And he took a few more steps towards the door. "I want to know you in a way no one has known you. I want to be close to you."

Margarete walked to him, grabbed him by the face, pulled him so close, he felt her sweet breath in his mouth. She stared into his eyes so intensely he felt helpless and naked inside, trying to look away, but he couldn't. She had gotten to him. She owned his heart. And she expressed her desire for him in an aggressive manner. Margarete reached for him with her lips and he kissed her back, hard. Back and forth they volleyed with affection. He embraced her in his arms. For once, she felt safe, warm. They were so lost in each other, time practically stood still.

And then... he stopped.

"I can't," he said. But then, he stared into her hungry eyes and couldn't help but to kiss her again... and again... and again. As he pulled away to say goodbye, he placed her face in his palms and kissed her lovely eyelids. He tasted the saltiness of her tears—yes, she was silently crying.

"Please, don't cry," he pleaded kindly.

Her lips quivered. The couple heard footsteps coming down the hallway.

The prince stepped away and opened the door. "I must leave."

She fell onto the bed, spellbound, watching as her prince retreated down the hallway. She closed her eyes and tried to catch her breath. She heard a man clearing his throat.

"Perhaps I'll finish the painting some other time. T'is late, my lady. I will walk you back to your room," said the painter as he stepped into the doorway to his room.

Whiter Than Snow

Chapter 39

The rehearsal dinner.

It was a glorious meal. Guests of the royal family found their names along the ornamented tables that lined the dining hall. Margarete felt rather out of place sitting next to Queen Viktoria near the head of the table, being served as a guest and not serving. And if that didn't make her uncomfortable enough, at the front table sat Queen Mary, just twenty feet away, staring her down. There were numbers at each place setting, and Margarete was number seven. How she received such a high number out of a couple hundred guests, she had no idea.

Within minutes of sitting down, servers brought appetizers to the guests. Margarete spotted Maria across the room, back from Spain once again, and waved her down.

Maria nervously eyed Margarete, not recognizing her at first in her royal attire, but then walked briskly from her appointed guests to hug her young friend, her face decorated with a beautiful smile.

"Magarete!" Maria said excitedly as she kissed each of her cheeks in typical Spanish fashion.

"You are speaking to a princess. I suggest you address her appropriately and learn your place!" Queen Viktoria interrupted, speaking sternly to Maria.

Maria nervously bowed and backed away from the Princess Margarete, escaping the cruel gaze of the queen and returning to the kitchen.

Queen Viktoria spoke through clenched teeth. "You are to act like a princess. You don't converse with the help, do you understand? You will not embarrass me like that again."

After the main course was devoured by the guests, luscious red and green apples from England were given for dessert. They were believed to cleanse the palette, freshen breath, and whiten teeth—an after meal staple. And while it was a common practice to eat apples after meals in most of Europe, no apple could compare to the size, sweetness, or juiciness of those grown in England. It was considered a true delicacy.

The apples were brought out on separate silver trays, one tray per family, and placed in front of the guests. However, the tray placed in front of Margarete and Queen Viktoria was gold plated. Queen Viktoria took notice of the difference and smirked at the other guests, feeling quite honored, placing her hand on her chest while deciding between the red or green one. She grabbed the larger of the two apples and took a bite, her lips touching the beautiful red fruit. It was heavenly, she thought to herself, as she savored the sweet piece in her mouth before swallowing.

Whiter Than Snow

The servant who carried the tray recognized Margarete as she served guests on the other side of the table. She wasn't just any help; Hannah, the head servant, was the apple deliverer, specifically ordered by Queen Mary to bring the golden tray to seat numbers six and seven. Hannah ached with worry as she backed away from the newly appointed princess and disappeared quickly into the kitchen.

She returned with a bottle of wine and rushed to Margarete's side. Hannah eyed the girl nervously, trying to communicate with her eyes. Heeding the warning of the queen, Margarete ignored Hannah, for she was just a servant, after all. The teenager lifted the golden-green apple to her lips, and as she did, Hannah poured the wine into the crystal in front of the young princess, knocking the crystal over and spilling the contents onto Margarete's lap.

"Oh!" Margarete cried as she arose from her seat and placed the apple back down onto the golden tray, the wet, sticky wine staining her dress.

"You stupid servant!" Queen Viktoria shouted at Hannah, standing up from her place at the table. "You stupid, stupid servant!" she yelled again, throwing her half-eaten apple at Hannah. "This will come out of your wages, do you understand! That was a very expensive dress!"

Hannah nodded, terror masking her usually tough demeanor.

"I'm sorry, my queen," Margarete said to Queen Viktoria, looking down at the beautiful dress the queen let her wear for the evening—the dress that was now ruined by red wine stains.

"You're no better than she is!" Viktoria addressed the teen, pointing at Hannah. "I knew better than to let you wear it!"

"I'll find a way to pay for it," Princess Margarete said timidly.

"You can't replace a dress like that—Made in Spain! It's worth more than your life!"

Margarete burst into tears and ran out of the dining hall.

Queen Viktoria glanced around the room, realizing all of the attention was on her. She offered the crowd a fake smile and sighed. "Accidents happen. Excuse me," she said softly as she retreated out of the room.

As Queen Viktoria exited the dining hall, she saw the handsome Prince Philip approaching. In her mind, she schemed a plan so devious she thought it was foolproof.

"Did you see Margarete run by?" she asked the prince, a concerned look on her face.

He wanted to avoid the crooked queen but the word *Margarete* from the queen's lips made him curious.

"No."

"She was very upset about something. I'm pretty sure she's in her room. Alone. She could use some comfort."

"I don't know what you are suggesting, but it's highly inappropriate."

Whiter Than Snow

"I'm just concerned for her well-being," the queen answered, then turned and re-entered the dining hall.

Prince Philip followed behind and took his place at the head table next to his bride-to-be. Queen Viktoria watched from her seat. From her view, she could see the worry in his eyes. It wasn't even a minute before he leaned over to the Queen of England, whispered into her ear, and disappeared again into the dark hallway.

The Princess Margarete Von Waldeck was on her knees, praying unintelligible words to her Maker in her dimly lit room—the candle almost completely burnt out. Her tears poured down her arms from her hands that were tightly clasped over her face.

Hearing her cry, Prince Philip slowly entered her room and knelt beside her, wanting to be close to her. It was the first time he'd found himself on his knees in perhaps a decade. There was something healing and humbling about it. It felt good. It felt right, although, unlike her, he wasn't kneeling to pray. His heart simply ached for hers. He wanted to help her. He wanted to heal her. It nauseated him that he was perhaps the cause of her pain. He was overwhelmed by this feeling of affection for her—pure affection. He wanted to hold her. He felt clean and innocent, like a child. There was something in the atmosphere of the room that stole him—something he had never felt before. He wanted to cry. He wanted to confess his sins. He wanted to be a new person. And he wanted nothing more than to be with Margarete, touching her, caressing her soft face, sharing his love with her. And in that moment, he was completely consumed with the present. The thoughts of the rehearsal dinner and his future wedding faded far away from his mind.

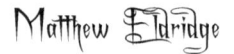

And as he stared at her in this delicate moment, Margarete never looked more beautiful, innocent, and wholesome. Perhaps it was her transparency. There was beauty in authentic tears. Or perhaps it was the anointing of her desperate prayer. Either way, God appeared to be in the room. Not that either of them could see God, but they could feel something spiritual touching them. A warmth enveloped the couple—a supernatural experience in this English cold. Prince Philip placed his hand gently on the back of the weeping young woman. It took her a full minute to recognize his presence. When she did, she fell into him and he held her tightly as she continued to sob. She leaned up to him and nuzzled her face against his, her tears wetting his cheeks. He offered her a soft kiss on her cheek and she returned it with a soft kiss of her own on his face. He returned the kiss again, as did she, until his lips met the corner of her lips.

She looked into his eyes and traced his face with her delicate hand, as if she was memorizing what it felt like. He returned her affection by painting her face with sweet, soft kisses, starting with each of her cheeks, then kissing the tip of her nose. Then he kissed each eyelid, from her right to her left. He softly touched her face with his hand and lifted her head, kissing the center of her chin. He followed her jaw line with his lips until he reached her ear and then moved down to her tender, bare neck. She moaned. It was her sensitive spot; her weakness. She'd never been kissed on the neck before; still she welcomed it nervously.

She lifted his hand and kissed his fingers. He pulled back and took a long stare at her lovely wrecked face—and she stared back, her eyes never leaving him. His eyes were cesspools of love pulling her in. He, on the other hand, could see her wounds, her fear, her wanting for him. And while his heart was beating wildly for the moment, he ached for the fragile child. She softly kissed him on the corner of the lips and pulled away.

Her vulnerability during her prayer time left her heart exposed, and he intruded into it like a warrior. In unison, the couple leisurely stood to their feet as they continued to enjoy the warmth, passion, and affection of the other, arms and legs becoming tangled in a tight embrace.

Slowly, they swayed together, as if dancing to an unheard melody—a soft, sweet melody they could hear only in their hearts. She felt warm and alive—safe in his arms. And he found everything he ever longed for in hers. The shadows from the candle danced over their faces as they slowly rotated in a circle—and yet, the lovely couple never left their stares on one another. She was finally dancing with the prince.

"Margarete... I..."

She put her finger over his lips and hushed him. For there was nothing worth saying, she felt. He could only make matters worse by his words and ruin the moment. And when she thought he would talk again, she kissed him to stop him from speaking. And the kiss worked.

Philip gently lowered the princess to the bed. He was over her, prostrate, his body against hers. He gazed into her oceanic, tear-stained eyes; her hair wildly fallen around her, spread out on the bed. He could almost swear he could see her soul through her eyes. There was no mistaken, the girl wanted him. She was willing to love him as he longed to be loved.

He kissed her hard and then sat up.

From the flat of her back, she watched him as he hesitated. She laced her fingers with his and tugged at him, trying to pull him back down on top of her, but he wouldn't move.

"What?" she asked softly, her hand on his chest.

"I really must go. I shouldn't be here."

She looked at him with sad, desperate eyes, and for a moment, he could do nothing but to observe her lovely frown. He leaned down for one last, small kiss. She cupped his face with her palms and attacked his lips with a memorable kiss, a token of her love for him to remember in the days to come. He didn't want the affection to stop. And as they broke for air, she continued with moist, tender kisses across his face and lips, refusing to let him pull away.

"I really must…" he started, but was stopped by her fingers on his lips again. He took one final look into her eyes. He leaned forward and pressed his lips hard against hers, stealing her breath. His body tensed as he continued to kiss her aggressively, his hands moving wildly around her body. This was passion, she thought. Or lust. Or perhaps both. Whatever it was—whatever it became, it wasn't the same feeling she felt just fifteen minutes earlier, and it scared her.

"What?" he asked endearingly, looking into her eyes—sensing something was upsetting her.

"Do you love me?" she asked like an insecure child.

He stopped kissing her, stunned by the question. And although he didn't answer, she could see it in his eyes—he did.

She kissed him softly a few more times, hoping to return to the beauty of the innocence of the previous kisses exchanged earlier in the night. But it was too late. She had crossed the line. They both had, and he appeared disinterested in a common kiss—although she could stay there forever.

Deep in distracted thought, she blurted out hastily, "I will sleep with you," while stealing a few more kisses. "I will give you all of me, now—not just my heart, if you promise…promise me that you will end the massacre of the Protestant Christians. Promise me that you will convince that bloody Mary to stop this bloodshed. Please. I beg of you."

He kissed her hard. Once again, they found themselves in a passionate embrace, arms, legs, and lips entangled. His hand slid against her leg and she jumped. He kept touching her, but she squirmed so he moved his hand to her stomach. She was breathless—whether in a good way or a bad way she couldn't tell, but she wanted it to stop. She needed to clear her head, and if she was honest with herself, she was quite frightened.

She pushed him back off of her, and he supported himself on his elbows, looking down on her. She searched his eyes.

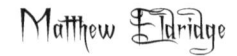

"Promise me?" she begged.

"I am a Catholic, Margarete. How can I disagree with her actions?" he said carelessly, trying to kiss her again.

"Catholic or Protestant, killing another man because he doesn't believe in your religion is wrong."

He paused, looking at her intently. He could see that she was heavy burdened. His face fell. He sat up on the bed, the intimate moment forever gone. "I cannot stop what my father has started. He would disown me."

"Yes, but…even your father was friends with King Henry, a Protestant, was he not?" she said, trying to win his affection again, taking his hand and kissing it.

"Those were the early years. It was all for political reasons, I believe." He looked into her eyes again. "You don't understand. I've already let my father down enough. He was the world's greatest Holy Roman Emperor… and I am just… a failure," he said while lowering his head. She had gotten to him. He was vulnerable.

"Does my heart belong to you?" she asked, kissing one of his fingers, then, taking his hand and placing it over her heart.

"What?"

"Does my heart belong to you?" she asked again.

"Have you given it to me?" he asked.

"Yes…" she said, kissing his hand again. "And I am a Protestant—the very person your fiancé wants to kill. You have already won me over. You can win the heart of the queen, and of the people as well. You are an amazing man, my prince. Please. I'm begging you."

She took his hand off her heart and placed it on her face, allowing him to feel the wetness of her tears.

"Margarete," he whispered softly. And then he choked.

The prince of Spain stood to his feet and stared at the ceiling, still holding her hand. "I'm responsible for the bloodshed of a number of the Protestant Christians myself." He turned to her. "But I want you to know that I only did it to please my father—to prove something to him." He looked away from her and let go of her hand. It's as if his mind was traveling back in time and he became troubled. "In my earlier years, I was against his crusade, and it cost us our friendship for a while. I was an arrogant, horrible young leader to him, and he gave half of his kingdom to my brother, Ferdinand. He wanted to give it to me."

Margarete propped herself up. She saw tears forming in his eyes and tried to take his hand, but he was lifeless—his fingers numb to what she was doing.

"I'm such a disappointment," he said in a monotone voice, then, acknowledged her by looking at her again.

"My God, is the prince actually crying?" she said, almost in disbelief. He was confiding in her.

"I just wanted the approval of my father. It's what every boy wants... And here I am, about to make the mistake of a lifetime, once again, to please my father." The revelation hit him like a rock in his stomach. His marriage to the Queen of England was his father's idea.

Prince Philip knelt on the bed beside the luscious princess and clasped his hands tightly over hers. "I feel like a fool. The Prince of Spain is blubbering like a baby to a beautiful servant girl. Maybe I've had too much wine."

"No, it's ok. I understand," she said with a soft voice, rubbing her fingers between his.

"My kingdom—his old kingdoms are falling apart. I joined in the crusade to make him proud of me. I'm responsible for innocent blood."

"It's not too late. Will you please try to stop them?" she said, placing his face in her hands.

"For you—I will try," he said as he breathed deeply. She pulled his face to her and warmed him with another kiss.

He touched her face, rubbing his thumb against her swollen lips. They were his—completely given to him, willingly, as he desired. He kissed her again, joyful in his revelation of her love. He looked deeply into her eyes—they were soft; sincere. He would die for them. He would die protecting them. He thought about Jesus and his deep love for his children—the love so real, he was willing to endure a shameful death on a cross for them—just to be with them for an eternity. Yes, this is the same love he was feeling for Margarete—or perhaps he thought he was feeling. He was willing to die to himself, to destroy everything he ever hoped to achieve, for this one love alone. He would fight the queen and put an end to the genocide.

He belonged to Margarete—at this moment anyways. His kisses were never-ending. At times she returned the kiss…and at times she shied away and her thoughts were elsewhere. She wanted to cry. She didn't want this. Ok, she *did* want it—the kiss that is, but not what she thought would come next…at least not like this. She wanted to be his wife. Her body would belong to her future husband; and him only, she always said. She made a vow to God.

But she had crossed the line. Her body burned in pleasure and she wanted to be touched by him. She made a proposition—a sacrifice of her purity to save Protestants from martyrdom in the prince's territory—and perhaps save those in the land belonging to the Queen of England. Perhaps she couldn't break up the wedding, but she could convince the Prince to make a promise and follow through on it. Her thoughts moved from delicious love to the saving of innocent lives, and he could sense that her mind was elsewhere.

Queen Viktoria watched the Queen of England fidget nervously, wondering the whereabouts of her future husband. He had been gone for at least twenty minutes or more. Viktoria felt an uneasiness in her stomach and didn't know if it was from the food or from what she was about to do. It's not every day she was able to exploit a princess and a prominent prince—a man who was to be wed to a queen, on the night before his wedding.

Viktoria stood from her chair and tried to move gracefully to the queen. However, the cramping in her stomach was more than she could handle and she stumbled into the guard standing by the queen's table. He caught her as she fell, and helped her regain her balance.

Queen Mary turned in Viktoria's direction. "Are you alright?" she asked with a smirk.

"I'm sure I'll be alright. Perhaps too much wine."

"Perhaps," the Queen of England said with a fraudulent smile.

Queen Viktoria sighed. "I'm sure you're looking for the prince?"

Queen Mary showed concern, tilting her head and lifting an eyebrow.

"I can't be too sure, but...I believe I saw him heading to Margarete's..." she backtracked her words, "to *Princess* Margarete's room."

Queen Mary leaned in and spoke through thin lips, "You may be a guest in my kingdom, but if you aren't careful, I will take your head, and the head of your so-called princess."

"I'm only speaking from experience. Why don't you go see for yourself?" said Queen Viktoria, hunched over and grasping her stomach, which ached greatly.

Queen Mary led three guards down the dimly lit hallway towards the princess's room. Queen Viktoria followed closely, almost unable to keep up. Just before they reached the room, Viktoria fell onto her knees, hunched over. Her face turned pale and she began to cough. Queen Mary stopped and turned back around, facing the ill woman.

Viktoria looked up at the Queen of England, her eyes turning black and filling with blood as she tremored. Blood purged from her stomach and filled her lips. She grasped at the mighty queen's dress. She coughed a few more times, blood expelling from her mouth and painting the ground beneath her. Queen Mary jerked her dress back from the dying woman, stimulated with curiosity as the Queen of Brussels took her last few breaths.

"How did it taste?"

"What?" Queen Viktoria gasped curiously, looking up at the Queen of England, her mouth now covered in blood, drops of the crimson red fluid dripping down her face and onto her glorious gown.

"The apple… It is to die for, isn't it?" answered the Queen of England as she laughed wickedly and held up the other apple from the golden tray—the apple destined for Margarete. She brought it with her to Margarete's room.

Queen Viktoria fell over, face first into the puddle of blood on the hallway floor.

One of the soldiers turned the woman over. Her dead, open eyes stared at him.

Satisfied by the death of Queen Viktoria, Queen Mary and her soldiers turned around and continued their journey to the princess's room.

Prince Philip stopped kissing Margarete's luscious lips and studied her face. Her blue eyes beckoned him to kiss her again, but yet, he couldn't. Instead, he lifted himself off of her and off the bed.

"What are you doing? What's wrong?" she beckoned.

He scurried to the door and opened it partially, then, turned around to face her. "I can't believe I'm doing this."

She smiled at him, propping herself up on her elbows, amused.

"I'm sorry," he apologized, shaking his head. "I can't do this."

"You don't want me?"

"That's the point. I do want you. I want you so badly. I've never, *not* done this before. But I'm crazy for you. It's because I'm crazy for you that I'm not going to do this... I can't hurt you anymore."

He evaded her dreamy eyes by rolling his, talking to himself. "I must be nuts. The most beautiful girl in the world is offering herself to me, and I'm declining." With his final statement, he exited the room.

The most beautiful girl in the world? She repeated it to herself in her mind. She had never heard such a compliment in all her life, and from the prince, no doubt. She was grinning as she lied back on the bed, burying her face in the soft pillow.

He stepped back in the room and she felt self conscious.

"Tomorrow I marry the queen. I'm sorry. I have no choice."

His words hit her in the chest like a hammer. And although she knew it to be true, she mustered up the courage to fire back. "There's something I need to tell you…"

He stood in the doorway and leaned against the frame. "What?"

She cleared her throat. He would know. He *had* to know. And she had to tell him. And she felt brave enough to tell him.

"I'm not really…I mean…I might not be who you think I am."

He heard a sound in the distance and was distracted, glancing behind him and down the hallway.

"I'm sorry?"

"What if…"

The sounds grew nearer.

"I'm sorry, love, another time. I need to go," the prince said softly. And with those words he exited the room.

She fell back into the bed, her face in her hands, frustrated. She wanted to tell him, but then again, she didn't want to tell him. To be rejected as a servant girl was one thing. But if he rejected her as a princess and still married Queen Mary, it would destroy her heart, and she wasn't prepared for that type of rejection. Perhaps not telling him was the better option.

The guards thrust the door open and entered Margarete's room, Queen Mary at the threshold giving her approval. But the room was empty. The candle was out; the wick still glowing with smoke rising from it. The young woman couldn't have been gone for more than a couple of minutes. Queen Mary walked to the bedside table and placed the golden-green apple down on it, next to the candle. She searched the room with her eyes, finding nothing of interest, and exited the room.

"Check the prince's chambers. Check everywhere until you find him," the queen addressed her guards.

Chapter 40

Prince Philip entered the room of his long-time friend and painter, Anthonis Mor. Anthonis was busy in the corner, touching up the painting of Margarete. He was so lost in his work, he didn't even notice the Spanish prince standing over him.

"And you, my dear…truly are the most beautiful subject I've ever painted," he said out loud to the painting, touching up the blue in her eyes on the canvas.

Philip exhaled, torn and staring at the beautiful portrait before him.

Without turning around, Anthonis addressed the prince. "Sad, isn't it? Have you ever painted someone with a broken heart?"

"I thought you were painting Elizabeth tonight—as a gift for the wedding tomorrow?"

"I was referring to *my* broken heart. It's almost impossible for me to work right now." He continued to paint as Philip watched.

"But you're painting…"

"There's a difference! Paid work is not the same as painting art." He continued, adjusting several of the many candles that lit his cluttered room.

"You're going to burn this place down with so many candles," said the prince.

"Did you know that the beauty in a person comes from the light?" He painted a few more strokes. "She's amazing, isn't she?"

"Since when do you paint servants?" the Prince asked.

"Aren't all royalty called to serve?" the painter fired back.

Prince Philip fidgeted with his sleeve and paced the small space of the room. "You know, don't you?"

"About your love for the young girl? I'm a painter—I see things many can't. And that's why you came to me, just now."

Prince Philip scratched his chin and smiled, for it was true. "What would you do?"

"Follow your heart, my prince. God gave it to you for a reason."

"It's complicated."

"Yes. It always is."

The prince suggested, "Why don't you move your paintings to my room. You'd have much more room to paint in there and plenty of lighting and privacy. I'm hardly in there. You can use it any time you want."

"And you could enjoy the painting of her in your room, I presume?" the artist joked.

"I'll have some guards move everything for you."

The blue moon glistened off the freshly fallen snow, illuminating the square. Margarete wandered aimlessly into the streets, her mind captured by the thought of a love lost, for tomorrow she would have to swallow the wretched pill of truth: the prince who stole her heart would be married to the Queen of England in less than twenty-four hours—all for the sake of political power. She clenched her chest, trying to soothe the ache deep within from the outside of her skin. The more she walked and the more she thought about it, the more the tears fell from her eyes.

She really hadn't been paying attention to her direction, but the strange smell of burnt flesh caused her to look up. In front of her, less than ten feet away, were the remnants of a public burning. Four charred bodies were tied to wooden posts placed in the market square. The smell and sight made Margarete nauseous, and yet, she couldn't stop looking at the poor souls left for the town to witness. She wondered about their deaths…why? What wrong had they done? And why was the town being forced to witness such atrocities? Who were they?

And perhaps because she wasn't a city girl, it bothered her a little more than the average Englander who strolled the streets underneath the open sky. A swarm of people surrounded the square, ignoring the bodies and the stench as if they didn't exist, or as if the sight was so common they no longer noticed. She was sure the new Queen of England made it a regular practice to burn bodies in public for the sport of it. She had heard horrific stories of such events.

Her heart ached for the four beings who had to endure the fire to the point of death, even if they were criminals. But for some reason she couldn't pull away from looking at them. And then, under the dim lighting of the moon, she read the sign beneath one of the bodies: *Protestants be warned! Your lies are intolerable in this Kingdom!*

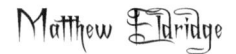

She looked near the feet of the other victims for signs, and that's when she saw it. Near the fourth burned body, just beneath the feet was a wooden musical instrument in the shape of a guitar, charred black from the fire. In fact, several barely recognizable musical instruments were used as firewood beneath all of the bodies. Margarete looked back to the fourth body and she trembled. It started deep within her soul and protruded through her veins to every inch of her being. She shook violently. She grew pale and leaned over as dry heaves worked their way up from inside of her.

"Jack!" she cried, barely able to get the word out as she fell to her knees. She wobbled to a standing position, tried to run but stumbled again, then crawled a few yards before climbing to a stand again. "Nooooo!" she screamed as she ran as fast as she could, stumbling a few more times, her heart racing, her eyes bloodied with tears. She vomited just as she reached the castle gates.

"What have I done?" Margarete cried out. "Jack, dear Jack; the blood of my love—the blood of your family is on my hands." She sobbed heavily, throwing her body on the cold ground. "If only I could have but one more day… If I could share but one more kiss—to touch your face…to feel your embrace…my love…dear Jack."

Whiter Than Snow

She thought about the stolen kisses by the endearing Prince Philip. Her stomach knotted as she wiped her lips aggressively with the back of her hands, as if wiping them could remove what she had done. She felt cheap, like a prostitute. She betrayed Jack, her true love. She kissed another man—a soon-to-be married man! She clenched her chest tightly in pain.

She heard the screams and saw a glow from behind the castle. Through blurred vision, she watched in horror as fire licked the walls in the direction of the prince's chambers. She screamed again, hoping and wishing he wasn't in his room. She couldn't lose both lovers in one night, she thought. The flames furiously shot through his windows and consumed the roof.

Margarete ran through the lower bailey and into the courtyard. She tried to get to the path that would lead to the prince's chamber, but several guards blocked anyone from entering that area.

"Please," she pleaded, crying, but the guard was unmoved.

The prince's quarters weren't connected to the rest of the castle, so Margarete was free to return to her wing.

Upon entering her room, Margarete threw herself onto the floor, drowning in tears, fear, and confusion. She leaned against her bed and looked to Heaven.

"Why, God? Please tell me the prince still lives."

But it didn't matter, because she didn't want to live. She lost Jack, and more than likely, the prince too. And even if he lived, he would belong to Queen Mary, and she would suffer greatly for simply falling in love with him. Aching in guilt and sorrow, she scanned the room for something—anything to take this pain away; to take her life away. But her eyes refused to see in the blackness of the room. She felt for the bedside table and felt the candle, but had no flint or fire-steel to strike it. She crawled to her bed and smothered herself in her pillow, wetting it with her tears.

Jack was dead. If the prince was still alive, he would marry the Queen of England by morning. More than likely, she assumed he was murdered. Her heart was numb.

She stilled herself in the quiet of the room—her eyes transfixed on the light shadows dancing on the wall. Her head was spinning—or was it the room? The walls seemed to close in on her. And yet, she remained motionless; silent, until she lost track of time caused by the drowsiness that seemed to bring her in and out of consciousness. She was hungry, and perhaps her hunger drew her out of the vegetated state that controlled her.

She slowly felt the bedside table again. The lone green apple awaited. She reached for it with her right arm. Her finger tips barely touching it. She scooted closer to the apple and palmed it with her hand, drawing it to her face and twirling it around mindlessly. It was plump and beautiful, she could feel. England's finest.

Chapter 41

"The guards said the prince wasn't in his room during the fire, praise God. Only his painter, who escaped unharmed."

"Still, we need to find him quickly," answered the King of Brussels.

"I will find him and tell him myself. It's not kingly for you to approach him. Besides, your intentions may be questioned," said Samuel.

"No, I will go. He knows me, and t'is my daughter he loves. I need to explain…"

"No, I…"

"Don't argue with me, Samuel, I am the king," he interrupted.

"Where you go, I will follow, my king."

Margarete felt the cool, tight skin of the apple in her hands. She thought about Adam and Eve. Oh, how the temptation of a simple piece of fruit changed the entire future. How one bite brought cursing and death. Funny. How she wished for death that very moment. *Wished* was too light of a word. She longed for it with all her being. She desired death with the aching of her soul.

She whispered to herself, "To taste death, would be to kiss Heaven."

Perhaps Jack would be waiting for her on the other side. But then again, perhaps he knew about the prince as well. She betrayed her first love and was grieved with guilt. One thing was for certain, though. Jack was in Heaven and was probably making beautiful music for his Maker. She had never met a man so in love with God before. Nor had she met a man so passionate about his faith. The thought warmed her. He was a sensitive soul who loved deeply, because God loved *him* deeply. She didn't think about God without thinking of Jack, and she didn't think about Jack without thinking of God. She envied Heaven for enjoying him. She thought warily about her own sins and how they separated her from God. Would God forgive her? Would he love her the way he loves Jack? Then again, did she love God the way that Jack loved him? Jack spoke often of the grace of God, and how his love for his children wasn't based on performance. She was hopeful of his words.

"Jesus," she whimpered. She hungered to see him now. But he was silent. "Jesus, forgive me!" she cried. She felt responsible for Jack's death and for her deceptive heart which longed for the prince. "Forgive me!" she cried again, hitting her fist against the bed. "I can't take this! I can't take this anymore." Her desperate crying turned into coughing and wheezing. She felt as if her chest was caving in. She moaned in anguish.

After searching the bleak, black room one more time with her eyes, she concluded there was no way to take her own life. Of course, she could run to the river and try to drown herself—but it was too cold this time of year, and especially at night. She wasn't brave enough to do such a thing.

She would endure the wedding. She would be dying inside, but she would do it. She suffered worse in the forest as a child, she reminded herself. She could survive this.

"He's nowhere to be found. They almost arrested me for even asking about him," answered Samuel. "Suspicions are always high the day before a royal wedding…and after the fire."

"Are you sure Micah made it safely here with my daughter?" asked the King of Brussels.

"There is word that your daughter is here, yes."

"Let's find my daughter then. I have an idea where she may be staying."

The King of Brussels and the prophet Samuel walked the halls of the servant's quarters. Most of the servants were still cleaning up after the rehearsal dinner and preparing for the wedding. However, a few lingered in the area, and none had heard of Margarete or knew her whereabouts. There were so many guests. It was getting late and both Margarete and the prince would soon be asleep. Time was running out.

The dining hall was littered with more servants, all whom knew nothing about the Princess Margarete. There were literally hundreds of royal guests staying at Whitehall Castle for the wedding. Finding Margarete was nearly impossible. And the prince was heavily guarded, they were certain.

"How may I assist you," the head servant, Hannah, said to the king, watching the two men question her helpers.

"We're looking for a servant from Brussels who goes by the name Margarete," said Samuel. "Do you know of her?"

"Yes. But Margarete, the servant, hasn't served here since the jousting tournament," Hannah answered with a tilt in her brow.

"Oh," said the king, as his face fell.

"But I do believe, Margarete, the queen's stepdaughter from Brussels, accompanied her at the rehearsal dinner tonight, but left early." She bowed and winked.

The king's face lit up. "Thank you, thank you."

"Has the king not spoken to his wife tonight?"

"No, not yet," he answered her. "We just arrived."

A guard led the King of Brussels and his companion to the queen's quarters, the place where his wife was staying. The king recognized the queen's luggage, but the room appeared unused. The candle was cold and hadn't been lit since the night before. The bed was perfectly made.

"You wouldn't happen to know the whereabouts of my queen, would you?" the king asked the guard, concerned.

"There are hundreds of guests at the castle. My duty is to simply show guests to their room."

"I understand," he answered.

Whiter Than Snow

As the guard began to walk away, he turned back to the king. "The queen also requested another smaller room, for a princess, I believe?"

The prince paced the halls of the guests, confused and desperate. Should he go back to Margarete's room? Or would that make things more complicated? Should he confess his love to her, or of his tainted devotion to keep her as his, protected in another kingdom far away? His heart ached to be with her, but he didn't want to hurt her anymore.

The words of Anthonis echoed in his mind. "Aren't all royalty called to serve?"

Yes. He was called to serve. His heart may long for Margarete, but in the end, that would be pure selfishness—to deny this union for the sake of his own heart's pleasure. To resist this marriage would cause fears of wars, and may even lead to war. Queen Mary was a vexed person who took pleasure in merciless killings. It was no secret that his father's hand was slipping from power, that his kingdoms were losing strength, and that England was growing in power. Marriage was the right thing to do. He must go on with it. He must crucify his heart, his feelings, his love for Margarete. He must break her heart so she would never want him again. But he knew, the second he looked into her kind eyes he wouldn't be able to do it. He would want her. He would want to kiss her again.

Who was he fooling? He could be with Margarete! He could run away, far away. He could even fake his own death for her sake, and they could live as commoners, happily in love. He was willing to sacrifice it all—the joining of the kingdoms, his land, his money, even being crowned as King. She may be just a servant, but she was a miracle to Prince Philip. She brought him from death to life. He had been born again. He was a new person, all because of her, and he swore he would never look at another woman ever again, if she would just be his forever. But now, he was going to die again—inwardly, if he married Mary.

The prince's heart leaped. He made his decision. He left the wing he was pacing in and entered the wing where Margarete was staying. He was nearly to her door when he noticed the dried blood splattered on the floor from Queen Viktoria's death. Of course, her body had been long removed. As he curiously eyed the stain, three other men approached the hallway from the other direction.

"Prince Philip!" the King of Brussels called out.

"Praise God!" Samuel said to himself, out loud.

"I'm sorry, I'm distracted at the moment. Would you please excuse me?" the prince said.

"Wait, we need to talk to you…" Samuel interjected.

"And whom might you be?" the prince addressed the prophet of God.

"He's someone who can change your entire future," the King of Brussels answered, kindly. "Please. Listen."

"Alright. I'm listening," he said.

Whiter Than Snow

Samuel and the king looked back and forth, not exactly knowing how to share the secret information.

"Would you excuse us, please?" the king said to the guard, knowing he was loyal to the Queen of England, and wanting him to leave.

Prince Philip nodded his approval of the king's request. The guard bowed out and returned the way he entered the hallway.

"I understand you love my daughter?" said the king to the prince.

"Your daughter?"

"Yes," Samuel interjected. "The princess Margarete—the servant girl."

"How? How is she your daughter?"

Samuel bowed his head in shame.

"You tell me this now, right before my wedding day?"

The prince was a well of emotions; anger sautéed with relief and joy. Anger, because it was too late. Relief and joy because as a prince, he could legally marry the daughter of a king and it would be widely accepted by the kingdoms surrounding him. Besides, not everyone was happy about his union to the Queen of England. But perhaps, choosing Magarete, a beautiful princess, over Queen Mary might make their life even more difficult. It would be almost easier to run away and live as commoners. His father would say his choice of a small kingdom princess would prove his weakness, and would be seen as an invitation for enemies to attack. He was at a crossroads.

Prince Philip looked into the tender eyes of Margarete's father. He could now see the resemblance to Margarete. Why didn't he see it before? And the tenderness of this king made him wish he was his father as well.

Margarete's stomach growled. She returned her thoughts to the luscious green apple in her hand and pulled it towards her lips. Her teeth sunk deep into the green flesh, the juices spilling on her lips and tongue. The taste was sweet, perhaps the sweetest apple she ever tasted. She savored the flavor for a moment as she held the piece of apple in her mouth, slowly chewing it, the juices flooding her taste buds.

"And I have your blessing?" the Prince of Spain asked the King of Brussels, referring to his daughter.

"Yes, of course. That is why we found you. To tell you, before you made the biggest mistake you've ever made in your entire life."

He sighed with relief. He was in love. And it was no longer a forbidden love. He wanted to shout it across the mountain tops.

"Do you know where she is?" Samuel asked.

"Perhaps," the prince answered. "Her room is around this corner."

Whiter Than Snow

"Margarete," the prince whispered as he entered her room, the king and prophet behind him. "Margarete," he whispered again. He could barely see her in the dark, except by the light that spilled from the hallway into the room, illuminating her silhouette.

Samuel took the candle out of the room, lit it with the torch attached to the hallway wall, and returned it to its position on the bedside table.

Prince Philip stared at the beautiful princess lying on the bed, glowing in the candlelight. She looked serene. Her shiny black hair covered her pillow, spread out, resembling the tail of a peacock. Her contrasting, soft, porcelain skin looked flawless, almost like a china doll. Her lips were pouty, colored with the touch of cherries one would presume.

"Margarete," the prince whispered again, hoping not to startle her. He gently touched her hand to hold it. And as he slid it into his, it felt cold and clammy. "Margarete!" he said anxiously, this time much louder.

He reached for her face and placed his hand on her dead cheek. He bent down and placed his ear next to her mouth—she wasn't breathing.

"Dear God, no!" he cried. "No! Margarete!" he yelled again. "Wake up, wake up, my love! Wake up!" Tears welled up in his eyes and poured down his face, dripping onto his lifeless beauty. "No! Wake up, please, my love, my true love!"

Both the King of Brussels and Samuel stood behind him, watching in disbelief.

"Nooooo!" the prince yelled again. "Please. Just be sleeping. Please!" he begged her. "Wake up, my love!" He looked to her soft, ruby lips and rubbed his fingers across them, blood smearing on his fingers. She was bleeding from the inside of her mouth.

"Wake up, my princess!" he said again, this time softer, more desperately. He bent over and pressed his lips against hers, his face pressed into her for a full thirty seconds, his tears covering her. He could taste the blood in her mouth, but he didn't care.

The King of Brussels placed his hand on the prince's back to comfort him, and the prince sat up. Prince Philip gently placed the princess's hand across her chest, and then grabbed her other hand which dangled off the side of the bed, and placed that hand across her chest as well. And that's when he saw it. The prince looked down to the floor and saw a half-eaten apple that had fallen from the princess's hand. Poisoned.

Chapter 42

It was the coldest day of the year so far. The queen waited in her bridal chambers, pampered by Sir John Gage, her lord chamberlayne, and fitted to her train prepared by the Marquesse of Win Chester.

She stared out the window, the streets soon to be lined with peasants, lords, and ladies. Her original plan was to march from her bridal chambers to the church, allowing guests a beautiful view of her dress, but the cold winds kept her from doing so. She would have to travel by carriage.

Had she more time to prepare, she would have made the wedding a much bigger production, and perhaps a better season of the year. It's not everyday the two most powerful people in the world were wed. She loved the attention she was receiving. She thought about the guests who would admire and envy her. She thought little of the prince this morning. Odd, she thought to herself, considering she was marrying him in less than ten hours.

John Gage was putting lotion on her hand when a guard knocked on the door of the bridal room. The queen pulled her hand from the man and rubbed her fingers along his cheek.

"Would you get that, sweetie?" she said, then puckered up and blew him a kiss. John got up from his seat while the Marquesse continued working on her dress.

Sir John opened the door and a guard handed him a note. "A message for the queen," the guard said.

Sir John closed the door and walked the note to the queen.

"Read it for me?" she asked as he sat down across from her again to continue his pampering. She gave him her hand to continue his duties.

"The prince is very ill," he said, concerned, looking up at her. "He will marry you, but not today."

Epilogue

Guards escorted Thomas Wyatt through the prison.

"I didn't do anything! I swear!" Thomas yelled, the guards pushing him along, his hands tied behind his back.

"You've been charged with starting a fire at Whitehall Castle in the prince's chambers," one of the guards shouted back at him.

"That's crazy," Thomas yelled, struggling to stay on his feet as they pushed him past Elizabeth's cell, the little sister to Queen Mary. "Who told you that?"

"John Dee. The queen's spiritual advisor. God showed him in a dream."

"That's ludicrous. Why would I do that?"

Elizabeth looked up at Wyatt as he was dragged by, pretending not to recognize him. He gave her a quick double wink and she understood what he was communicating. She blinked back and lowered her head. The rebellion was coming soon.

It was a solemn journey. A caravan of carriages paraded through the streets. Most of the carriages were of Spanish design and belonged to the dear Prince Philip. A few belonged to the King of Brussels.

As the entourage exited the castle walls and traveled through the lower bailey, peasants lined the streets to bid farewell to the body of the stunning princess. Prince Philip paid for her funeral, refusing the offer by her father, and purchased a custom made casket with a glass top to display her body as they traveled to the gravesite. He believed her beauty was too compelling to cover in a wooden box, and wanted people to be exposed to her as long as possible.

Prince Philip stared forward, choked with emotion, the terrain of the trail jerking the carriage from side to side. He ignored the waving peasants, many who were crying at the sight of the beautiful bride in the bed of the open carriage behind him. Yes, the princess was a beautiful bride. The prince had her placed in a wedding dress for her burial, and he hired the best make up artists he could find in the kingdom to touch up her face and hair. When they finished with her, she was the most striking woman the world had ever seen. And yet she was dead.

The prince was making a point. She was and always would be his bride, no matter what the future held for him. Princess Margarete was his love, his true love; his choice for a bride—not his father's and certainly not Spain or England or the surrounding territories. He would let the world know, the woman he truly loved is dead. Any other woman he married would be second to her.

As they traveled into the countryside, the line of viewers dissipated and it was only those traveling with the royal men who were present. Upon reaching the gravesite, Prince Philip exited his carriage, followed by the king of Brussels. His royal guards lined themselves on each side of Margarete's casket and removed it from the following carriage, carrying the body and placing it in front of the shallow grave.

"Stop," the young prince said, walking over to the glass casket.

The men stepped away.

Prince Philip leaned down on one knee to gaze upon his bride. Even in death, she was breathtaking. He placed his hand on the glass cover and rested for a moment, exhaling heavily. Someone so young and beautiful should never face death, he thought to himself. With his head bent over and his eyes closed, he fought the emotions welling up in his throat, but he was losing the battle. Tears fell from his face and splashed onto the casket. He opened his sodden eyes to look upon her youthful face once more. She was just a child, really; so young, so pretty. He surveyed her small frame, remembering every detail; her dress, her arms, her tiny hands, her soft neck, her flawless face, and of course, those cherry lips. He looked at her eyelids and thought about the time he kissed them so sweetly. How he wished he could do it again. He wanted to touch her, to see her laugh, to hear her voice. He wanted to feel each delicate finger of hers intertwined with his fingers. He wanted to make her smile again, for it was her smile that stole his heart in the first place. He was overcome with anguish, searching the skies for emotional freedom as he lifted his head to the heavens.

He looked back down to Margarete's face through the glass and whispered, "If only I could kiss you one more time." And with those words, he leaned down and pressed his lips against the glass casket. "Goodbye, my love," the prince said, as he dropped a single red rose onto her casket.

He stood and backed away from her as his men stepped forward. They lowered the casket into the dirt as he watched on. As they began to cover it with earth, the prince turned away and was greeted by Margarete's father, the king.

"You are welcome to stay in my kingdom, anytime…son," said the king, still numb from losing both his wife and the daughter he never really knew.

The prince nodded and stepped into his carriage, resting a moment—his face in his hands. Through wet eyes, he watched the sun descending on the hill outside of the carriage, just behind Margarete's grave. It was beautiful. God painted the sky with hues of orange and pink. And as he watched, it occurred to him, in all of his years as an adult, he never noticed a sunset before. Sure, he encountered many of them, but he never truly noticed one. He imagined the words of Margarete telling him how lovely it was. And it was in that moment, he swore he heard her voice speaking to him. He rested in it—albeit nothing but the wind.

Trinkets of light danced over Margarete's buried casket, catching his attention. *Was it angels?* He thought. The lights flittered from the casket and slowly reached his carriage. One of them landed on his hand. He held his hand up to his face and watched the little lighted creature as it crawled on him.

Whiter Than Snow

"What a marvelous bug you are," he said to the firefly, observing it wondrously. As quickly as it came, it lifted from his finger and flew away into the night.

He felt the jerking of the carriage as it started to move again. He looked back one last time in the direction of his love, his true love; his bride. And while he may never marry her, she was to be a bride, after all. She was the bride of Christ, according to his Catholic beliefs, and perhaps to her Protestant beliefs as well, and she was on her way to meet the great and glorious groom, the one who loved her unconditionally; the one who gave his life for her: Jesus the Messiah. And she would live with her groom in Paradise for an eternity. This was Christianity—and perhaps to some it was just a fairy tale, but to him it was true.

It was warm thoughts of Margarete in Heaven that gave Philip the closure he needed. Protestant or Catholic, it didn't matter. His heart knew this to be true. She was a lover of God. He knew it by the tenderness in her eyes. He could sense it in her innocence. He felt it in her purity. He saw it in her smile and laughter. She walked the narrow road—the road of love and grace, peace and joy, the truest gifts from God. It permeated through her life, and he felt honored just to know her, if even for a moment.

Matthew Eldridge

Whiter Than Snow

About the Author:

Matthew Eldridge lives with his lovely wife and three beautiful daughters in Atlanta, Georgia. Besides writing fiction, Matthew works in the film industry as an actor, body double, and stand-in. He is also a singer/songwriter and enjoys creating music to share with others. Interesting fact: Matthew is highly allergic to apples.

Blood Sisters, the sequel to Whiter Than Snow, releases in 2015. Blood Sisters is about the rivalry between sister Queens Elizabeth and Mary of England, and of course, the handsome Prince of Spain, Philip II.

Matthew is available for speaking engagements, book interviews (including print, radio, vlogs, blogs, etc.) and more. Please contact him at meldridge@cheerful.com

Made in the USA
Charleston, SC
11 November 2014